DRIVER
OF
THE
WAYWARD
BUS

The passengers on the bus from the inland
California valley didn't know it, but their
driver, Juan Chicoy, was headed for Mexico.
He had a sharp homesickness in him for the
smell of burning pine knots in the high
mountains, the popcorn smell of frying
tortillas, the warm perfume of his own kind
of woman.

Juan was tired of his California wife, tired
of living in an alien land, tired of his bus
and its passengers.

So when the bus broke down in a raging storm,
Juan simply walked away from it. He didn't
know that the quiet girl on the bus wanted
him enough to come after him . . .

THE WAYWARD BUS, the story of a
group of widely diverse people whose
emotions are stripped raw in an elemental
crisis, is one of John Steinbeck's
greatest and most famous novels.

THE WAYWARD BUS

BY JOHN STEINBECK

BANTAM BOOKS | NEW YORK

THE WAYWARD BUS

A Bantam Book published by arrangement with
The Viking Press, Inc.

Printing History

Viking edition published February 1947
2nd printing January 1947
3rd printing February 1947
Book-of-the-Month Club edition published March 1947
Armed Services Edition published April 1947
Material from this book appeared in *Omnibook* August 1947
Condensation appeared in The New York *Post* October 1947
Grosset & Dunlap Edition published February 1948
Bantam edition published January 1950
2nd printing February 1950
3rd printing April 1950
4th printing November 1952
5th printing (new edition) April 1957

Bantam Books are published by Bantam Books, Inc. Its
trade mark, consisting of the words "Bantam Books"
and the portrayal of a bantam, is registered in the U. S.
Patent Office and in other countries. *Marca Registrada*

PRINTED IN THE UNITED STATES OF AMERICA
Bantam Books, 25 West 45th Street, New York 36, N. Y.

For
Gwyn

I pray you all gyve audyence,
And here this mater with reverence,
By fygure a morall playe;
The somonynge of Everyman called it is,
That of our lyves and endynge shewes
How transytory we be all daye.

—EVERYMAN

Chapter 1

FORTY-TWO miles below San Ysidro, on a great north-south highway in California, there is a crossroad which for eighty-odd years has been called Rebel Corners. From here a country road goes at right angles toward the west until, after forty-nine miles, it connects with another north-south highway, that leads from San Francisco to Los Angeles and, of course, Hollywood. Anyone who wishes to go from the inland valley to the coast in this part of the state must take the road that begins at Rebel Corners and winds through hills and a little desert and through farmland and mountains until, at last, it comes to the coastal highway right in the middle of the town of San Juan de la Cruz.

Rebel Corners got its name in 1862. It is said that a family named Blanken kept a smithy at the crossroads. The Blankens and their sons-in-law were poor, ignorant, proud, and violent Kentuckians. Having no furniture and no property, they brought what they had with them from the East—their prejudices and their politics. Having no slaves, they were ready, nevertheless, to sell their lives for the free principle of slavery. When the war began, the Blankens discussed traveling back across the measureless West to fight for the Confederacy. But it was a long way and they had crossed once, and it was too far. Thus it was that in a California which was preponderantly for the North, the Blankens seceded a hundred and sixty acres and a blacksmith shop from the Union and joined Blanken Corners to the Confederacy. It is also said that they dug trenches and cut rifle slits in the blacksmith shop to defend this rebellious island from the hated Yankees. And the Yankees, who were mostly Mexicans and Germans and Irish and Chinese, far from attacking the Blankens, were rather proud of them. The Blankens had never lived so well, for the enemy

1

brought chickens and eggs and pork sausage in slaughter time, because everyone thought that, regardless of the cause, such courage should be recognized. Their place took the name of Rebel Corners and has kept it to this day.

After the war the Blankens became lazy and quarrelsome and full of hatreds and complaints, as every defeated nation does, so that, pride in them having evaporated with the war, people stopped bringing their horses to be shoed and their plows for retipping. Finally, what the Union Armies could not do by force of arms the First National Bank of San Ysidro did by foreclosure.

Now, after eighty-odd years, no one remembers much about the Blankens except that they were very proud and very unpleasant. In the following years the land changed hands many times before it was incorporated into the empire of a newspaper king. The blacksmith shop burned down and was rebuilt and burned again, and what was left was converted into a garage with gas pumps and then into a store-restaurant-garage and service station. When Juan Chicoy and his wife bought it and got the franchise to run a public conveyance between Rebel Corners and San Juan de la Cruz, it became all these and a bus station too. The rebel Blankens have, through pride and a low threshold of insult which is the test of ignorance and laziness, disappeared from the face of the earth, and no one remembers what they looked like. But Rebel Corners is well known and the Chicoys are well liked.

There was a little lunchroom in back of the gas pumps, a lunchroom with a counter and round, fixed stools, and three tables for those who wanted to eat in some style. These were not used often for it was customary to tip Mrs. Chicoy when she served you at a table and not to if she served you at the counter. On the first shelf behind the counter were sweet rolls, snails, doughnuts; on the second, canned soups, oranges, and bananas; on the third, individual boxes of cornflakes, riceflakes, grapenuts, and other tortured cereals. There was a grill at one end behind the counter and a sink beside it, beer and soda spouts beside that, ice-cream units beside those, and on the counter itself, between the units of paper-napkin containers, juke-box coin slots, salt, pepper, and ketchup, the cakes were displayed under large plastic covers. The walls, where there was room, were well decorated with calendars and posters showing bright,

improbable girls with pumped-up breasts and no hips—
blondes, brunettes and redheads, but always with this bust
development, so that a visitor of another species might judge
from the preoccupation of artist and audience that the seat of
procreation lay in the mammaries.

Alice Chicoy, Mrs. Juan Chicoy, that is, who worked among
the shining girls, was wide-hipped and sag-chested and she
walked well back on her heels. She was not in the least jealous
of the calendar girls and the Coca-Cola girls. She had never
seen anyone like them and she didn't think anyone else ever
had. She fried her eggs and hamburgers, heated her canned
soup, drew beer, scooped ice cream, and toward evening her
feet hurt and that made her cross and snappish. And as the day
went on the flat curl went out of her hair so that it hung damp
and stringy beside her face, and at first she would brush it aside
with her hand and finally she would blow it out of her eyes.

Next to the lunchroom was a garage converted from the
last blacksmith shop, its ceiling and beams still black from the
soot of the old forge, and here Juan Chicoy presided when he
was not driving the bus between Rebel Corners and San Juan
de la Cruz. He was a fine, steady man, Juan Chicoy, part
Mexican and part Irish, perhaps fifty years old, with clear black
eyes, a good head of hair, and a dark and handsome face. Mrs.
Chicoy was insanely in love with him and a little afraid of
him too, because he was a man, and there aren't very many of
them, as Alice Chicoy had found out. There aren't very many
of them in the world, as everyone finds out sooner or later.

In the garage Juan Chicoy fixed flat tires, got the air locks
out of gas lines, cleaned the diamond-hard dust from choked
carburetors, put new diaphragms in tubercular gasoline pumps,
and did all the little things that the motor-minded public
knows nothing whatever about. These things he did except
during the hours from ten-thirty until four. That was the time
he drove the bus, carrying passengers who had been deposited
at Rebel Corners by the big Greyhound busses to San Juan de
la Cruz and bringing passengers back from San Juan de la
Cruz to Rebel Corners, where they were picked up either by
the Greyhound bus going north at four-fifty-six or by the Greyhound going south at five-seventeen.

While Mr. Chicoy was gone on his route his duties at the
garage were carried out by a succession of overgrown boys or

immature young men who were more or less apprentices. None of them lasted very long. Unwary customers with dirty carburetors could not know in advance the destruction these apprentices could heap on a carburetor, and while Juan Chicoy himself was a magnificent mechanic, his apprentices usually were cocky adolescents who spent their time between jobs putting slugs in the juke box in the lunchroom and quarreling mildly with Alice Chicoy. To these young men opportunity beckoned constantly, drawing them ever southward toward Los Angeles and, of course, Hollywood, where, eventually, all the adolescents in the world will be congregated.

Behind the garage were two little outhouses with trellises, one of which said "Men" and the other "Ladies." And to each one a little path led, one around the right-hand side of the garage and one around the left-hand side of the garage.

What defined the Corners and made it visible for miles among the cultivated fields were the great white oaks that grew around the garage and restaurant. Tall and graceful, with black trunks and limbs, bright green in summer, black and brooding in winter, these oaks were landmarks in the long, flat valley. No one knows whether the Blankens planted them or whether they merely settled near to them. The latter seems more logical first, because the Blankens are not known to have planted anything they could not eat, and second, because the trees seemed more than eighty-five years old. They might be two hundred years old; on the other hand, they might have their roots in some underground spring which would make them grow large quickly in this semidesert country.

These great trees shaded the station in summer so that travelers often pulled up under them and ate their lunches and cooled their overheated motors. The station itself was pleasant too, brightly painted green and red, a deep row of geraniums all around the restaurant, red geraniums and deep green leaves thick as a hedge. The white gravel in front and around the gas pumps was raked and sprinkled daily. In the restaurant and in the garage there was system and order. For instance, on the shelves in the restaurant the canned soup, the boxed cereals, even the grapefruits, were arranged in little pyramids, four on the bottom level, then three, then two, and one balanced on top. And the same was true of the cans of oil in the garage, and the fan belts hung neatly in their sizes on nails. It was a very well-kept place. The windows of the restaurant were screened against flies, and the screen door banged shut after every entrance or exit. For Alice Chicoy hated flies. In a world that was not easy for Alice to bear or to understand, flies were the final and malicious burden laid upon her. She hated them with a cruel hatred, and the death of a fly by swatter, or slowly smothered in the goo of fly paper, gave her a flushed pleasure.

Just as Juan usually had a succession of young apprentices to help him in the garage, so Alice hired a succession of girls to help her in the lunchroom. These girls, gawky and romantic and homely—the pretty ones usually left with a customer within a few days—seemed to accomplish little in the way of work. They spread dirt about with damp cloths, they dreamed over movie magazines, they sighed into the juke box—and the most recent one had reddening eyes and a head cold and wrote long and passionate letters to Clark Gable. Alice Chicoy suspected every one of them of letting flies in. Norma, this most recent girl, had felt the weight of Alice Chicoy's tongue many times about flies.

The routine of the Corners in the morning was invariable. With the first daylight or, in the winter, even before, the lights came on in the lunchroom, and Alice steamed up the coffee urn (a great godlike silver effigy which may, in some future archaeological period, be displayed as an object of worship of the race of Amudkins, who preceded the Atomites, who, for some unknown reason, disappeared from the face of the earth). The restaurant was warm and cheerful when the first truck drivers pulled wearily in for their breakfast. Then came the salesmen, hurrying to the cities of the south in the dark so as to have a full day of business. Salesmen always spotted trucks and stopped, because it is generally believed that truck drivers are great connoisseurs of roadside coffee and food. By sun-up the first tourists in their own cars began to pull in for breakfast and road information.

The tourists from the north did not interest Norma much, but those from the south or those who came over the cutoff from San Juan de la Cruz and who might have been to Hollywood fascinated her. In four months Norma personally met fifteen people who had been to Hollywood, five who had been on a picture lot, and two who had seen Clark Gable face to face. Inspired by these last two, who came in very close together, she wrote a twelve-page letter which began, "Dear Mr. Gable," and ended, "Lovingly, A Friend." She often shuddered to think that Mr. Gable might find out that she had written it.

Norma was a faithful girl. Let others, featherbrains, run after the upstarts—the Sinatras, the Van Johnsons, the Sonny Tufts'. Even during the war, when there had been no Gable pictures, Norma had remained faithful, keeping her dream warm with a colored picture of Mr. Gable in a flying suit with two belts of 50-caliber ammunition on his shoulders.

She often sneered at Sonny Tufts. She liked older men with interesting faces. Sometimes, wiping the damp cloth back and forth on the counter, her dream-widened eyes centered on the screen door, her pale eyes flexed and then closed for a moment. Then you could know that in that secret garden in her head, Gable had just entered the restaurant, had gasped when he saw her, and had stood there, his lips slightly parted and in his eyes the recognition that this was his woman. And around him the flies came in and out with impunity.

It never went beyond that. Norma was too shy. And, besides, she didn't know how such things were done. The actual love-making in her life had been a series of wrestling matches, the aim of which was to keep her clothes on in the back seat of a car. So far she had won by simple concentration. She felt that Mr. Gable not only would not do things like that, but wouldn't like them if he heard about them.

Norma wore the wash dresses featured by the National Dollar Stores, though, of course, she had a sateen dress for parties. But if you looked closely you could always find some little bit of beauty even on the wash dresses. Her Mexican silver pin, a representation of the Aztec calendar stone, was left to her in her aunt's will after Norma had nursed her for seven months and really wanted the sealskin stole and the ring of baroque pearls and turquoise. But these went to another branch of the family. Norma had also a string of small amber beads from her mother. She never wore the Mexican pin and the beads at the same time. In addition to these, Norma possessed two pieces of jewelry which were pure crazy and which she knew were pure crazy. Deep in her suitcase she had a gold-filled wedding ring and a gigantic Brazilian-type diamond ring, the two of which had cost five dollars. She wore them only when she went to bed. In the morning she took them off and hid them in her suitcase. No one in the world knew that she owned them. In bed she went to sleep twisting them on the third finger of her left hand.

The sleeping arrangements at the Corners were simple. Directly behind the lunchroom there was a lean-to. A door at the end of the lunch counter opened into the Chicoys' bed-sitting room, which had a double bed with an afghan spread, a console radio, two overstuffed chairs and a davenport—which group is called a suite—and a metal reading lamp with a marble green glass shade. Norma's room opened off this room, for it was Alice's theory that young girls should be watched a little and not let to run wild. Norma had to come through the Chicoys' room to go to the bathroom—that, or slip out the window, which she ordinarily did. The apprentice-mechanic's room was next to the Chicoys' on the other side, but he had an outside entrance and used the vine-covered cubicle marked "Men" behind the garage.

It was a nice compact grouping of buildings, functional and pleasant. The Rebel Corners of the Blankens' time had been a miserable, dirty, and suspicious place, but the Chicoys flour-ished here. There was money in the bank and a degree of security and happiness.

This island covered by the huge trees could be seen for miles. No one ever had to look for road signs to find Rebel Corners and the road to San Juan de la Cruz. In the great valley the grain fields flattened away toward the east, to the foothills and to the high mountains, and toward the west they ended nearer in the rounded hills where the live oaks sat in black splotches. In the summer the yellow heat shimmered and burned and glared on the baking hills, and the shade of the great trees over the Corners was a thing to look forward to and to remember. In the winter when the heavy rains fell, the restaurant was a warm place of coffee and chili beans and pie.

In the deep spring when the grass was green on fields and foothills, when the lupines and poppies made a splendid blue and gold earth, when the great trees awakened in yellow-green young leaves, then there was no more lovely place in the world. It was no beauty you could ignore by being used to it. It caught you in the throat in the morning and made a pain of pleasure in the pit of your stomach when the sun went down over it. The sweet smell of the lupines and of the grass set you breathing nervously, set you panting almost sexually. And it was in this season of flowering and growth, though it was still before daylight, that Juan Chicoy came out to the bus carrying an electric lantern. Pimples Carson, his apprentice-mechanic, stumbled sleepily behind him.

The lunchroom windows were still dark. Against the eastern hills not even a grayness had begun to form. It was so much night that the owls were still shrieking over the fields. Juan Chicoy came near to the bus which stood in front of the garage. It looked, in the light of the lantern, like a large, silver-windowed balloon. Pimples Carson, still not really awake, stood with his hands in his pockets, shivering, not because it was cold but because he was very sleepy.

A little wind blew in over the fields and brought the smell of lupine and the smell of a quickening earth, frantic with production.

Chapter 2

THE electric lantern, with a flat downward reflector, lighted sharply only legs and feet and tires and tree trunks near to the ground. It bobbed and swung, and the little incandescent bulb was blindingly blue-white. Juan Chicoy carried his lantern to the garage, took a bunch of keys from his overalls pocket, found the one that unlocked the padlock, and opened the wide doors. He switched on the overhead light and turned off his lantern.

Juan picked a striped mechanic's cap from his workbench. He wore Headlight overalls with big brass buttons on bib and side latches, and over this he wore a black horsehide jacket with black knitted wristlets and neck. His shoes were round-toed and hard, with soles so thick that they seemed swollen. An old scar on his cheek beside his large nose showed as a shadow in the overhead light. He ran fingers through his thick, black hair to get it all in the mechanic's cap. His hands were short and wide and strong, with square fingers and nails flattened by work and grooved and twisted from having been hammered and hurt. The third finger of his left hand had lost the first joint, and the flesh was slightly mushroomed where the finger had been amputated. This little overhanging ball was shiny and of a different texture from the rest of the finger, as though the joint were trying to become a fingertip, and on this finger he wore a wide gold wedding ring, as though this finger was no good for work any more and might as well be used for ornament.

A pencil and a ruler and a tire pressure gauge protruded from a slot in his overalls bib. Juan was clean-shaven, but not since yesterday, and along the corners of his chin and on his neck the coming whiskers were grizzled and white like those of an old Airedale. This was the more apparent because the rest of his beard was so intensely black. His black eyes were squinting and humorous, the way a man's eyes squint when he is smoking and cannot take the cigarette from his mouth. And Juan's mouth was full and good, a relaxed mouth, the underlip slightly protruding—not in petulance but in humor and self-confidence—the upper lip well formed except left of center where a deep scar was almost white against the pink tissue. The lip must have been cut clear through at one time, and now this thin taut band of white was a strain on the fullness of the lip and made it bunch in tiny tucks on either side. His ears were not very large, but they stood out sharply from his head like seashells, or in the position a man would hold them with his hands if he wanted to hear more clearly. Juan seemed to be listening intently all the time, while his squinting eyes seemed to laugh at what he heard, and half of his mouth disapproved. His movements were sure even when he was not doing anything that required sureness. He walked as though he were going to some exact spot. His hands moved with speed and precision and never fiddled with matches or with nails. His teeth were long and the edges were framed with gold, which gave his smile a little fierceness.

At his workbench he picked tools from nails on the wall and laid them in a long, flat box—wrenches and pliers and several screwdrivers and a machine hammer and a punch. Beside him Pimples Carson, still heavy with sleep, rested his elbow on the oily wood of the bench. Pimples wore the tattered sweater of a motorcycle club and the crown of a felt hat cut in saw teeth around the edge. He was a lank and slender-waisted boy of seventeen, with narrow shoulders and a long foxy nose and eyes that were pale in the morning and became greenish-brown later in the day. A golden fuzz was on his cheeks, and his cheeks were riveted and rotted and eroded with acne. Among the old scars new pustules formed, purple and red, some rising and some waning. The skin was shiny with the medicines that were sold for this condition and which do no good whatever.

Pimples' blue jeans were tight, and so long that they were turned up ten inches on the bottoms. They were held to his narrow middle by a broad, beautifully tooled leather belt with a fat and engraved silver buckle in which four turquoises were set. Pimples kept his hands at his sides as much as he could, but in spite of himself his fingers would move to his pitted cheeks until he became conscious of what he was doing and put his hands down again. He wrote to every company that advertised an acne cure, and he had been to many doctors, who knew that they could not cure it but who also knew that it would probably go away in a few years. They nevertheless gave Pimples prescriptions for salves and lotions, and one had put him on a diet of green vegetables.

His eyes were long and narrow and slanted like the eyes of a sleepy wolf, and now in the early morning they were almost sealed shut with mucus. Pimples was a prodigious sleeper. Left to his own devices, he could sleep nearly all the time. His whole system and his soul were a particularly violent battle-ground of adolescence. His concupiscence was constant, and when it was not directly and openly sexual it would take to channels of melancholy, of deep and tearful sentiment, or of a strong and musky religiosity. His mind and his emotions were like his face, constantly erupting, constantly raw and irritated. He had times of violent purity when he howled at his own depravity, and these were usually followed by a melancholy laziness that all but prostrated him, and he went from the depression into sleep. It was opiatic and left him drugged and dull for a long time.

He wore pierced white and brown saddle oxfords on bare feet this morning, and his ankles, where they showed below the turned-up jeans, were streaked with dirt. In his periods of depression Pimples was so prostrated that he did not bathe nor even eat very much. The felt hat crown notched so evenly was not really for beauty but served to keep his long light brown hair out of his eyes and to keep the grease out of it when he worked under a car. Now he stood stupidly watching Juan Chicoy put the tools in his box while his mind rolled in great flannel clouds of sleepiness, almost nauseating in their power.

Juan said, "Get the work light on the long cord connected. Come on, Pimples. Come on now, wake up!"

Pimples seemed to shake himself like a dog. "Can't seem to come out of it," he explained.

"Well, get the light out there and take my back board out. We've got to get going."

Pimples picked up the hand light, basketed for protection of the globe, and began unwinding the heavy rubber-guarded cable from around its handle. He plugged the cord into an outlet near the door and the hand light leaped into brilliance. Juan lifted his toolbox and stepped out of the door and looked at the darkened sky. A change had come in the air. A little wind was stirring the young leaves of the oaks and whisking among the geraniums and it was an uncertain, wet wind. Juan smelled it as he would smell a flower.

"By God, if it rains," he said, "that would be one too many."

To the east the tops of the mountains were just becoming visible in outline with the dawn. Pimples came out carrying the lighted hand lamp and unkinking the cable behind him on the ground. The light made the great trees stand out, and it was reflected on the yellow-green of the new little oak leaves. Pimples took his light to the bus and went back to the garage for the long board with casters on the bottom on which a man could lie and wheel himself about when he worked under a car. He flung the board down beside the bus.

"Well, it's like to rain," he said. "Take nearly every year in California it rains this season."

Juan said, "I'm not complaining about the season, but with this ring gear out and the passengers waiting, and the ground is pulpy with rain—"

"Makes good feed," said Pimples.

Juan stopped and looked around at him. His eyes crinkled with amusement. "Sure," he said, "it sure does."

Pimples looked shyly away.

The bus was lighted by the hand lamp now and it looked strange and helpless, for where the rear wheels should have been were two heavy sawhorses, and instead of resting on axles the rear of the bus rested on a four-by-four which extended from one horse to the other.

It was an old bus, a four-cylinder, low-compression engine with a special patented extra gear shift which gave it five speeds ahead instead of three, two below the average ratio, and two speeds in reverse. The ballooning sides of the bus, heavy and shining with aluminum paint, showed nevertheless the bumps and bends, the wracks and scratches, of a long and violent career. A home paint job on an old automobile somehow makes it look even more ancient and disreputable than it would if left in honorable decay.

Inside, the bus was rebuilt too. The seats which had once been woven of cane were now upholstered in red oilcloth, and while the job was neatly done, it was not professionally done. There was the slightly sour smell of oilcloth in the air and the frankly penetrating odor of oil and gasoline. It was an old, old bus, and it had seen many trips and many difficulties. Its oaken floorboards were scooped and polished by the feet of passengers. Its sides were bent and straightened. Its windows could not be opened, for the whole body was slightly racked out of shape. In the summer Juan removed the windows and in the winter put them back again.

The driver's seat was worn through to the springs, but in the worn place was a flowered chintz pillow which served the double purpose of protecting the driver and holding down the uncovered springs. Hanging from the top of the windshield were the penates: a baby's shoe—that's for protection, for the stumbling feet of a baby require the constant caution and aid of God; and a tiny boxing glove—and that's for power, the power of the fist on the driving forearm, the drive of the piston pushing its connecting rod, the power of person as responsible and proud individual. There hung also on the windshield a little plastic kewpie doll with a cerise and green ostrich-feather headdress and a provocative sarong. And this was for the pleasures of the flesh and of the eye, of the nose, of the ear. When the bus was in motion these hanging items spun and jerked and swayed in front of the driver's eye.

Where the windshield angled in the middle and the center of support went up, sitting on top of the dashboard was a small metal Virgin of Guadalupe painted in brilliant colors. Her rays were gold and her robe was blue and she stood on the new

moon, which was supported by cherubs. This was Juan
Chicoy's connection with eternity. It had little to do with religion as connected with the church and dogma, and much to
do with religion as memory and feeling. This dark Virgin was
his mother and the dim house where she, speaking Spanish
with a little brogue, had nursed him. For his mother had made
the Virgin of Guadalupe her own personal goddess. Out had
gone St. Patrick and St. Bridget and the ten thousand pale
virgins of the North, and into her had entered this dark one
who had blood in her veins and a close connection with
people.

His mother admired her Virgin, whose day is celebrated
with exploding skyrockets, and, of course, Juan Chicoy's
Mexican father didn't think of it one way or another. Skyrockets were by nature the way to celebrate Saints' Days.
Who could think otherwise? The rising, hissing tube was
obviously the spirit rising to Heaven, and the big, flashing bang
at the top was the dramatic entrance to the throne room of
Heaven. Juan Chicoy, while not a believer in an orthodox sense,
now he was fifty, would nevertheless have been uneasy driving
the bus without the Guadalupana to watch over him. His
religion was practical.

Below the Virgin was a kind of converted glove box, and
in it were a Smith & Wesson 45-caliber revolver, a roll of
bandage, a bottle of iodine, a vial of lavender smelling salts,
and an unopened pint of whisky. With this equipment Juan
felt fairly confident that he could meet most situations.

The front bumpers of the bus had once borne the inscription,
still barely readable, *"el Gran Poder de Jesus,"* "the great power
of Jesus." But that had been painted on by a former owner.
Now the simple word "Sweetheart" was boldly lettered on
front and rear bumpers. And the bus was known as "Sweetheart" to all who knew her. Now she was immobilized, her rear
wheels off, her end sticking up in the air and resting on a four-
by-four set between two sawhorses.

Juan Chicoy had the new ring and pinion gears and he was
rolling them carefully together. "Hold the light close," he said
to Pimples, and he turned the pinion in the ring all the way
around. "I remember once I put a new ring on an old pinion
and she went out right away."

"Busted tooth sure makes a noise," said Pimples. "It sounds

like it's coming through the floor at you. What do you suppose knocked that tooth out?"

Juan held the ring gear up sideways and in front of the light turned the pinion slowly, inspecting the fit of tooth against tooth as he went. "I don't know," he said. "There's lots nobody knows about metal and about engines too. Take Ford. He'll make a hundred cars and two or three of them will be no damn good. It's not just one thing that's bad, the whole car's bad. The springs and the motor and the water pump and the fan and the carburetor. It just breaks down little by little and there don't nobody know what makes them. And you'll take another car right off the line, you'd say it was just exactly the same as the others, but it's not. It's got something the others haven't got. It's got more power. It's almost like a guy with a lot of guts. It won't bust down no matter what you do."

"I had one of them," said Pimples. "Model A. I sold her. Bet she's still running. Had her three years and never spent a dime on her."

Juan laid his ring gear and pinion on the step of the bus and picked up the old ring from the ground. With his finger he traced the raw place where the tooth had broken out. "Metal's funny stuff," he said. "Sometimes it seems to get tired. You know, down in Mexico where I came from they used to have two or three butcher knives. They'd use one and stick the others in the ground. 'It rests the blade,' they said. I don't know if it's true, but I know those knives would take a shaving edge. I guess nobody knows about metal, even the people that make it. Let's get this pinion on the shaft. Here, hold the light back here."

Juan put his little platform behind the bus and he lay on it on his back and scooted himself under with his feet. "Hold the light a little more to the left. No, higher. There. Now shove me my toolbox, will you?"

Juan's hands worked busily and a little oil dropped down on his cheek. He rubbed it off with the back of his hand. "This is a mean job," he said.

Pimples peered underneath the bus at him. "Maybe I could hook the light over that nut," he said.

"Oh, you'd just have to move it in a minute," said Juan.

Pimples said, "I sure hope you get her going today. I'd like to sleep in my own bed tonight. You don't get no rest in a chair."

Juan chuckled. "Did you ever see madder people in your life when we had to come back after that tooth broke out? You'd think I did it on purpose. They were so mad they gave Alice hell about the pie. I guess they thought she made it. When people are traveling they don't like anything to interrupt them."

"Well, they got our beds," Pimples observed. "I don't see what they got to squawk about. You and me and Alice and Norma were the ones slept in chairs. And them Pritchards was the worst. I don't mean Mildred, the girl, but her old man and old lady. They figure they've been getting gypped someway. He tells me a hundred times how he's a president or something and he's going to make somebody suffer for this. Outrage, he says it was. And him and his wife had your bed. Where'd Mildred sleep?" Pimples' eyes glowed a little.

"On the davenport, I guess," said Juan. "Or maybe with her father and mother. That fellow from the trick company got Norma's room."

"I kinda liked that guy," Pimples said. "He didn't say nothing much. He said he'd just as soon set up. He didn't say what line he was in. But them Pritchards made up for it, all except Mildred. You know where they're going, Mr. Chicoy? They're going on a trip down to Mexico. Mildred's been studying Spanish in college. She's going to interpret for them."

Juan drove a key pin into the shaft and pounded it gently into place. He pulled himself from under the bus. "Let's get that rear-end assembly now."

Light was creeping up the sky and over the mountains. The colorless dawn of grays and blacks moved in so that white and blue things were silver and red and dark green things were black. The new leaves on the big oaks were black and white, and the mountain rims were sharp. Lumpish, heavy clouds that rolled in the sky like dumplings were beginning to take on a faint rose-pink color on their eastern edges.

Suddenly the lights in the lunchroom sprang on and the geranium border around the building leaped into being. Juan glanced toward the lights. "Alice is up," he said. "Won't be long till the coffee's ready. Come on, let's move the rear end in now."

The two men worked together well. Each understood what was to be done. Each did his piece. Pimples lay on his back too, tightening the housing nuts, and in the teamwork a good feeling came to him.

Juan strained a tight forearm against a nut and his wrench slipped and he took skin and flesh off his knuckle. The blood ran thick and black out of his greasy hand. He put the knuckle in his mouth and sucked it and made a line of grease around his mouth.

"Hurt it bad?" Pimples asked.

"No, it's good luck, I guess. You can't finish a job without blood. That's what my old man used to say." He sucked the blood again and already the flow was lessening.

The warmth and pinkness of the dawn sneaked in about them so that the electric light seemed to lose some of its brilliance.

"I wonder how many will come in on the Greyhound," Pimples asked idly. And then a strong thought came to him out of the good feeling from Mr. Chicoy. It was a thought so sharp that it almost hurt him. "Mr. Chicoy," he began uncertainly, and his tone was fawning, craven, begging.

Juan stopped turning the nut and waited for the request for a day off, for a raise, for something. There was going to be a request. That was inherent in the tone, and to Juan it was trouble. Trouble always started this way.

Pimples was silent. He couldn't get the words.

"What do you want?" Juan asked guardedly.

"Mr. Chicoy, could we fix it—I mean—could you fix it so you don't call me Pimples any more?"

Juan took his wrench from the nut and turned his head sideways. The two were lying on their backs, their faces toward each other. Juan saw the craters of old scars and the coming eruptions and one prime, tight, yellow-headed pustule about to burst on the cheek. As he looked, Juan's eyes softened. He knew. It came on him suddenly, and he wondered why he had not known before.

"What's your name?" he asked roughly.

"Ed," said Pimples. "Ed Carson, distant relative of Kit Carson. Before I got these in grammar school, why, they used to call me Kit." His voice was studied and calm, but his chest rose and fell heavily and the air whistled in his nostrils.

Juan looked away from him and back at the bulbous lump of the rear-end housing. "O.K.," he said, "let's get the jacks underneath." He rolled out from under the bus. "Get the oil in there now."

Pimples went quickly into the garage and brought out the pressure gun, trailing the air hose behind him. He turned the petcock and the compressed air hissed into the gun behind the oil. The gun clicked as he filled the housing with the oil until a little ran thickly out. He screwed in the plug.

Juan said, "Kit, wipe your hands and see if Alice has got any coffee ready, will you?"

Pimples went toward the lunchroom. Near the door where one of the great oaks stood there was a patch of near darkness. He stood there for a moment, holding his breath. He was shaking all over in a kind of a chill.

Chapter 3

W HEN the rim of the sun cleared the mountains to the east, Juan Chicoy stood up from the ground and brushed the dirt from the legs and seat of his overalls. The sun flashed on the windows of the lunchroom and lay warm on the green grass that edged the garage. It blazed on the poppies in the flat fields and on the great islands of blue lupines.

Juan Chicoy went to the entrance door of the bus. He reached in, turned the ignition key, and pushed down the starter with the heel of his hand. For a while the starter whined rustily, and then the engine caught and roared for a moment until Juan throttled it down. He pushed down the clutch with his hand, put the gear in compound low, and let up the clutch. The rear wheels turned slowly in the air and Juan went around to the rear to listen to the action of the gears, to try to hear any uneven matching of the assembly.

Pimples was washing his hands in a flat pan of gasoline in the garage. The sun warmed a brown leaf left by the past year and blown into a corner of the garage doorframe. After a while a little night-laden fly crawled heavily out from under the leaf and stood in the clear sun. Its wings were muddily iridescent and it was sluggish with night cold. The fly rubbed its wings with its legs and then it rubbed its legs together and then it rubbed its face with its forelegs while the sun, slanting under the great puffed clouds, warmed its juices. Suddenly the fly took off, circled twice, fluttered under the oaks and crashed against the screen door of the lunch room, fell on its back and buzzed against the ground, upside down for a second. Then it righted itself and flew up and took its position on the frame beside the lunchroom door.

Alice Chicoy, haggard from the night of sitting up, came to the door and looked out toward the bus. The screen door opened only a few inches, but the fly flung himself through the opening. Alice saw him come through and whacked at him with the dish towel she carried in her hand. The fly buzzed crazily for a moment and then settled under the edge of the counter. Alice watched the rear wheels of the bus idly turning in the air and then she went in back of the counter and turned off the steam valve of the coffee urn.

The brown fluid in the glass pipe on the side of the urn looked thin and pale. She ran her towel over the counter and in doing so noticed that the big white coconut cake in its transparent plastic cover was ragged on one edge with a "V" cut out of it. She took a knife from the silver tray, lifted the cover, trimmed the cake's edge, and put the crumbs in her mouth. And just before the cover went back into place the fly lunged under the edge and flung himself on the coconut filling. He clung under a slight overhang so that he was not visible from above, and he dug and struggled hungrily into the sweet filling. He had a high, huge mountain of cake and he was very happy.

Pimples came in, smelling of gasoline and grease, and he took his place on one of the round stools. "Well, we got that done," he said.

"You and who else?" Alice asked satirically.

"Well, of course, Mr. Chicoy done the expert work. I'd like to have a cup of coffee and a piece of cake."

"You been in that cake already, before I got up." She brushed her hair out of her eyes with one hand. "You can't cover up," she said.

"Well, charge it to me," said Pimples. "I'm paying for my feed, ain't I?"

"What do you want to eat all that sweet stuff for?" Alice said. "You're at the candy tray all day long. You don't get hardly any pay. All goes for sweet stuff. I bet that's what makes all them pimples. Why don't you lay off for a while?"

Pimples looked shyly down at his hands. The nails were rimmed with black where the gasoline had not reached. "It's rich in food energy," he said. "Fellow's going to work, he needs food energy. Take about three o'clock in the afternoon when you get a let-down. Why, you need something rich in food energy."

"It's rich in lead in the pants," Alice observed. "You need food energy about as much as I need a—" and she left it in the air. Alice was a very profane woman but she never said the words, she only led up to them. She drew a cup of coffee from the spout—a thick, flat-bottom cup with no saucer—spurted in some milk and slipped the cup across the counter.

Pimples, looking hazily at the Coca-Cola girl who swung provocatively over the juke box, put in four spoonfuls of sugar and stirred the coffee around and around with the spoon straight up.

"I like to have a piece of cake," he repeated patiently.

"Well, it's your funeral. You're going to have a can on you like a balloon."

Pimples looked at Alice's well-formed behind and then quickly away. Alice took the knife from behind the counter and cut a wedge of coconut cake. The cliff of cake toppled on the fly and pressed him down. Alice shoveled the cake onto a saucer and slid it along the counter. Pimples went at it with his coffee spoon.

"Those folks didn't get up yet?" he asked.

"No, but I heard them stirring around. One of them must have used up all the hot water. I haven't got a bit in the lunchroom."

"That must be Mildred," said Pimples.

"Huh?"

"The girl. Maybe she took a bath."

Alice looked at him levelly. "You get to your food energy and keep your mind where it belongs," she said sharply.

"I never said nothing. Hey, there's a fly in this cake!"

Alice stiffened. "You had a fly in your soup yesterday. I think you carry flies in your pocket."

"No, look here. He's still kicking."

Alice came near. "Kill him," she cried. "Squash him! You

want him to get loose?" She picked up a fork from behind the counter and mashed the fly and cake crumbs together and scraped the whole thing into the garbage can.

"How about my cake?" Pimples asked.

"You'll get another piece of cake. I don't know why you always get flies. Nobody else does."

"Just lucky, I guess," Pimples said softly.

"Huh?"

"I said I was—"

"I heard what you said." She was unrested and nervous. "You watch your mouth or you'll go out of here so fast you'll think you're on fire. I don't care if you are a mechanic. To me you're just a punk. A pimple-faced punk." Pimples had withered. His chin had settled lower and lower against his chest as her anger rose. And he didn't know that she was making him the depository of a number of things.

"I didn't say nothing," he said. "Can't a guy even make a joke?"

Alice had reached a point where she had either to go on into a crazy, hysterical rage that tore the living daylights out of herself and everyone else around her, or she had to begin to taper off quickly, for she could feel the uncontrollable pressure rising in her chest and throat. In a second she appraised the situation. Things were tight. The bus had to get out. Juan had not rested either. The people who were using the beds would hear her rage and come out and Juan might hit her. He had once. Not hard, but accurately, and timed so perfectly that she imagined he had nearly killed her. And then the black fear that was always on the edge of her mind—Juan might leave her. He had left other women. How many she didn't know because he'd never spoken of it, but a man of his attractiveness must have left other women. All of this happened in a split second. Alice decided on no rage. She forced the pressure down in her chest. Woodenly she raised the plastic cake cover and cut an oversized wedge and put it on a saucer and she carried this down the counter and set it in front of Pimples.

"Everybody's nervous," she said.

Pimples looked up from his fingernails. He saw how the little lines of age were sneaking down her neck, and he noticed the thickness of her upper eyelids. He saw that her hands had lost the tightness of skin of young girls. He was very sorry for her.

Unblessed with beauty as he was, he thought that youth was the only thing in the world worth having and that one who had lost youth was already dead. He had won a great victory this morning, and now when he saw the weakness and indecision in Alice he pressed for a second victory.

"Mr. Chicoy says he ain't going to call me Pimples no more," he said.

"Why not?"

"Well, I asked him not. My name's Edward. They used to call me Kit in school on account my last name's Carson."

"Is Juan calling you Kit?"

"Uh-huh."

Alice didn't really understand what it was about, and behind her in the bedroom there was movement, footsteps between the rugs and a little low talking. Now that she was aware of the strangers, Pimples became closer to her because he was not quite a stranger. "I'll see how it goes," she said.

The sun had been shining in through the front windows and the door, making five bright splashes on the wall, illuminating the grapenuts packages and the pyramids of oranges behind the counter. And now the bright squares dimmed and went out. There was a roll of thunder, and without warning the rain began. It whisked down on the roof.

Pimples went to the door and looked out. The rain sheeted down, obscuring the country, splashing high on the cement road. There was a steely look to the wet light. Pimples saw Juan Chicoy inside the bus for shelter. The back wheels were still turning around slowly. As he watched, Juan leaped to the ground and made a run for the lunchroom. Pimples held the door open for him and he bolted through, but even in the little run his overalls were dark with water and his shoes squidged sloppily on the floor.

"God Almighty," he said, "that's a real cloudburst."

The gray wall of water obscured the hills and there was a dark, metallic light with it. The heads of the lupines bent down, heavy with water. The petals of the poppies were beaten off and lay on the ground like gold coins. The already wet ground could absorb no more water, and little rivulets started immediately for the low places. The cloudburst roared on the roof of the lunchroom at Rebel Corners.

Juan Chicoy had taken one of the tables by the lunchroom

window and he drank well-creamed coffee and chewed a dough-nut and looked out at the downpour. Norma came in and began to wash the few dishes on the stainless steel sink behind the counter.

"Bring me another cup of coffee, will you?" Juan asked.

She came listlessly around the end of the counter. The cup was too full. A little stream of coffee dripped off the bottom of it. Juan pulled out a paper napkin and folded it as a blotter for the wet cup.

"Didn't get much rest, did you?" he asked.

Norma was drawn, and her dress was wrinkled. You could see now that she would be an old-looking woman long before she was old. Her skin was muddy and her thin hands were splotched. Many, many things gave Norma the hives.

"Didn't get any sleep at all," she said. "I tried the floor but I couldn't sleep."

"Well, we'll see it doesn't happen again," said Juan. "I should have got a car to take them into San Ysidro."

"Giving them our beds!" Alice said derisively. "Now, where did you get that idea? Where else do you suppose they could have got the owners' beds? They don't have to work today. They could just as well of sat up."

"Slipped up on me, I guess," said Juan.

"You don't care if your wife sleeps in a chair," Alice said. "You'd give away her bed any time." Again Alice could feel rage rising in her and it frightened her. She didn't want it to rise. She knew it would spoil things, and she was afraid of it, but there it was, rising and boiling in her.

A sheet of rain whisked over the roof like a heavy broom and left silence as it moved on, and almost immediately another flat of rain took its place. The drip and gurgle of water from the roof eaves and from the drains was loud again. Juan had been looking reflectively at the floor, a small smile tightening his mouth against the white band of the scar on his lip. And this was another thing Alice was frightened of. He had set her out to observe her. She knew that. All relations and all situations to Alice were person-to-person things in which she and the other were huge and all others were removed from the world. There was no shading. When she talked to Juan, there were only the two of them. When she picked at Norma, the whole world disappeared, leaving only Norma and her in a gray universe of cloud.

But Juan, now, he could shut everything out and look at each thing in relation to the other. Things of various sizes and importance. He could see and judge and consider and enjoy. Juan could enjoy people. Alice could only love, like, dislike, and hate. She saw and felt no shading whatever.

Now she tucked her loosening hair back. Once a month she used a rinse on her hair which was guaranteed to give it the mysterious and glamorous glints that capture and keep men in slavery. Juan's eyes were distant and amused. This was a matter of horror to Alice. She knew he was seeing her, not as an angry woman who darkened the world, but as one of thousands of angry women to be studied, inspected, and, yes, even enjoyed. This was the cold, lonely horror to her. Juan blotted out the universe to her and she sensed that she blotted out nothing to him. He could see not only around her but through her to something else. The remembered terror of the one time he had hit her lay not in the blow—she had been hit before, and far from hating it had taken excitement and exuberance from it—but Juan had hit her as he would a bug. He hadn't cared about it much. He hadn't even been very angry, just irritated. And he had hit a noisy thing to shut it up. Alice had only been trying to attract his attention in one of the few ways she knew. She was trying to do the same thing now, and she knew from the changed focus in his eye that he had slipped away from her.

"I try to make a nice little home for us; nice, and with a carpet and a velveteen suite, and you got to give it away to strangers." Her voice was losing its certainty. "And you let your own wife sit up in a chair all night."

Juan looked up slowly. "Norma," he said, "bring me another cup of coffee, will you? Plenty of cream."

Alice braced herself for the rage she knew was coming, and then Juan looked slowly toward her. His dark eyes were amused and warm, the focus changed again, and he was looking at her and she knew that he saw her.

"It didn't hurt you any," he said. "Make you appreciate the bed tonight."

Her breath caught. A hot wave flooded over her. Rage was

transmuted to hot desire. She smiled at him vacantly and licked her lips. "You bastard," she said very softly. And she took a huge, shuddering sigh of air. "Want some eggs?" she asked.

"Yeah. Two in the water, about four minutes."

"I know how you like them," she said. "Bacon on the side?"

"No. A piece of toast and a couple of doughnuts."

Alice went behind the counter. "I wish they'd come out of there," she said. "I'd like to use my own bathroom."

"They're stirring around," said Juan. "They'll be out in a little."

And they were stirring. There were footsteps in the bedroom. A door inside opened and a woman's voice said sharply, "Well, I think you could knock!" And a man replied, "I'm sorry, ma'am. The only other way was to go out the window."

Another man's voice with a brittle singsong of authority said, "Always a good idea to knock, my friend. Hurt your foot?"

"Yes."

The door at the end of the counter opened and a small man came out into the lunchroom. He was dressed in a double-breasted suit; his shirt was of that light brown color worn by traveling men and known as a thousand-miler because it does not show dirt. His suit was a neutral pepper-and-salt for the same reason, and he wore a knitted dark green tie. His face was sharp, like a puppy's face, and his eyes were bright and questioning, like a puppy's eyes. A small carefully trimmed mustache rode his upper lip like a caterpillar, and when he talked it seemed to hump its back. His teeth were white and even except for the two front uppers, and these were glittering gold. He had a brushed look about him, as though he had cleaned the lint from his suit with his hairbrush; and his shirt had the strained appearance that comes from washing the collar in the hand basin and patting it flat on the dresser top to dry. There was a kind of shy confidence in his manner and a wincing quality in his face, as though he protected himself from insult with studied techniques.

"Morning, folks," he said. "I just wondered where you all slept. And I'll bet you sat up all night."

"Well, we did," Alice said sourly.

"It's all right," said Juan. "We'll get to bed early tonight."

"Get the bus fixed? Think we'll make it in this rain?"

"Oh, sure," said Juan.

The man limped around the end of the counter and sat painfully down at one of the little tables. Norma brought a glass of water and a handful of silver wrapped in a paper napkin.

"Eggs?"

"Fried, with their eyes open, crisp bacon, and buttered toast. Buttered—get it? Hardest thing in the world is to get buttered toast. Now you butter that toast, plenty of butter, and let it melt in so there's no yellow lumps showing and you'll get yourself a nice tip." He lifted his foot shod in a perforated and decorated brown oxford and looked at it and grunted with pain.

"Sprain your ankle?" Juan asked.

The door at the end of the counter opened and a medium-sized man came out. He looked like Truman and like the vice-presidents of companies and like certified public accountants. His glasses were squared off at the corners. His suit was gray and correct, and there was a little gray in his face too. He was a businessman, dressed like one, looked like one. In his lapel buttonhole there was a lodge pin so tiny that from four feet away you couldn't see what it was at all. His vest was unbuttoned one notch at the bottom. Indeed, this bottom button was not intended to be buttoned. A fine gold watch and key chain crossed this vest and ducked in and out of a buttonhole on the way.

He said, "Mrs. Prichard will have scrambled eggs, moist if they're fresh, toast and marmalade. And Miss Pritchard only wants orange juice and coffee. I'll have grapenuts and cream, eggs turned over and well done—don't let the yolk be running—dry toast and Boston coffee—that's half milk. You can bring it all in on a tray."

Alice looked up with fury. "You better come out here," she said. "We haven't got tray service."

Mr. Pritchard looked at her coldly. "We got held up here," he said. "I've already lost one day of my vacation. It isn't my fault that the bus broke down. Now the least you can do is to bring that breakfast in. My wife isn't feeling so good. I'm not used to sitting on a stool and Mrs. Pritchard isn't either."

Alice lowered her head like an angry milk-cow. "Look, I want to go to the toilet and wash my face and you're holding up my bathroom."

Mr. Pritchard touched his glasses nervously. "Oh, I see." He turned his head toward Juan and the light reflected from his glasses so that there were two mirrors with no eyes behind them. His hand whipped his watch chain out of his vest pocket. He opened a little gold nail file and ran the point quickly under each nail. He looked about and a little shudder of uncertainty came over him. Mr. Pritchard was a businessman, president of a medium-sized corporation. He was never alone. His business was conducted by groups of men who worked alike, thought alike, and even looked alike. His lunches were with men like himself who joined together in clubs so that no foreign element or idea could enter. His religious life was again his lodge and his church, both of which were screened and protected. One night a week he played poker with men so exactly like himself that the game was fairly even, and from this fact his group was convinced that they were very fine poker players. Wherever he went he was not one man but a unit in a corporation, a unit in a club, in a lodge, in a church, in a political party. His thoughts and ideas were never subjected to criticism since he willingly associated only with people like himself. He read a newspaper written by and for his group. The books that came into his house were chosen by a committee which deleted material that might irritate him. He hated foreign countries and foreigners because it was difficult to find his counterpart in them. He did not want to stand out from his group. He would like to have risen to the top of it and be admired by it; but it would not occur to him to leave it. At occasional stags where naked girls danced on the tables and sat in great glasses of wine, Mr. Pritchard howled with laughter and drank the wine, but five hundred Mr. Pritchards were there with him.

And now, at the end of Alice's ugly statement about a toilet, he looked about the lunchroom and found that he was alone. There were no other Mr. Pritchards here. For a moment his glance rested on the little man in the business suit, but there was something queer about him. True, there was some kind of a pin in his buttonhole, a little blue enamel bar with white stars on it, but it was no club Mr. Pritchard recognized. He found himself hating these people and hating even his vacation. He wanted to go back to the bedroom and close the door, but here was this stout woman who wanted to go to the toilet. Mr. Pritchard cleaned his nails very rapidly with the gold nail file on his watch chain.

At bottom, and originally, Mr. Pritchard was not like this. He

had once voted for Eugene Debs, but that had been a long time
ago. It was just that the people in his group watched one another. Any variation from a code of conduct was first noted,
then discussed. A man who varied was not a sound man, and if
he persisted no one would do business with him. Protective
coloring was truly protective. But there was no double life in
Mr. Pritchard. He had given up his freedom and then had forgotten what it was like. He thought of it now as youthful folly.
He put his vote for Eugene Debs alongside his visit to a parlor
house when he was twenty. Both were things to be expected of
growing boys. He even occasionally mentioned at a club
luncheon his vote for Debs, to prove that he had been a spirited
young man and that such things were, like a kid's acne, a part
of the process of adolescence. But although he excused and
even enjoyed his prank in voting for Debs, he was definitely
worried about the activities of his daughter Mildred.

She was playing around with dangerous companions in her
college, professors and certain people considered Red. Before
the war she had picketed a scrap-iron ship bound for Japan, and
she had gathered money for medical supplies for what Mr. Pritchard called the Reds in the Spanish war. He did not discuss
these things with Mildred. She didn't want to talk it out with
him. And he had a strong feeling that if everyone was quiet and
controlled she would get over it. A husband and a baby would
resolve Mildred's political uneasiness. She would then, he said,
find her true values.

Mr. Pritchard's visit to the parlor house he did not remember
very well. He had been twenty and drunk, and afterward he had
had a withering sense of desecration and sorrow. He did remember the subsequent two weeks when he had waited in terror for
symptoms to develop. He had even planned to kill himself if
they did; to kill himself and make it look like an accident.

Now he was nervous. He was on a vacation he didn't really
want to take. He was going to Mexico which, in spite of the
posters, he considered a country not only dirty but dangerously
radical. They had expropriated the oil; in other words, stolen
private property. And how was that different from Russia?
Russia, to Mr. Pritchard, took the place of the medieval devil as
the source of all cunning and evil and terror. He was nervous this
morning because he hadn't slept either. He liked his own bed.
It took him a week to get used to a bed, and here he was in for

three weeks of a different bed practically every night, and God knew how some of them would be populated. He was tired and his skin felt grainy. The water was hard here so that when he shaved he knew he would have a ring of ingrown hairs around his neck within three days.

He took a handkerchief from his breast pocket, removed his glasses and polished them. "I'll tell my wife and daughter," he said. "We didn't know we were discommoding you so."

Norma liked that word and she said it over under her breath. "Discommode—I wouldn't want to discommode you, Mr. Gable, but I think you should know . . ."

Mr. Pritchard had gone back into the bedroom. His voice was audible, explaining the situation, and women's voices were questioning.

The man with the mustache got up from his chair and limped painfully to the counter, groaning under his breath.

He brought the sugar bowl back with him and sank, with grimaces, back into his chair.

"I would have got that for you," Norma said with concern.

He smiled at her. "I wouldn't want to trouble you," he explained bravely.

"It wouldn't discommode me none," said Norma.

Juan put down his coffee cup.

Pimples said, "I'd like to have a piece of that coconut cake."

Alice absently cut him a piece and slid the saucer down the counter and made a note on a pad.

"I guess there ain't never one on the house," said Pimples.

"I figure there's plenty on the house the house don't know about," Alice replied.

"Looks like a bad sprain you've got there," Juan observed to the little man.

"Crushed," he said, "toes crushed. Here, I'll show you."

Mr. Pritchard came out of the bedroom and took a seat at the remaining table.

The little man unlaced his oxford and took it off. He slipped his sock off and laid it carefully in the oxford. His foot was bandaged from the instep to the ends of the toes, and the bandage was spotted and soaked with bright red blood.

"You don't need to show us," Alice said quickly. Blood made her faint.

"I ought to change the bandage anyway," said the little man, and he unwound the gauze and exposed the foot. The big toe and the two next to it were horribly crushed, the nails blackened and the ends of the toes tattered and bloody and raw.

Juan had arisen. Pimples came close. Even Norma could not stay away.

"My God, that's an awful smash," Juan said. "Let me get some water and wash it. You ought to have some kind of salve. You'll get an infection. You might lose that foot."

Pimples whistled shrilly between his teeth to indicate interest and a kind of enthusiasm for the quality of the hurt. The little man was looking into Juan's face, his eyes shining with pleasure and anticipation.

"You think it's bad?" he demanded.

"You're damn right, it's bad," said Juan.

"You think I should get a doctor?"

"Well, I would if it was me."

The little man chuckled with delight. "That's all I wanted to hear," he said. He ran his thumbnail down his instep, and the top of his foot lifted off—the skin, the blood, the mashed toes —and underneath there was his foot whole and unhurt and his toes untouched. He put back his head and laughed with glee.

"Good, isn't it? Plastic. New product."

Mr Pritchard had come close, a look of disgust on his face.

"It's the 'Little Wonder Artificial Sore Foot,'" the man said. He pulled a flat box from his side pocket and handed it to Juan. "You've been so nice to me, I want you to have one. Compliments of Ernest Horton representing the Little Wonder Company." His voice raced with his enthusiasm. "It comes in three sizes—one, two, or three crushed toes. This one I'm giving you is the three-toe number, just like the one you just saw. It's got bandage and a bottle of artificial blood to keep the bandage looking terrible. Instructions inside. You've got to soften it in warm water the first time you put it on. Then it fits like skin and nobody can tell. You can have a barrel of fun with it."

Mr. Pritchard leaned forward. Way in the back of his mind he could see himself taking off his socks at a board meeting. He could do it right after he got back from Mexico, tell some story about bandits first.

"What do you get for them?" he asked.

"Dollar and a half, but I hardly ever sell for retail," Ernest Horton said. "The trade snaps them up as fast as I can get them. I sold forty gross to the trade in two weeks."

"No?" said Mr. Pritchard. His eyes were wide with appreciation.

"Show you my order book if you don't believe it. It's the fastest-selling novelty I've ever handled. Little Wonder is cleaning up with it."

"What is the mark-up?" Mr. Pritchard demanded.

"Well, I wouldn't like to say unless you're in the trade. Business ethics, you know."

Mr. Pritchard nodded. "Well, I'd like to try one at the retail price," he said.

"Get you one right after I eat. You got that buttered toast?" he asked Norma.

"Coming up," said Norma, and she went guiltily behind the counter and switched on the toaster.

"You see, it's the psychology that sells it," Ernest said exultantly. "We've stocked artificial cut fingers for years and they moved slow, but this—it's the psychology of taking off your shoe and sock. Nobody ever thinks you'd go to the trouble of doing that. The fellow that figured that out got himself a very nice fee."

"I guess you're making a little something out of it yourself," said Mr. Pritchard with admiration. He was feeling much better now.

"I do all right," said Ernest. "I got one or two other little things that might interest you in my sample case. Not for sale except to the trade, but I'll demonstrate them. It might give you a laugh."

"I'd like to take half a dozen of the sore feet," said Mr. Pritchard.

"All the three toes?"

Mr. Pritchard considered. He wanted them for gifts, but he didn't want competition. Charlie Johnson could sell the tricks better than Mr. Pritchard could. Charlie was a natural comic.

"Suppose you let me have one three-toe and three two-toe and two one-toe," he said. "That'd be about right for me, I guess."

The quality of the rain was changing. It came with great, gusty, drenching downpours and with short, drippy intervals between. Juan sat with his coffee by the window. Half a brown doughnut lay in the saucer.

"I think she's going to let up a little," said Juan. "I'd like to turn over that rear end some more before we start."

"I'd like to have a piece of that coconut cake," said Pimples.

"No you don't," Alice said. "I've got to keep a little cake for customers."

"Well, I'm a customer, ain't I?"

"I don't know if we'll get deliveries from San Ysidro today," said Alice. "I've got to keep a little cake on hand."

At the very end of the counter there was a candy tray arranged like steps, with wrapped and packaged candy bars in it. Pimples got up from his stool and stood in front of the display. He considered the bright little packages a long time before he made his selections. Finally he picked out three bars and put them in his pocket. "One Baby Ruth, one Love Nest, and one Coconut Sweetheart," he said.

"Coconut Sweethearts are a dime. They got nuts," said Alice.

"I know," said Pimples.

Alice picked up her pad from behind the counter. "You're one jump ahead of your pay now," she said.

Chapter 4

THE moment the Pritchards came out of the bedroom Norma said quickly, "I got to brush my hair and clean up a little bit." And she bolted for the door. Alice was right behind her.

"After me in the bathroom," Alice said coldly. Norma went across the bedroom of Mr. and Mrs. Chicoy and into her own bedroom. She closed the door behind her and, as there was no key, she snapped the little catch beside the lock to secure her privacy. Her narrow iron Army cot was unmade, and Ernest Horton's big sample case stood against the wall.

It was a very narrow room. A dresser with a bowl and pitcher stood against one wall, a silken pillow top, fringed and shiny, was tacked up over the dresser. It was pink and had a picture of crossed cannons in front of a bunch of red roses. And printed on the pillow top was a poem called "A Soldier's Prayer to His Mother."

> Midst shot and shell I think of you, Mother dear
> I hope your prayers will keep me clear
> And when the war is o'er and won,
> I will come back to you, my Number One.

Norma looked quickly at the window, murky with rainy light, and then she reached inside the neck of her dress and turned back the material. On a safety pin, fastened to the turned edge, was a small key. Norma unpinned it. She pulled her suitcase from under the dresser, unlocked and opened it. A shiny picture of Clark Gable in a silver frame lay on top, and it was signed "With Best Regards—Clark Gable." She had bought the picture and frame and signature in a gift shop in San Ysidro.

She ran her hand quickly to the bottom of the suitcase. Her fingers came on a little square ring box. She pulled it out and jerked it open, saw that the rings were there, and shoved the box back to the bottom of the suitcase. She closed and locked the case, pushed it under the dresser, and pinned the key back inside her dress. She opened the dresser drawer, lifted out a brush and comb, and went to the window. On the wall beside the red-and-green flowered cretonne drapes there was a framed mirror. Norma stood in front of it and looked at herself.

A lead-colored light came through the window and fell on her face. She widened her eyes with intensity and then she smiled, showing all her teeth, smiled vivaciously. She stood on her toes a little and waved to an immense crowd and smiled again. She ran the comb through her thin hair and tugged as the teeth caught in the marceled ends. She got a pencil from the dresser and worked the dull point through her pale eyebrows, accentuating the curve in the middle so that her face took on a surprised look. Then she began to brush her hair, ten strokes on one side and ten on the other. And while she brushed, she raised and flexed the muscles of one leg and then the other to develop the calves. It was a routine recommended by a picture star who had never willingly taken any exercise of any kind but who had beautiful legs.

Norma glanced quickly at the window as the light grew still dimmer. She would have hated to be observed in the grotesque dance. Norma was even more submerged than an iceberg. Only the tiniest part of Norma showed above the surface. For the greatest and best and most beautiful part of Norma lay behind her eyes, sealed and protected.

The doorknob of her bedroom turned and then there was pressure against the door. Norma stiffened and stood rigid. Only one hand moved, and it frantically rubbed at her eyebrows and succeeded in making gray smudges on her forehead. And now there came a knocking at the bedroom door. A light, courteous knocking. She put her brush on the dresser, smoothed down her dress, and went to the door. She pushed the catch and opened the door a crack. The face of Ernest Horton was looking in at her. His tight, hairy mustache arched over his mouth.

Norma still held the door open only a crack.

"You folks have been so nice and all," he went on. "I don't want to be any more nuisance than I have to."

Norma slowly relaxed, but she was still breathing a little hard. She opened the door and stepped back. Ernest, with a smile of embarrassment, came into the room. He went to the bed.

"I should have made this bed," he said, and he drew the sheet and blanket up and began to pat the wrinkles out.

"No, I'll do that," said Norma.

"You didn't even wait for your tip I promised you," said Ernest. "But I've got it for you." He made the bed neatly, as though he had done it many times before.

"I could have done that just as well," said Norma.

"Well, it's done now," he said. He went to his big sample case. "Mind if I open this? I want to get some stuff out."

"Go ahead," said Norma. Her eyes filled with interest.

He laid the big sample case on her bed and snapped the catch and threw back the lid. There were wonderful things in the case. There were cardboard tubes and handkerchiefs that changed color. There were exploding cigars and stinkbombs. There were voice-throwers and horns and paper hats for parties and pennants and funny buttons. There were silken pillows like the one on the wall. Ernest was extracting six of the artificial sore feet in their flat packages, and Norma had moved close to look into the wonderful sample case. Her eyes had been caught by a series of photographs of picture stars. They were not like any she had ever seen. The pictures were pressed and molded into thick sheets of sheer plastic at least a quarter of an inch through. And there was another curious thing about them. The pictures did not look flat. By some trick of bending, or possibly of refracted light, the faces were rounded and had depth. They seemed to be three-dimensional, and the frames were eight by ten inches in size.

On top was a lifelike, smiling picture of James Stewart, and projecting from under that was a second picture of which she could only see the hair and a part of the forehead, but she knew that hair and that forehead. Her lips parted and a shine came into her eyes. Slowly her hand moved into the case and lifted James Stewart aside. And there he was, Clark Gable, looking round and full. It was a serious, intense pose, the chin out, the eyes level and intent. It was such a picture as she had never seen. She sighed deeply and tried to control her breath so that it could not be heard. She lifted the picture out and stared into the eyes, and her own were wide and hypnotized.

Ernest watched her and saw her interest. "Isn't that a knock-out?" he said. "It's a new idea. Notice how it looks round, almost like a statue?"

Norma nodded, speechless.

"I make a prophecy," Ernest said. "I go down the line and lay my word on it. That little number is going to wipe every other kind of pictures right off the map. It's acid-proof, moisture-proof, lasts forever, won't ever turn brown. It's molded and baked right inside the frame. It'll last forever."

Norma's eyes never left the picture. Ernest reached for the picture and her fingers tightened on it like claws.

"How much?" Her voice came out a throaty, rasping growl.

"It's just a sample," said Ernest. "It's something to show to the trade. It's not for sale. You order them."

"How much?" Her fingers were white with pressure. Ernest looked at her closely. He saw her face intent and set, jaw muscles rigid and nostrils flaring a little with controlled breathing.

Ernest said, "They bring two bucks retail, but I said I was going to give you a nice tip. Would you rather have that than a nice tip?"

Norma's voice was hoarse. "Yes."

"Well, then, you can have it."

The whiteness went slowly out of her fingers. There was a light of glory in her eyes. She licked her lips. "Thanks," she said. "Oh, thanks, mister!" She turned the face of the picture toward her and pressed it against her. The plastic was not cold, like glass, but warm and soft-feeling.

"I guess I can get along with only one sample," Ernest said. "See, I'm swinging south. I won't go back to the head office for six weeks. I figured to spend two weeks in L. A. That's a great place for novelties."

Norma carried the picture to her dresser and opened the drawer and shoved the picture down under a pile of clothes and closed the drawer. "I suppose you'll get to Hollywood," she said.

"Oh, sure. That's even better than L. A. for novelties. Then, it's kind of like my vacation too. I've got a lot of friends there. I have my vacation and get around and see things and I see the trade too. Kills two birds. I don't lose any time. I got an Army friend works in a studio there. I always run around some with him. Last time we had a party it started out in the Melrose Grotto. That's over on Melrose, right next to RKO. And that really was a party! I wouldn't really like to tell you what we did do, but I never had so much fun in my life. And then my friend, of course, had to go back to work at the studio."

Norma had become as intent as a setter pup watching a bug. "You're friend works in a studio?" she asked casually. "Which one?"

"Metro-Goldwyn-Mayer," said Ernest. He was repacking his sample case and not looking up at her. He did not hear the rasp of breath in her throat or the unnatural tone that came into her voice.

"You go into the studio lots?"

"Yeah. Willie gets me a pass. I go and watch them shoot sometimes. Willie's a carpenter. Worked there before the war and now he's back there. I soldiered with him. Awful nice fellow. And what a guy at parties! He knows more dames, he's got more phone numbers than you ever saw. A big thick black book full of phone numbers. Even he can't remember who half the dames are he's got the phone numbers of."

Ernest was warming to his subject. He sat down on the little straight chair beside the wall. He chuckled. "Willie was stationed in Santa Ana first of the war, before I even knew him. Well, the officers got to know about his black book and they'd take Willie into Hollywood and he'd get dames for them and then Willie got a pass when he wanted it. He was making out good when they shipped his outfit out."

Norma's eyes took on a quick look of annoyance during this recital. Her fingers picked at her apron. Her voice became high and then low. "I wonder if it would discommode you to do a favor for me?"

"Sure," said Ernest. "What do you want?"

"Well, if I was to give you a letter and you was—er—were on the MGM lot and you happened to see Mr. Gable, why I wonder if you'd give it to him?"

"Who's Mr. Gable?"

"Mr. Clark Gable," said Norma sternly.

"Oh, him. You know him?"

"Yes," said Norma frostily, "I'm—I'm his cousin."

"Oh, I see. Well, sure I will. But maybe I don't go. Why don't you put it in the mail?"

Norma's eyes narrowed. "He don't get his mail," she said mysteriously. "There's a girl, a secretary like, that just takes it and burns it up."

"No!" said Ernest. "What for?"

Norma stopped to consider this. "They just don't want him to see it."

"Not even from his own relatives?"

"Not even from his cousin," said Norma.

"Did he tell you that?"

"Yes." Her eyes were wide and blank. "Yes. Course I'll go there pretty soon," she said. "I've had offers and once I was just about to go and my cousin—Mr. Gable, that is—he said, 'No, you've got to get experience,' he said. 'You're young. You're not in any hurry.' So I'm getting experience. You learn a lot about people in a lunchroom. I study them all the time."

Ernest looked at her a little skeptically. He knew the fantastic stories about waitresses who became dramatic stars overnight, but Norma didn't have the bubs for it, he thought, nor the legs. Norma's legs were like sticks. But, then, he knew about two or three picture stars who were so plain without make-up that no one would recognize them off the screen. He'd read about them. And Norma, even if she didn't look it—well, they could pad her out, and if her cousin was Clark Gable, why, that was an "in" you couldn't beat. That was the breaks.

"Well, I hadn't thought much about asking Willie to get me a pass this time," he said. "I've been out there quite a few times but—well, if you want me to I'll go right in, find him, and give him your letter. What do you suppose they throw away his mail for?"

"They just want to work him to death and then throw him away like an old shoe," said Norma passionately. Wave after wave of emotion swept over her. She was in an ecstasy, and at the the same time panic was crowding up on her. Norma was not a liar. She had never done anything like this before. She was going out on a long teetering plank and she knew it. One question, one bit of knowledge on Ernest's part, would throw her off and hurtle her into a chasm, and yet she couldn't stop.

"He's a great man," she said, "a great gentleman. He don't like the parts they make him do because he isn't like that. Even Rhett Butler—he didn't like to play that because he's not a rat and he don't like to play rat parts."

Ernest had lowered his eyes and was studying Norma through his eyelashes. And Ernest was beginning to understand. The key to it was creeping into his brain. Norma was as pretty now as she was ever likely to be. There was dignity in her face, courage, and a truly great flow of love. There were only two things for Ernest to do—to laugh at her or play along. If there'd been any other person in the room—another man, for instance—he probably would have laughed to protect himself from the other person's scorn, and he would have been ashamed and more boisterous because he could see that it was a powerful, pure, and overwhelming thing shining in this girl. This was the thing that kept the neophytes lying through the nights on the stone floors in front of the altars. This was an outpouring of an attar of love, of a naked intensity that Ernest had never seen before in anyone.

"I'll take the letter," he said. "I'll tell him it's from his cousin."

A look of fright came on Norma's face. "No," she said, "I'd rather surprise him. Just tell him it's from a friend. Don't tell him a single other thing."

"When do you think you'll be going down there to take a job?" Ernest asked.

"Well, Mr. Gable says I ought to wait another year. He says I'm young and need experience studying people. I get pretty tired of it sometimes, though. Sometimes I wish I was there in my own house with them—those—big, thick curtains and a long couch, like, and I'd see all my friends—Bette Davis and Ingrid Bergman and Joan Fontaine, because I don't mess around with that other kind that's always getting divorced and things like that. We just sit around and talk about serious things, and we study all the time because that's how you get ahead and be a great actress. And there's lots that treat their fans mean; won't sign autographs and things like that, but not us! Not our kind, I mean. We even have girls right off the streets sometimes in for a cup of tea and talk and just like they were us because we know we owe everything we got to the loyalty of our fans." She was quaking inside with fear and she couldn't stop. She was getting far out on the plank and she couldn't stop and it was about to throw her.

Ernest said, "I didn't understand at first. You've already been in pictures. Are you a star already?"

"Yes," said Norma. "But you wouldn't know me by the name I'm using here. I have another name I use in Hollywood."

"What it is?"

"I couldn't tell," said Norma. "You're the only person anywhere around here that knows anything about me. Now, you won't tell, will you?"

Ernest was shaken. "No," he said, "I won't tell if you don't want me to."

"Keep my secret inviolate," said Norma.

"Sure," said Ernest. "Just give me the letter and I'll see he gets it."

"You'll see who gets what?" said Alice from the doorway. "What are you two doing alone in a bedroom?" Her eyes roved suspiciously about for evidence, skimmed over the sample case on the bed, stopped on the pillow, inspected the spread, and then moved to Norma. Alice's eyes traveled up her feet and legs, lingered a moment on her skirt, hesitated on her waist, and then settled on her flaming face.

Norma was almost sick with embarrassment. Her cheeks were splotched with blood. Alice put her hands on her hips.

Ernest said placatingly, "I was just getting my sample case out of the way and she asked me to take a note to a cousin of hers in L. A."

"She's got no cousin in L. A."

"Yes, she has too," Ernest said angrily, "and I know her cousin."

And now the rage that had been trying to get out of Alice all morning burst from her. "You listen to me," she shouted. "I won't have you drummers diddling my hired girls."

"Nobody's touched her," Ernest said. "Nobody laid a hand on her."

"No? Well, then, what'cha doing in her bedroom? Take a look at her face." The hysteria boiled over in Alice. A heavy, throaty, screaming voice came from her throat. Her hair fell about her face and her eyes rolled and watered and her lips became cruel and tight, as a fighter's do when he is slugging a half-conscious opponent. "I won't have it. You think I want her knocked up? You think I want bastards all over the place? We give you our beds and our rooms!"

"I tell you nothing happened!" Ernest shouted at her. He was overwhelmed with hopelessness in the face of this craziness. His denials sounded in his ears almost like admissions. He didn't understand why she was doing it, and the injustice made him sick to his stomach and rage was rising in him too.

Norma's mouth was open and she was catching the microbe of hysteria. Whinnying cries came from her with every panting breath. Her hands fought in front of her as though they were trying to destroy each other.

Alice advanced on Norma and her right fist was doubled, not like a woman's fist, but with the fingers folded tightly and the knuckles up and outstuck, the thumb laid close against the first joints. Her words were thick and moist. "Get out of here! Get out of the whole place! Get out in the rain!" Alice descended on Norma and Norma backed away and a terrified scream came from her mouth.

There were quick steps in the doorway and Juan said sharply, "Alice!"

She stopped. Her mouth sagged open and her eyes grew afraid. Juan came slowly into the room. His thumbs were hooked in his overalls pockets. He moved toward her as lightly as a creeping cat. The gold ring on his amputated finger glimmered in the leaden light from the window. Alice's rage poured over into terror. She cringed away from him, passed the end of the bed and into the blind alley until she came up against the wall, and there she was stopped.

"Don't hit me," she whispered. "Oh, please don't hit me."

Juan came close to her and his right hand moved slowly to her arm just above the elbow. He was looking at her, not through her or around her. He swung her gently about and led her across the room and through the door and he closed the door on Norma and Ernest.

They stared at the closed door and hardly breathed. Juan led Alice to the double bed and turned her gently and she sagged down like a cripple and fell back, staring wildly up at him. He picked a pillow from the top of the bed and put it under her head. His left hand, the one with the stump finger and the wedding ring, stroked her cheek gently. "You'll be all right now," he said.

She crossed her arms over her face and her sobs were strangled and harsh and dry.

Chapter 5

BERNICE Pritchard and her daughter Mildred and Mr. Pritchard sat at the small table to the right of the entrance door of the lunchroom. The little group had drawn closer together. The two older people because they felt that in some way they were under attack, and Mildred in a kind of protective sense toward them. She often wondered how her parents had survived in a naughty and ferocious world. She considered them naïve and unprotected little children, and to a certain extent she was right about her mother. But Mildred overlooked the indestructibility of the child and the stability, its pure perseverance to get its own way. And there was a kind of indestructibility about Bernice. She was rather pretty. Her nose was straight and she had for so long worn pince-nez that the surfaces between her eyes were shaped by the pressure. The high, gristly part of her nose was not only very thin from the glasses, but two red spots showed where the springs regularly pressed. Her eyes were violet-colored and myopic, which gave her a sweet, inward look.

She was feminine and dainty and she dressed always with a hint of a past period. She wore jabots occasionally and antique pins. Her shirtwaists had always some lace and some handwork, and the collars and cuffs were invariably immaculate. She used lavender toilet water so that her skin and her clothing and her purse smelled always of lavender, and of another, almost imperceptible, acid odor which was her own. She had pretty ankles and feet, on which she wore very expensive shoes, usually of kid and laced, with a little bow over the instep. Her mouth was rather wilted and childlike, soft, and without a great deal of character. She talked very little but had in her own group gained a reputation for goodness and for sagacity; the first by saying only nice things about people, even people she did not know, and the second by never expressing a general idea of any kind beyond perfumes or food. She met the ideas of other people with a quiet smile, almost as though she forgave them for having ideas. The truth was that she didn't listen.

There had been times when Mildred wept with rage at her mother's knowing, forgiving smile after one of Mildred's political or economic deliveries. It took the daughter a long time to discover that her mother never listened to any conversation that had not to do with people or places or material things. On the other hand, Bernice never forgot a detail about goods or colors or prices. She could remember exactly how much she had paid for black suede gloves seven years ago. She was fond of gloves and rings—any kind of rings. She had a rather large collection, but she wore with anything else, always, her small diamond engagement ring and her gold wedding band. These she removed only to bathe. She left them on when she washed her combs and brushes in ammonia water in the band basin. The ammonia cleaned the rings and made the little diamonds shine brightly.

Her married life was fairly pleasant and she was fond of her husband. She thought she knew his weaknesses and his devices and his desires. She herself was handicapped by what is known as a nun's hood, which prevented her experiencing any sexual elation from her marriage; and she suffered from an acid condition which kept her from conceiving children without first artificially neutralizing her body acids. Both of these conditions she considered normal, and any variation of them abnormal and in bad taste. Women of lusty appetites she spoke of as "that kind of woman," and she was a little sorry for them as she was for dope fiends and alcoholics.

Her husband's beginning libido she had accepted and then gradually by faint but constant reluctance had first molded and then controlled and gradually strangled, so that his impulses for her became fewer and fewer, until he himself believed that he was reaching an age when such things did not matter.

In her way she was a very powerful woman. She ran an efficient, clean, and comfortable house and served meals which were nourishing without being tasty. She did not believe in the use of spices, for she had been told long ago that they had an aphrodisiac effect on men. The three—Mr. Pritchard, Mildred, and herself—did not take on any weight, probably because of the dullness of the food. It did not stimulate any great appetite.

Bernice's friends knew her as one of the sweetest, most unselfish people you will ever meet, and they often referred to her as a saint. And she herself said often that she felt humbly lucky, for she had the finest, most loyal friends in the whole world. She loved flowers and planted and pinched and fertilized and cut them. She kept great bowls of flowers in her house always, so that her friends said it was like being in a florist's shop, and she arranged them herself so beautifully.

She did not take medicines and often suffered in silence from constipation until the accumulated pressure relieved her. She had never really been ill nor badly hurt, and consequently she had no measuring rod of pain. A stitch in her side, a backache, a gas pain under her heart, convinced her secretly that she was about to die. She had been sure she would die when she had borne Mildred, and she had arranged her affairs so that everything would be easy for Mr. Pritchard. She had even written a letter to be opened after her death, advising him to marry again so that the child could have some kind of mother. She later destroyed this letter.

Her body and her mind were sluggish and lazy, and deep down she fought a tired envy of the people who, so she thought, experienced good things while she went through life a gray cloud in a gray room. Having few actual perceptions, she lived by rules. Education is good. Self-control is necessary. Everything in its time and place. Travel is broadening. And it was this last axiom which had forced her finally on the vacation to Mexico.

How she reached her conclusions not even she knew. It was a long, slow process built up of hints, suggestions, accidents, thousands of them, until finally, in their numbers, they forced the issue. The truth was that she didn't want to go to Mexico. She just wanted to come back to her friends having been to Mexico. Her husband didn't want to go at all. He was doing it for his family and because he hoped it would do him good in a cultural way. And Mildred wanted to go, but not with her parents. She wanted to meet new and strange people and through such contacts to become new and strange herself. Mildred felt that she had great covered wells of emotion in her, and she probably had. Nearly everyone has.

Bernice Pritchard, while denying superstition, was nevertheless profoundly affected by signs. The bus breaking down so early in the trip frightened her, for it seemed to portend a series of accidents which would gradually ruin the trip. She was sensitive to Mr. Pritchard's unrest. Last night, lying sleepless in the Chicoys' double bed, listening to the sighing breaths of her husband, she had said, "This will turn into an adventure when it's over. I can almost hear you telling it. It will be funny."

"I suppose so," Mr. Pritchard answered.

There was a certain fondness between these two, almost a brother-and-sister relationship. Mr. Pritchard considered his wife's shortcomings as a woman the attributes of a lady. He never had to worry about her faithfulness. Unconsciously he knew that she was without reaction, and this was right in his mind. His nerves, his bad dreams, and the acrid pain that sometimes got into his upper abdomen he put down to too much coffee and not enough exercise.

He liked his wife's pretty hair, always waved and clean; he liked her spotless clothes; and he loved the compliments she got for her good housekeeping and her flowers. She was a wife to be proud of. She had raised a fine daughter, a fine, healthy girl. Mildred was a fine girl; a tall girl, two inches taller than her

father and five inches taller than her mother. Mildred had inherited her mother's violet eyes and the weakness that went
with them. She wore glasses when she wanted to see anything
clearly. She was well formed, with sturdy legs and strong, slender
ankles. Her thighs and buttocks were hard and straight and
smooth from much exercise. She played tennis well and was
center on her college basketball team. Her breasts were large
and firm and wide at the base. She had not inherited her
mother's physiological accident, and she had experienced two
consummated love affairs which gave her great satisfaction and
a steady longing for a relationship that would be constant.

Mildred's chin was set and firm like her father's, but her
mouth was full and soft and a little frightened. She wore heavy
black-framed glasses, and these did give her a student look. It
was always a surprise to new acquaintances to see Mildred at a
dance without glasses. She danced well, if a little precisely, but
she was a practicing athlete and perhaps she practiced dancing
too carefully and without enough relaxation. She did have a
slight tendency to lead, but that could be overcome by a partner
with strong convictions.

Mildred's convictions were strong too, but they were variable.
She had undertaken causes and usually good ones. She did not
understand her father at all because he constantly confused her.
Telling him something reasonable, logical, intelligent, she often
found in him a dumb obtuseness, a complete lack of thinking
ability that horrified her. And then he would say or do something so intelligent that she would leap to the other side. When
she had him catalogued rather smugly as a caricature of a businessman, grasping, slavish, and cruel, he ruined her peace of
conception by an act or a thought of kindliness and perception.

Of his emotional life she knew nothing whatever, just as he
knew nothing of hers. Indeed, she thought that a man in middle
age had no emotional life. Mildred, who was twenty-one, felt
that the saps and juices were all dried up at fifty, and rightfully
so, since neither men nor women were attractive at that age. A
man or a woman in love at fifty would have been an obscene
spectacle to her.

But if there was a chasm between Mildred and her father,
there was a great gulf between Mildred and her mother. The
woman who had no powerful desires to be satisfied could not
ever come close to the girl who had. An early attempt on

Mildred's part to share her strong ecstasies with her mother and to receive confirmation had met with a blankness, a failure to comprehend, which hurled Mildred back inside herself. For a long time she didn't try to confide in anyone, feeling that she was unique and that all other women were like her mother. At last, however, a big and muscular young woman who taught ice hockey and softball and archery at the university gained Mildred's confidence, her whole confidence, and then tried to go to bed with her. This shock was washed away only when a male engineering student with wiry hair and a soft voice did go to bed with her.

Now Mildred kept her own counsel, thought her own thoughts, and waited for the time when death, marriage, or accident would free her from her parents. But she loved her parents, and she would have been frightened at herself had it ever come to the surface of her mind that she wished them dead.

There had never been any close association among these three although they went through the forms. They were dear and darling and sweet, but Juan and Alice Chicoy regularly established a relationship which Mr. or Mrs. Pritchard could not have conceived. And Mildred's close and satisfying friendships were with people of whose existence her parents were completely ignorant. They had to be. It had to be. Her father considered the young women who danced naked at stags depraved, but it would never have occurred to him that he who watched and applauded and paid the girls was in any way associated with depravity.

Once or twice, on his wife's insistence, he had tried to warn Mildred against men just to teach her to protect herself. He hinted and believed that he had considerable knowledge of the world, and his complete knowledge, besides hearsay, was his one visit to the parlor house, the stags, and the dry, unresponding acquiescence of his wife.

This morning Mildred wore a sweater and pleated skirt and low, moccasin-like shoes. The three sat at the little table in the lunchroom. Mrs. Pritchard's three-quarter-length black fox coat hung on a hook beside Mr. Pritchard. It was his habit to shepherd this coat, to help his wife on with it and to take it from her, and to see that it was properly hung up and not just thrown down. He fluffed up the fur with his hand when it showed evidence of being crushed. He loved this coat, loved the fact that it was expensive, and he loved to see his wife in it and to hear other women speculate upon it. Black fox was comparatively rare, and it was also a valuable piece of property. Mr. Pritchard felt that it should be properly treated. He was always the first to suggest that it go into summer storage. He had suggested that it might be just as well not to take it to Mexico at all, first, because that was a tropical country, and second, because of bandits who might possibly steal it. Mrs. Pritchard held that it should be taken along, because, in the first place, they would be visiting Los Angeles and Hollywood where everyone wore fur coats, and second, because it was quite cold in Mexico City at night, so she had heard. Mr. Pritchard capitulated easily; to him, as well as to his wife, the coat was the badge of their position. It placed them as successful, conservative, and sound people. You get better treatment everywhere you go if you have a fur coat and nice luggage.

Now the coat hung beside Mr. Pritchard, and he ran his fingers deftly up through the hairs to clear the long guard hairs from the undercoat. Sitting at the table, they had heard through the bedroom door Alice's hoarse, screaming attack on Norma, and the animal vulgarity of it had shocked them deeply, had driven them as nearly close together as they could be. Mildred had lighted a cigarette, avoiding her mother's eye. She had done this only in the six months since she had turned twenty-one. After the initial blow-up the subject had never verbally come up again, but her mother disapproved with her face every time Mildred smoked in front of her.

The rain had stopped and only the drips from the white oaks fell on the roof. The land was soggy, water-beaten, sodden. The grain, fat and heavy with the damp, rich springtime, had lain heavily down under the last downpour, so that it stretched away in tired waves. The water trickled and ran and gurgled and rushed to find low places in the fields. The ditches beside the state highway were full, and in some places the water even invaded the raised road. Everywhere there was a whisper of water and a rush of water. The golden poppies were all stripped of their petals now, and the lupines lay down like the grain, too fat, too heavy, to hold up their heads.

The sky was beginning to clear. The clouds were tattering, and there were splashes of lovely clear sky with silks of cloud skittering across them. Up high a fierce wind blew, spreading and mixing and matting the clouds, but on the ground the air was perfectly still, and there was a smell of worms and wet grass and exposed roots.

From the area of the lunchroom and garage at Rebel Corners the water ran in shallow ditches to the large ditch beside the highway. The bus stood shining and clean in its aluminum paint, and the water still dripping from its sides and its windshield flecked with droplets. Inside the lunchroom it was a little overwarm.

Pimples was behind the counter, trying to help out, and this would never have occurred to him before today. Always, in other jobs, he had hated the work and automatically hated his employer. But the experience of the morning was still strong in him. He could still hear Juan's voice saying in his ears, "Kit, wipe your hands and see if Alice got the coffee ready yet." It was the sweetest-sounding sentence he had ever heard. He wanted to do something for Juan. He had squeezed orange juice for the Pritchards and carried coffee to them, and now he was trying to watch the toaster and scramble eggs at the same time.

Mr. Pritchard said, "Let's all have scrambled eggs. That'll make it easier. You can leave mine in the pan and get them good and dry."

"O.K.," said Pimples. His pan was too hot and the eggs were ticking and clicking and sending up an odor of wet chicken feathers that comes from too fast frying.

Mildred had crossed her legs and her skirt was caught under her knee, so that the side away from Pimples must be exposed. He wanted to get down that way and look. His darting, narrow eyes took innumerable quick glances at what he could see. He didn't want her to catch him looking at her legs. He planned it in his mind. If she didn't move he would serve the eggs and he would take a napkin over his arm. Then, after he set down their plates, he would pass their table and go on about ten feet and drop the napkin as though by accident. He would lean down and look back under his arm, and then he would be able to see Mildred's leg.

He had the napkin ready and he was mixing the eggs to get them done before she moved. He stirred the eggs. They were stuck by now so he scooped shallowly to leave the burned crust in the pan. The odor of burning eggs filled the lunchroom. Mildred looked up and saw the flash in Pimples' eye. She looked down, noticed how her skirt was caught, and pulled it clear. Pimples saw her without looking directly at her. He knew that he had been caught and his cheeks stung with blood.

A dark smoke rose from the egg pan and a blue smoke rose from the toaster. Juan came in quietly from the bedroom and sniffed.

"God Almighty," he said, "what are you doing, Kit?"

"Trying to help out," said Pimples uneasily.

Juan smiled. "Well, thanks, but I guess you'd better not help out with eggs." He came to the gas stove, took the hot pan of burned eggs, put the whole thing into the sink, and turned the water on. It hissed and bubbled for a moment and then subsided, complaining, in the water.

Juan said, "Kit, you go out and try to start the engine. Don't choke her if she won't start. That'll only flood her. If she doesn't start right away, take off the distributor head and dry the points. They may have got wet. When you get her started, put her in low for a few minutes and then shift her to high and let the wheels turn over. But be careful she doesn't shake herself off those sawhorses. Just let her idle."

Pimples wiped his hands. "Should I open the grease cock first and see if she's still full?"

"Yeah. You know your stuff. Yeah, take a look. That gudgeon grease was pretty thick this morning."

"It might of shook down," said Pimples. He had forgotten the last look at Mildred's leg. He glowed under Juan's praise.

"Kit, I don't figure anybody would steal her, but keep an eye on her." Pimples laughed in sycophantic amusement at the boss's joke and went out the door. Juan looked over the counter. "My wife's not feeling very well," he said. "What can I get for you folks? More coffee?"

"Yes," said Mr. Pritchard. "The boy was trying to scramble some eggs and he burned them up. My wife likes her moist—"

"If they're fresh," Mrs. Pritchard interposed.

"If they're fresh," said Mr. Pritchard. "And I like mine dry."

"They're fresh, all right," said Juan. "Right fresh out of the ice."

"I don't think I could eat a cold-storage egg," said Mrs. Pritchard.

"Well, that's what they are, I wouldn't lie to you."

"I guess I'll just have a doughnut," said Mrs. Pritchard.

"Make mine the same," said Mr. Pritchard.

Juan looked frankly and with admiration at Mildred's legs. She looked up at him. Slowly his eyes rose from her legs, and his dark eyes were filled with so much pleasure, were so openly admiring, that Mildred blushed a little. She warmed up in the pit of her stomach. She felt an electric jar.

"Oh—!" She looked away from him. "More coffee, I guess. Well, maybe I'll take a doughnut too."

"Only two doughnuts left," said Juan. "I'll bring two doughnuts and a snail and you can fight over them."

The engine of the bus exploded into action outside and in a moment was throttled down to a purr.

"She sounds good," said Juan.

Ernest Horton came quietly, almost secretly, out of the bedroom door and closed it softly behind him. He walked over to Mr. Pritchard and laid the six thin packages on the table. "There you are," he said, "six of them."

Mr. Pritchard pulled out his billfold. "Got change for twenty?" he asked.

"No, I haven't."

"You got change for twenty?" Mr. Pritchard asked Juan.

Juan pushed the "No Sale" button on the cash register and raised the wheel weight on the bill compartment. "I can give you two tens."

"That will do," said Ernest Horton. "I've got a dollar bill or so. You owe me nine dollars." He took one of the tens and gave Mr. Pritchard a dollar.

"What are they?" Mrs. Pritchard asked. She picked one up but her husband snatched it out of her hand. "No you don't," he said mysteriously.

"But what are they?"

"That's for me to know," said Mr. Pritchard playfully. "You'll find out quick enough."

"Oh, a surprise?"

"That's right. Little girls better keep their noses out of what doesn't concern them." Mr. Pritchard always called his wife "little girl" when he was playful, and automatically she fell into his mood.

"When do iddle girls see pretty present?"

"You'll find out," he said, and he stuffed the flat packages in his side pocket. He wanted to come in limping when he got the chance. He had a variation on the trick. He would pretend that his foot was so sore that he couldn't take off his shoe and sock himself. He would get his wife to take off the sock for him. What a kick that would be to watch her face! She'd nearly die when she saw that sore foot on him.

"What is it, Elliott?" she asked a little peevishly.

"You'll find out, just keep your pretty hair on, little girl."

"Say," he went on to Ernest, "I just thought up a new wrinkle. Tell you about it later."

Ernest said, "Yup, that's what makes the world tick. You get a new wrinkle and you're fixed. You don't want to go radical. Just a wrinkle, like they call it in Hollywood, a switcheroo. That's with a story. You take a picture that's made dough, and you work a switcheroo—not too much—not too much, just enough, and you've got something then."

"That makes sense," said Mr. Pritchard. "Yes, sir, that makes good sense."

"It's funny about new wrinkles," said Ernest. He sat down on a stool and crossed his legs. "Funny how you get a wrong idea. Now, I've got a kind of invention and I figured I could sit back and count my money, but I was wrong. You see, there's a lot of fellows like me traveling around living out of a suitcase. Well, maybe there's a convention or you've got a date that's pretty fancy. You'd like to have a tuxedo. Well, it takes a lot of room to pack a tuxedo and maybe you only use it twice on a whole trip. Well, that's when I got this idea. Suppose, I said, you've got a nice dark business suit—dark blue or almost black or oxford—and suppose you got little silk slipcovers like little lapels and silk stripes that just snap on the pants. In the afternoon you've got a nice dark suit and you slip on the silk covers to the lapels and snap on the strips and you've got a tuxedo. I even figured out a little bag to carry them in."

"Say!" cried Mr. Pritchard, "that's a wonderful idea! Say, why I've got to take up room in my suitcase right now for a tuxedo. I'd like to get in on a thing like that. If you get up a patent and put on a campaign, a big national advertising campaign, why, you might get a big movie star to endorse—"

Ernest held up his hand. "That's just the way I figured," he said. "And I was wrong and you're wrong. I drew it all out on paper and just how it would go on and how the trousers leg would have little tiny silk loops for the hooks for the stripes to go on, and then I had a friend who travels for a big clothes manufacturer"—Ernest chuckled—"he put me right mighty quick. 'You'd get every tailor and every big manufacturer right on your neck,' he said. 'They sell tuxedoes anywhere from fifty to a hundred and fifty bucks and you come along with ideas to take that business away with a ten-dollar gadget. Why, they'd run you right out of the country,' he said."

Mr. Pritchard nodded gravely. "Yes, I can see the point. They have to protect themselves and their stockholders."

"He didn't make it sound too hopeful," said Ernest. "I figured I'd just sit and count the profits. I figured that a fellow, say, traveling by air—he's got the weight limitations. He's got the right to save room in his suitcase. It'd be like two suits for the weight of one. And then I figured maybe the jewelry companies might take it up. Set of studs and cuff links and my lapels and stripes all in a nice package. I haven't got around to that yet. Haven't asked anybody. Might still be something in it."

"You and I ought to get together for a good talk," said Mr. Pritchard. "Have you got it patented?"

"Well, no. I didn't want to go to the expense until I could see if anybody was interested."

"Oh," said Mr. Pritchard. "I guess maybe you're right. Patent attorneys and all, they cost quite a bit of money. Maybe you're right." Then he changed the subject. "What time can we get started?" he asked Juan.

"Well, the Greyhound gets in around ten. They bring regular freight and some passengers. We should get started at ten-thirty. That's the schedule. Can I get you folks any thing else? Some more coffee?"

"Some more coffee," said Mr. Pritchard.

Juan brought it to him and looked out the window at the bus with its wheels turning over in the air. Mr. Pritchard looked at his watch.

"We've still got an hour," he said.

A tall, stooped old man came around the side of the building. The man who had slept in Pimples' bed. He opened the door to the lunchroom, came in, and sat down on a stool. He had his head bent permanently forward on the arthritic stalk of his neck so that the tip of his nose pointed straight at the ground. He was well over sixty, and his eyebrows overhung his eyes like that of a Skye terrier. His long, deeply channeled upper lip was raised over his teeth like the little trunk of a tapir. The point over his middle teeth seemed to be almost prehensile. His eyes were yellowish gold, so that he looked fierce.

"I don't like it," he said without preliminaries. "I didn't like it yesterday when you broke down, and I like it even less today."

"I've got the rear end fixed," said Juan. "Turning over right now."

"I think I'll cancel and go on back to San Ysidro on the Greyhound," said the man.

"Well, you can do that."

"I've got a feeling," said the man. "I just don't like it. Something's trying to give me a warning. I've had 'em before a couple of times. I didn't pay any mind to them once and I got into trouble."

"The bus is all right," said Juan, his voice rising a little in exasperation.

"I'm not talking about the bus," said the man. "I live in this county, native of it. The ground's full of water. San Ysidro River will be up. You know how the San Ysidro rises. Right under Pico Blanco it comes down that Lone Pine Canyon and makes a big loop. Ground gets full of water and every drop runs off into the San Ysidro. She'll be raging right now."

Mrs. Pritchard began to look alarmed. "Do you think there's danger?" she asked.

"Now, dear," said Mr. Pritchard.

"I've got a feeling," said the man. "The old road used to go around that loop of the river and never cross it. Come thirty years ago Mr. Trask got himself made roadmaster of the county. The old road wasn't good enough for him. He put in two bridges and saved what? Twelve miles, that's what he saved. It cost the county twenty-seven thousand dollars. Mr. Trask was a crook."

He turned his stiff neck and surveyed the Pritchards. "A crook. Just about to indict him for another job when he died, three years ago. Died a rich man. Got two boys in the University of California right now living on the taxpayers' money." He stopped and his upper lip waggled from side to side over his long yellow teeth. "If those bridges get any real strain on them they'll go out. The concrete isn't stout enough. I'll just cancel and go back to San Ysidro."

"The river was all right day before yesterday," said Juan. "Hardly any water in it."

"You don't know the San Ysidro River. She can get up in a couple of hours. I've seen her half a mile wide and covered with dead cows and chickenhouses. No, once I get this kind of feeling I won't go. I'm not superstitious, either."

"You think the bus might go through the bridge?"

"I don't say what I think. I know Trask was a crook. Left an estate of thirty-six thousand five hundred dollars. His boys are up at college spending it right now."

Juan came out from behind the counter and went to the wall phone. "Hello," he said. "Give me Breed's Service Station out on the San Juan road. I don't know the number." He waited a while and then he said, "Hello. Say, this is Chicoy down at the Corners. How's the river? Oh, yeah? Well, is the bridge all right? Yeah. Well, O.K., I'll see you pretty soon." Juan hung up. "The river is up pretty high," he explained. "They say the bridge is all right."

"That river can rise a foot an hour when Pine Canyon dumps a cloudburst into it. Time you get there the bridge might be gone."

Juan turned a little impatiently to him. "What do you want me to do? Not go?"

"You do just as you like. I only want to cancel and get back to San Ysidro. I'm not going to fool around with this kind of nonsense. Once I had a feeling like this and I didn't pay attention and I broke both legs. No, sir, I got that feeling when you broke down yesterday."

"Well, consider yourself canceled," said Juan.

"That's what I want, mister. You're not an old-timer here. You don't know what I know about Trask. Salary of fifteen hundred a year and he leaves thirty-six thousand five hundred and a clear title to a hundred and sixty acres of land. Tell me!"

Juan said, "Well, I'll see you get on the Greyhound."

"Well, I'm not telling you anything about Trask, I'm just telling you what happened. You figure it out for yourself. Thirty-six thousand five hundred dollars."

Ernest Horton asked, "Suppose the bridge is out?"

"Then we won't go across it," said Juan.

"Then what'll we do? Turn around and come back?"

"Sure," said Juan. "We'll either do that or jump it."

The stooped man smiled about the room in triumph. "You see?" he said. "You'll come back here and there'll be no bus here for San Ysidro. You'll sit around here for how long? Months? Wait for them to build a new bridge? You know who the new roadmaster is? A college boy. Just out of college. All books and no practice. Oh, he can draw a bridge, but can he build one? We'll see."

Suddenly Juan laughed. "Fine," he said. "The old bridge isn't washed out yet and already you're having trouble with the new one that isn't built."

The man turned his aching neck sideways. "Are you getting lippy?" he demanded.

For a moment a dark red light seemed to glow in Juan's black eyes. "Yes," he said. "I'll get you on the Greyhound, don't you worry. I wouldn't want you on this run."

"Well, you can't kick me off, you're a common carrier."

"O.K.," said Juan wearily. "Sometimes I wonder why I keep the bus. Maybe I won't much longer. Just a headache. You've got a feeling! Nuts!"

Bernice had been following this conversation very closely. "I don't believe in these things," she said, "but they say it's the dry season down in Mexico. It's like autumn. Summer's when it rains."

"Mother," said Mildred, "Mr. Chicoy knows Mexico. He was born there."

"Oh, were you? Well, it's the dry season, isn't it?"

"Some places," said Juan. "I guess it is where you'll be going. Other places there isn't any dry season."

Mr. Pritchard cleared his throat. "We're going to Mexico City and to Puebla and then to Cuernavaca and Taxco, and we may take the trip to Acapulco and we'll go to the volcano if it's all right."

"You'll be all right," said Juan.

"You know those places?" Mr. Pritchard demanded.

"Sure."

"How are the hotels?" Mr. Pritchard asked. "You know how the travel agencies are—everything is wonderful. How are they really?"

"Wonderful," Juan said, smiling now. "They're great. Breakfast in bed every morning."

"I didn't mean to cause trouble this morning," said Mr. Pritchard.

"Sure, it's all right." He leaned his arms on the counter and spoke confidentially. "I get fed up a little sometimes. I drive that damn bus back and forth and back and forth. Sometime I'd like to take and just head for the hills. I read about a ferryboat captain in New York who just headed out to sea one day and they never heard from him again. Maybe he sunk and maybe he's tied up on an island some place. I understand that man."

A great red truck with a trailer slowed down on the highway outside. The driver looked in. Juan moved his hand rapidly from side to side. The truck went into second gear, gathered speed, and went away.

"I thought he was coming in," said Mr. Pritchard.

"He likes raspberry pie," said Juan. "He always stops when we got some. I just told him we haven't got any."

Mildred was looking at Juan, fascinated. There was something in this dark man with his strange warm eyes that moved her. She felt drawn to him. She wanted to attract his attention, his special attention, to herself. She had thrown back her shoulders so that her breasts were lifted.

"Why did you leave Mexico?" she asked, and she took off her glasses so that when he answered he would see her without them. She leaned on the table, and put her forefinger to the corner of her left eye, and pulled the skin and eyelid backward. This changed the focus of her eye. She could see his face more clearly that way. It also gave her eyes a long and languorous shape, and her eyes were beautiful.

"I don't know why I left," Juan said to her. His warm eyes seemed to surround her and to caress her. Mildred felt a little weak and sirupy in the pit of her stomach. "I'll have to stop this," she thought. "This is crazy." A quick and sexual picture had formed in her mind.

Juan said, "People down there, unless they're rich, have to work too hard and for too little money. I guess that's the main reason I left."

"You speak very good English," Bernice Pritchard said as though it were a compliment.

"Why not? My mother was Irish. I got both languages at once."

"Well, are you a Mexican citizen?" Mr. Pritchard asked.

"I guess so," said Juan. "I never did anything about it."

"It's a good idea to take out your first papers," said Mr. Pritchard.

"What for?"

"It's a good idea."

"It doesn't make any difference to the government," said Juan. "They can tax me and draft me."

"It's still a pretty good idea," said Mr. Pritchard.

Juan's eyes were playing with Mildred, touching her breasts and sliding down over her hips. He saw her sigh and arch her back a little, and deep in Juan an imp of hatred stirred. Not strongly because there wasn't much of it in him, but the Indian blood was there, and in the dark past lay the hatred for the *ojos claros,* the light eyes, the blonds. It was a hatred and a fear of a complexion. The light-eyed people who had for centuries taken the best land, the best horses, the best women. Juan felt the stirring like a little heat lightning, and he felt a glow of pleasure knowing that he could take this girl and twist her and outrage her if he wanted to. He could disturb her and seduce her mentally, and physically too, and then throw her away. The cruelty stirred and he let it mount in him. His voice grew softer and more rich. He spoke directly into Mildred's violet eyes.

"My country," he said, "even if I don't live there, it is in my heart." He laughed inside at this, but Mildred did not laugh. She leaned forward a little and pulled back the corners of both eyes so that she could see his face more clearly.

"I remember things," said Juan. "In the square of my town there were public letter-writers who did all the business for the people who couldn't read or write. They were good men. They had to be. The country people would know if they weren't. They know many things, those people of the hills. And I remember one morning when I was a little boy I was sitting on a bench. There was a fiesta in this town in honor of a saint. The church was full of flowers and there were candy stands and a ferris-wheel and a little merry-go-round. And all night the people shot off skyrockets to the saint. In the park an Indian came to the letterwriter and said, 'I want you to write a letter to my patron. I will tell you what to say and you will put it in

good and beautiful form so he will not find me discourteous.'
'Is it a long letter?' the man asked. 'I don't know,' said the
Indian. 'That will be one peso,' said the man. And the little
Indian paid him, and he said, 'I want you to say to my patron
that I cannot go back to my town and my fields for I have seen
great beauty and I must stay behind. Tell him I am sorry and I
do not wish to give him pain, nor my friends, either, but I
could not go back. I am different and my friends would not
know me. I would be unhappy in the field and restless. And
because I would be different my friends would reject me and
hate me. I have seen the stars. Tell him that. And tell him to
give my chair to my friend brother and my pig with the two
little ones to the old woman, who sat with me in fever. My pots
to my brother-in-law, and tell the patron to go with God, with
loveliness. Tell him that.'"

Juan paused and saw that Mildred's lips were open a little,
and he saw that she was taking his story as an allegory for
herself.

"What had happened to him?" she asked.

"Why, he had seen the merry-go-round," said Juan. "He
couldn't leave it. He slept beside it, and pretty soon his money
was gone and he was starving, and then the owner let him turn
the crank that ran the merry-go-round and fed him. He couldn't
ever leave. He loved the merry-go-round. Maybe he's still
there." Juan had become foreign in the telling. A trifle of accent
had come into his speech.

Mildred sighed deeply. Mr. Pritchard said, "Let me get this
straight. He gave away his land and all his property and he
never went home because he saw a merry-go-round?"

"He didn't even own his land," said Juan. "Little Indians
never own their land. But he gave away everything else he
had."

Mildred glared at her father. This was one of the times when
she found him stupid to the point of nausea. Why couldn't he
see the beauty in this story? Her eyes went back to Juan to tell
him silently that she understood, and she thought she saw
something in his face that had not been there before. She
thought there was a cruel, leering triumph in his face, but it
was probably her eyes, she thought. Her damnable eyes that
couldn't see very well. But what she saw was a shock to her.

.

She looked quickly at her mother and then at her father to see whether they had noticed anything, but they were regarding Juan vacantly.

Her father was saying in his slow and, to Mildred, maddening way, "I can understand how he would think it was fine if he had never seen a merry-go-round before, but you get used to anything. A man would get used to a palace in a few days and then he'd want something else."

"It's just a story," Mildred said with so much fierceness that her father turned surprised eyes on her.

Mildred could almost feel Juan's fingers on her thighs. Her body tingled with desire, aroused and unsatisfied. She itched with a pure sexual longing, and her anger arose against her father as though she had been interrupted in the midst of connection. She put on her glasses, looked quickly at Juan and then away, for his eyes were veiled although he looked at all of them. He was enjoying a kind of triumph. He was laughing at her and also at the thing her father and mother did not know was happening. And suddenly her desire hardened into a knot in her stomach and her stomach ached and she felt a revulsion. She thought she would be sick.

Ernest Horton said, "I always intended to get down Mexico way. Thought I might ask the head office about it some time. Might make some pretty valuable contacts down there. Like these fiestas they have. They sell novelties, don't they?"

"Sure," said Juan. "They sell little rosaries and holy pictures and candles and things like that, candy and ice cream."

"Well, if a guy went down and got a line on that stuff, why, we could probably turn it out a lot cheaper than they can. We could stamp out those rosaries—well, nice ones—out of pot metal. And skyrockets. My company supplies some of the biggest celebrations, all kinds of fireworks. It's an idea. I think I'll write a letter."

Juan looked at the increasing pile of dirty dishes in the sink. He stared over his shoulder at the door to the bedroom and then he opened the door and looked in. The bed was empty. Alice had got up, but the bathroom door was shut. Juan came back and began to scrub the dirty dishes in the sink.

The sky was clearing fast now, and the clean yellow sun was shining on the washed land. The young leaves of the oaks were almost yellow in the new light. The green fields looked incredibly young.

Juan smiled shortly. He cut two slices of bread.

"I think I'll walk around a little bit," said Mr. Pritchard. "Want to come, dear?" he asked his wife. She looked quickly at the bedroom door.

"Pretty soon," she said, and he understood her.

"Well, I'll just go outside," he said.

Chapter 6

AFTER Juan left her Alice lay a long time on her back with her arms crossed over her face. Her sobbing stopped gradually, like a child's. She could hear the murmuring talk out in the lunchroom. The inside of her arm was warm and wet over her eyes. She was flooded with a kind of comfort, and the release from tension was as though a tight mesh had been loosened from her body. As she lay in relaxed comfort, her mind jumped back to what had happened. She didn't remember the woman who had screamed at Norma. The morning was beginning to be hazy to her. She had not yet found her own rationalization for her action. Now that she thought of it, she knew she had not really suspected Norma of misconduct, and if she had she really wouldn't have cared very much. She did not love Norma. She didn't care a thing for Norma. Poor little washed-out cat.

When Norma had come to work, Alice, of course, put her senses on the girl and on Juan like a stethoscope, and when she had found no reaction on Juan's part, no quickening, no little creeping and trailing with the eye, Alice had lost interest in Norma except as an organism for carrying coffee and washing dishes. Alice was not very aware of things or people if they did not in some way either augment or take away from her immediate life. And now, as she lay relaxed and warm and quiet, her mind began to work and terror came with her thoughts.

She went back over the scene. Her terror grew out of Juan's gentleness. He should have hit her. His failure to do so worried her. Maybe he didn't care about her any more. Casual kindness in a man she had found to be the preliminary to a brush-off. She tried to remember what the Pritchard women looked like, and she tried to remember whether Juan had looked with warmth on either of them. She knew Juan. His eyes heated up like a stove when his interest was aroused. Then, with a little shock, she remembered that he had given up their bed to the Pritchards. She could smell the lavender on the bed-clothes right now. A hatred and a distaste for that odor came to her.

She listened to the murmur of voices through the door. Juan was feeding them. He wouldn't have done it if he hadn't been interested. Juan would say the hell with it and go on out to work on the bus. A restless fear arose in Alice. She had mis-treated Norma. That was easy. With Norma's kind you showed weakness, and Norma would melt and run down over herself. Take a girl like that, why, she'd had so little love that even a stink of it on a wind would knock her ass over teacup. Alice was contemptuous of this starvation for love. She could not tie her own up with Norma's. Alice was big in herself and everyone else was very little, everyone, that is, except Juan. But, then, he was an extension of herself. She thought it might be just as well to put Norma on her feet before anything else. She needed Norma to run the lunchroom, because Alice intended to get drunk just as soon as Juan went away in the bus. She would tell him when he came back that she had a toothache that was killing her.

She didn't do it very often, but she looked forward to it now. And if she was going to do it, she'd better begin covering her tracks. Juan didn't like drunk women. She uncrossed her arms from over her face. Her eyes were sunken from the pressure and it took a moment to get them to track. She saw how the sun was flooding sweetly over the green plain behind the bed-room, and how it flowed over the rising hills far to the west. A sweet day.

She struggled her body upright and went to the bathroom. There she dampened one end of a bath towel in cold water and patted it against her face to take out the creases where her arms had pressed down against her plump cheeks. She rubbed the

end of the towel around her face and over her nose and along
the edge of her hairline. A brassière strap was broken. She
slipped open her dress and found that the little safety pin that
held it was still there, so she pinned the strap to the brassière
again. It was a little tight but she'd sew it after Juan had gone.
She wouldn't, of course. When enough of the strap was broken
she'd buy a new brassière.

Alice brushed her hair and put on lipstick. Her eyes were
still red. She put some eyedrops in the corners with a medicine
dropper and rubbed the lids against her eyeballs with her
fingers. For a moment she inspected herself in the medicine-
chest mirror and then went out. She slipped off her wrinkled
dress and put on a clean print.

Quickly she crossed the bedroom to Norma's door and
knocked softly. There was no answer. She knocked again. From
inside the room came a rustling of paper. Norma came to the
door and opened it. Her eyes were glazed, and she seemed to
have been just awakened. In her hand she held the stub pencil
she had used for the eyebrows earlier.

When she saw Alice a look of alarm came upon her face.
"I didn't do nothing wrong with that fellow," she said quickly.

Alice stepped into the room. She knew how to handle the
Normas when she had her wits. "I know you didn't, honey,"
Alice said. She cast down her eyes as though she were ashamed.
She knew how to handle girls.

"Well, you shouldn't of said it. Suppose somebody heard it
and believed it? I'm not that kind. I'm just trying to make my
living and no trouble." Her eyes suddenly swam in tears of
self-pity.

Alice said, "I shouldn't of done it but I just felt so bad. It's
my time of the month. You know yourself how miserable you
feel. Sometimes you go kind of crazy."

Norma inspected her with interest. This was the first time
she'd ever found softness in Alice. This was the first time that
Alice had ever needed to enlist Norma. She didn't like women
and girls. There was a streak of cruelty in Alice toward other
women, and when she saw Norma's eyes brim with tears of
sympathy she felt triumphant.

"You know how it is," Alice said. "You just get a little
crazy."

"I know," said Norma. Soft tentacles of warmth stretched

out from her. She ached for love, for association, for some human being in the world to be friendly with. "I know," she said again, and she felt older and stronger than Alice and a little protective too, which was what Alice wanted.

Alice had seen the pencil in her hand. "Maybe you had better come out now and help. Mr. Chicoy's doing it all alone."

"I will in just a moment," said Norma.

Alice closed the door and listened. There was a pause, a slipping sound, and then the sharp sound of the bureau drawer closing. Alice pushed back her hair with her hand and walked softly toward the door into the lunchroom. She felt fine. She had gathered a great deal of information about Norma. She knew how Norma felt about things. She knew where Norma had put the letter.

Alice had tried to get into Norma's suitcase before but it was always locked, and while she could have taken it apart with her fingers—it was only cardboard—the marks would have showed tampering. She would wait. Sooner or later, if she was careful, Norma would neglect to lock her suitcase. Alice was clever, but she didn't know that Norma was clever too. Norma had worked for Alices before. When Alice went through Norma's dresser drawers and looked at her things and read the letters from her sister, she didn't notice the paper match carelessly lying on the drawer's edge. Norma always put it there, and when it was displaced she knew someone had been going through her things. She knew it couldn't be Juan or Pimples, so it must be Alice.

Norma was not likely to leave her suitcase unlocked. For all her dreams Norma was not stupid. In a toothpaste box in her locked suitcase there was twenty-seven dollars. When she had fifty dollars Norma would go to Hollywood and get a job in a restaurant and wait her chance. The fifty dollars would rent her a room for two months. Food she would get where she worked. Her high, long-legged dreams were one thing, but she could take care of herself too. Norma was no fool. True, she didn't understand Alice's hatred of all women. She didn't know that this apology was a trick. But she would probably find it out in time to save herself. And while Norma believed that only the best and most noble thoughts and impulses resided in Clark Gable, she had a knowledge of and a lack of respect for the impulses of the people she met and came in contact with in everyday life.

When Pimples came scratching softly at her window at night she knew how to take care of that. She locked her window. He wouldn't dare make too much noise trying to get in for fear Juan in the next room would hear him. Norma was nobody's fool.

Now Alice stood in front of the door between the bedroom and the lunchroom. She ran her finger down either side of her nose and then she opened the door and went behind the counter as though nothing at all had happened.

Chapter 7

THE big and beautiful Greyhound bus was pulled in under the loading shed at San Ysidro. Helpers put gasoline into the tank and checked the oil and the tires automatically. The whole system worked smoothly. A Negro man cleaned between the seats, brushing the cushions and picking up gum wrappers and matches and cigarette butts from the floor. He ran his fingers behind the last seat, which stretched across the rear. Sometimes he found coins or pocket-knives behind this seat. Loose money he kept, but most other articles he turned in to the office. People made an awful stink about things they left, but not about small change. Sometimes the swamper managed as much as a couple of dollars behind that seat. Today he had dug out two dimes, a fifty-cent piece, and a hip-pocket wallet with a draft card, driver's license, and a Lions Club membership card.

He glanced inside the bill section. Two fifty-dollar bills and a certified check for five-hundred dollars. He put the wallet in his shirt pocket and brushed the seat with his whisk broom. He breathed a little hard. The money was easy. He could take it out and leave the wallet behind the seat for some other swamper to find down the line. The check would be left too.

There was too much danger in checks. But those two sweet fifties—those sweet, sweet fifties! His throat was tight and would be until he got those sweet fifties out and the wallet behind the seat.

But he couldn't get to them because the punk kid was washing the outside of the windows where they were splashed with dirty mist from the highway. The swamper had to wait. If they caught him they'd put him away.

There was a little rip in the cuff of his blue serge trousers. He figured he would slip those two sweet fifties in there, inside the cuff, before he got off the bus. Then he'd get sick before he went off the job. He'd be sick, all right. Like enough he wouldn't be back for a week. If he got sick on the job and still stayed out the day till quitting time, they wouldn't figure anything if he didn't show up for a few days and it would save his job. He heard a step on the bus and stiffened a little. Louie, the driver, looked in.

"Hi, George," he said. "Say, did you find a wallet? Guy says he lost it."

George mumbled.

"Well, I'll come back and look," said Louie.

George swung around, still on his knees. "I found it," he said. "I was going to turn it in as soon as I finished."

"Yeah?" said Louie. He took the wallet from George's hand and opened it. The punk kid looked in through the window Louie smiled sorrowfully at George and flicked his eyes toward the punk.

"Too bad, George," Louie said. "I guess they've got 'em stacked against us. Two fifties the guy said and two fifties it is." He pulled out the bills and the check so the punk looking through the window could see them. "Better luck next time, George," Louie said.

"Suppose the guy pays a reward," said George.

"You'll get half," said Louie. "If it's under a buck, you'll get it all."

Louie moved out of the bus and into the waiting room. He handed the wallet in at the desk.

"George found it. He was just bringing it in," said Louie. "That's a good guy."

Louie knew the wallet's owner was right beside him so he said to the cashier, "If it was me that lost this, I'd give George a nice little present. Nothing don't turn a guy bad like no appreciation. I remember a guy found a grand and he turned it in and he didn't even get a thank-you. The next thing you know he robbed a bank and killed a coupla guards." Louie lied easily and without strain.

"How many going south?" Louie asked.

"You're full up," said the clerk. "You got one for Rebel Corners, and don't forget the pies like you did last week. I never had so much trouble with fifty pies in my life. Here's your wallet, sir. Will you inspect it to see if it's all right?"

The owner paid a five-dollar reward. Louie figured to give George a buck sometime. He knew George wouldn't believe him, but what the hell. It was a stinker's game and a muddy track. Everybody had to take his chance. Louie was big, a little on the stout side, but a dresser. His party friends called him "meat-face." He had a fast line and was smart and liked to be known as a horse player. He called race horses dogs and spoke of all situations as parlays. He would have liked to be Bob Hope or, better, Bing Crosby.

Louie saw George looking in from the loading platform doors. An impulse of generosity seized him. He walked over and gave George a dollar bill. "Cheap son of a bitch!" he said. "Here, you take the buck. Over five hundred dollars he gets back and he put out a buck!"

George looked into Louie's face, just one quick, brown flash of the eyes. He knew it was a lie and he knew there wasn't anything he could do about it. If Louie was mad at him he could make it tough. And George had wanted that drunk. He had almost felt the liquor take hold of him. If only that punk kid had kept his big nose out of it.

"Thanks," said George.

The kid went by with his bucket and sponge. George said, "You call those windows clean?" And Louie made it up to George. He said to the kid, "You want to get any place, you better get on the ball. Those windows stink. Do them again."

"I ain't taking orders from you. I'll wait till I get some kind of complaints from the super."

Louie and George exchanged glances. It was just a punk. In less than a week he'd be out on his ass if Louie thought of it.

The big Greyhounds came in and out of the covered loading shed heavy and high as houses. The drivers slipped them smoothly and beautifully into place. The station smelled of oil and diesel exhaust fumes and candy bars and a powerful floor cleaner that got in the nose.

Louie went back toward the front. His eyes had caught a girl coming in from the street. She was carrying a suitcase. All in one flash Louie caught her. A dish! A dish like that he wanted to ride in a seat just behind his own raised driver's chair. He could watch her in the rear-view mirror and find out about her. Maybe she lived somewhere on his route. Louie had plenty of adventures that started like this.

The light from the street was behind the girl so he couldn't see her face, but he knew she was a looker. And he didn't know how he knew it. There might have been fifty girls come in with a light behind them. But how did he know this one was a looker? He could see a nice figure and pretty legs. But in some subtle way this girl smelled of sex.

He saw that she had carried her suitcase over to the ticket window so he did not go directly toward her. He went into the washroom. And there he stood at the wash basin and dipped his hands in water and ran them through his hair. From his side pocket he took a little comb and combed his hair back smoothly and patted it behind where the suggestion of a duck tail stood out. And he combed his mustache, not that it needed combing for it was very short. He settled his gray corduroy jacket, tightened his belt, and pulled his stomach in a little bit.

He put the comb back in his pocket and inspected himself again in the mirror. He ran his hand over the sides of his hair. He felt behind to see that no strands were out and that the duck tail was lying down. He straightened his regulation black ready-made bow tie and he took a few grains of sen-sen out of his inner shirt pocket and threw them in his mouth. And then he seemed to shake himself down in his coat.

Just as his right hand went to the brass knob of the washroom door, Louie's left hand flipped fingers up and down his fly to be sure he was buttoned up. He put on his face a little crooked smile, half worldliness and half naïveté, an expression that had been successful with him. Louie had read someplace that if you looked directly into a girl's eyes and smiled it had an effect. You must look at her as though she were not only the most beautiful thing in the world, but you must keep looking into her eyes until she looked away. There was another trick too. If it bothered you to look into people's eyes, you should look at a point on the bridge of the nose right between the eyes. To the person looked at it appeared that you were looking into the eyes, only you weren't. Louie had found this a very successful approach.

Nearly all his waking hours Louie thought about girls. He liked to outrage them. He liked to have them fall in love with him and then walk away. He called them pigs. "I'll get a pig," he would say, "and you get a pig, and we'll go out on the town."

He stepped through the door of the washroom with a kind of lordliness, and then had to back up because two men came down between the benches carrying a long crate with slats to let air in. The side of the crate said in large white letters MOTHER MAHONEY'S HOME-BAKED PIES. The two men went in front of Louie and through to the loading platform.

The girl was sitting on a bench now, her suitcase beside her on the floor. As he moved across the room Louie took a quick look at her legs and then caught her eyes and held them as he walked. He smiled his crooked smile and moved toward her. She looked back at him, unsmiling, and then moved her eyes away.

Louie was disappointed. She hadn't been embarrassed as she should have been. She had simply lost interest in him. And she was a looker too—fine well-filled legs with rounded thighs and no stomach whatever and large breasts which she made the most of. She was a blonde and her hair was coarse and a little broken at the ends from a too-hot iron, but well-brushed hair that had good lights in it and a long, curling bob that Louie liked. Her eyes were made up with blue eye-shadow and some cold cream on the eyelids and plenty of mascara on the lashes. No rouge, but a splash of lipstick that was put on to make her mouth look square, like some of the picture stars. She wore a suit, a tight skirt and a jacket with a round collar. Her shoes were tan saddle-leather with white stitching. Not only a looker but a dresser. And the stuff looked good.

Louie studied her face as he walked. He had a feeling that he had seen her someplace before. But then, she might look like someone he knew, or he might have seen her in a movie. That had happened. Her eyes were wide-set, almost abnormally wide-set, and they were blue with little brown specks in them and with strongly marked dark lines from the pupils to the outer edge of the iris. Her eyebrows were plucked and penciled in a high arch so that she looked a little surprised. Louie noticed that her gloved hands were not restless. She was not impatient nor nervous, and this bothered him. He was afraid of self-possession, and he did feel that he had seen her somewhere. Her knees were well-covered with flesh, not bony, and she kept her skirt down without pulling at it.

As he strolled by Louie punished her for looking away from his eyes by staring at her legs. This usually had the effect of making a girl pull down her skirt, even if it was not too high, but it hadn't any effect on this girl. Her failure to react to his art made him uneasy. Probably a hustler, he said to himself. Probably a two-dollar hustler. And then he laughed at himself. Not two dollars with that stuff she's wearing.

Louie went on to the ticket window and smiled his sardonic smile at Edgar, the ticket clerk. Edgar admired Louie. He wished he could be like him.

"Where's the pig going?" Louie asked.

"Pig?"

"Yeah. The broad. The blonde."

"Oh, yes." Edgar exchanged a secret man-look with Louie. "South," he said.

"In my wagon?"

"Yeah."

Louie tapped the counter with his fingers. He had let the little fingernail on his left hand grow very long. It was curved, like half a tube, and sanded to a shallow point. Louie didn't know why he did this, but he was gratified to notice that some of the other bus drivers were letting their little fingernails grow too. Louie was setting a style and he felt good about it. There was that cab driver who had tied a raccoon's tail on his radiator cap and right overnight everybody had to have a piece of fur flapping in the breeze. Furriers made artificial fox tails, and high-school kids wouldn't be seen in a car without a tail whipping around. And that cab driver could sit back and have the satisfaction of knowing he had started the whole thing. Louie had been letting his little fingernail grow for five months and already he'd seen five or six other people doing it. It might sweep the country, and Louie would have started the whole thing.

He tapped the counter with the long, curved nail, but

gently, because when a nail gets that long it breaks easily. Edgar looked at the nail. He kept his left hand below the counter. He was growing one too, but it wasn't very long yet, and he didn't want Louie to see it until it was much longer. Edgar's nails were brittle, and he had to put colorless nail polish on his to keep it from breaking right off. Even in bed it broke once. Edgar glanced toward the girl.

"Figure to make some time with the—pig?"

"No harm trying," said Louie. "Probably a hustler."

"Well, what's wrong with a good hustler?" Edgar's eyes flicked up. The girl had recrossed her legs.

"Louie," he said apologetically, "before I forget, you'd better see to the loading of that crate of pies yourself. We had a complaint last week. Someplace along the line somebody dropped the crate and a raspberry pie got all mixed up with a lemon pie and there was raisins all over hell. We had to pay the claim."

"It never happened on my run," said Louie truculently. "It goes to San Juan, don't it? That jerk line from Rebel Corners done it."

"Well, we paid the claim," said Edgar. "Just kind of check it, will you?"

"There wasn't no pies dropped on my run," Louie said dangerously.

"I know. I know you didn't. But the front office told me to tell you to check it."

"Why don't they come to me?" Louie demanded. "They got complaints, why don't they call me up instead of sending messages?" He tended his anger as he would a fire. But he was angry at the blonde. The god-damned hustler. He looked up at the big clock on the wall. A hand two feet long jerked seconds around the dial, and in the reflection of the glass Louie could see the girl sitting with crossed legs. Although he couldn't be sure because of the curve of the glass, he thought she was looking at the back of his head. His anger melted away.

"I'll check the pies," he said. "Tell them there won't be any raspberries in the lemon pie. I guess I'll make a little time with the pig." He saw the admiration in Edgar's eyes as he turned slowly and faced the waiting room.

He was right. She had been looking at the back of his head, and when he was turned she was looking in his face. There was no interest, no nothing, in her glance. But she had beautiful eyes, he thought. God-damn, she was a looker! Louie had read in a magazine that wide-set eyes meant sexiness, and there was no doubt that this girl put out a strong, strong feeling of sex. She was the kind of girl everybody watched walk by. Why, she walked in a place and everybody turned and looked at her. You could see their heads turn, like watching a horse race. It was something about her, and it wasn't make-up and it wasn't the way she walked, although that was part of it too. Whatever it was, it projected all around her. Louie had felt it when she came in from the street and the light was behind her so he couldn't see her then. And now she was looking in Louie's face, not smiling, not putting out anything, just looking, and he still felt it. A tightness came into his throat and a little flush rose out of his collar. He knew that in a moment his glance would slide away. Edgar was waiting, and Edgar had faith in Louie.

There were a few lies in Louie's reputation but actually he did have a way, he did make time with pigs. Only now he wasn't easy. This pig was getting him down. He wanted to slap her face with his open hand. His breath was rising painfully in his chest. The moment was going to be over unless he did something. He could see the dark raylike lines in her irises and the fullness of her jowls. He put on his embracing look. His eyes widened a little and he smiled as though he had suddenly recognized her. At the same time he moved toward her.

Carefully he made his smile a little respectful. Her eyes held onto his, and a little of the coldness went out of them. He stepped near to her. "Man says you're going south on my bus, ma'am," he said. He almost laughed at that "ma'am," but it usually worked. It worked with this girl. She smiled a little.

"I'll take care of your bag," Louie went on. "We leave in about three minutes."

"Thanks," said the girl. Her voice was throaty and sexy, Louie thought.

"Let me take your suitcase. I'll put it on now and then you'll have a seat."

"It's heavy," said the girl.

"I ain't exactly a midget," said Louie. He picked up her suitcase and walked quickly out to the loading platform. He climbed into the bus and put the suitcase down in front of the seat that was right behind his seat. He could watch the girl in his mirror and he could talk to her some when they got rolling. He came out of the bus and saw the punk and another swamper putting the crate of pies on top of the bus.

"Careful of that stuff," Louie said loudly. "You bastards dropped one last week and I got the beef."

"I never dropped nothing," said the punk.

"The hell you didn't," said Louie. "You watch your step." He went through the swinging doors to the waiting room.

"What's eating him?" the other swamper asked.

"Oh, I sort of jammed him up," said the punk. "George found a wallet and I seen it, so they figured they got to turn it in. It was a big roll of jack too. They're both sore at me 'cause I seen it. Louie and George was gonna split them up a coupla half centuries and I guess I jammed it for 'em. Course they had to turn it in when they seen I saw 'em."

"I could use some of that," said the swamper.

"Who couldn't," said the punk.

"I can take me a century and I can go out and I can get very nice stuff for that there." They went on for a time with ritual talk.

In the waiting room there was a little burst of activity. The crowd for the southbound bus was beginning to collect. Edgar was busy behind his counter, but not too busy to keep his eye on the girl. "A pig," he said under his breath. It was a new word to him. From now on he would use it. He glanced at the little fingernail on his left hand. It would be long before he would have as good a one as Louie's. But why kid himself? He couldn't make time like Louie anyway. He always ended up by going down the line.

There was a last-minute flurry of customers at the candy counter, at the peanut vending machines, at the gum dispensers. A Chinese bought copies of *Time* and *Newsweek* and rolled them carefully together and put them in his black broadcloth overcoat pocket. An old lady restlessly turned over magazines on the newsstand without any intention of buying one. Two Hindus with gleaming white turbans and shining black curly beards stood side by side at the ticket window. They glanced fiercely about as they tried to make themselves understood.

Louie stood by the entrance to the loading platform and glanced continually at the girl. He noticed that every man in the room was doing the same thing. All of them were watching her secretly, and they didn't want to get caught at it. He turned and looked through the swinging glass doors and saw that the punk and the swamper had got the crate of pies safely on top of the bus and the tarpaulin pulled down over it. The light in the waiting room dimmed to dusk. A cloud must have covered the sun. And then the light rose again as though controlled by a rheostat. The big bell over the glass doors clamored. Louie looked at his watch and went through the door to his big bus. And the passengers in the waiting room got up and shuffled toward the door.

Edgar was still trying to make out where the Hindus wanted to go. "The god-damned rag heads," he said to himself. "Why'nt they learn English before they start running around?"

Louie climbed into the high seat enclosed by a stainless steel bar and glanced at the tickets as the passengers got on. The Chinese in the dark coat went directly to the back seat, took off his coat, and laid the *Times* and *Newsweek* in his lap. The old lady clambered breathlessly up the step and sat down in the seat directly behind Louie.

He said, "I'm sorry, ma'am, that seat's taken."

"What do you mean, taken?" she said belligerently. "There aren't any reserved seats."

"That seat's taken, ma'am," Louie repeated. "Don't you see the suitcase beside it?" He hated old women. They frightened him. There was a smell about them that gave him the willies. They were fierce and they had no pride. They never gave a damn about making a scene. They got what they wanted. Louie's grandmother had been a tyrant. She had got whatever she wanted by being fierce. From the corners of his eyes he saw the girl on the lower step of the bus, waiting behind the Hindus to get in. He was pushed into a spot. Suddenly he was angry.

"Ma'am," he said, "I'm boss on my bus. There's plenty of good seats. Now will you move back?"

The old woman set her chin and scowled at him. She switched her behind a little, settling into the seat. "You've got that girl in this seat, that's what you've got," she said. "I've got a mind to report you to the management."

Louie blew up. "All right, ma'am. You just get out and report me. The company's got lots of passengers, but it hasn't got many good drivers." He saw that the girl was listening, and he felt pretty good about it.

The old woman saw that he was angry. "I'm going to report you," she said.

"Well, report me then. You can get off the bus," Louie said loudly, "but you're not going to sit in that seat. The passenger in that seat got a doctor's order."

It was an out, and the old woman took it. "Why didn't you say so?" she said. "I'm not unreasonable. But I'm still going to report you for discourtesy."

"All right, ma'am," Louie said wearily. "That I'm used to."

The old woman moved back one seat.

"Going to hang out her big ear and catch me off base," Louie thought. "Well, let her. We got more passengers than drivers." The girl was beside him now, holding out her ticket. Involuntarily Louie said, "You only going as far as the Corners?"

"I know, I've got to change," said the girl. She smiled at his tone of disappointment.

"That's your seat right there," he said. He watched the mirror while she sat down and crossed her legs and pulled down her skirt and put her purse beside her. She straightened her shoulders and fixed the collar of her suit.

She knew Louie was watching every move. It had always been that way with her. She knew she was different from other girls, but she didn't quite know why. In some ways it was nice always to get the best seat, to have your lunches bought for you, to have a hand on your arm crossing the street. Men couldn't keep their hands off her. But there was always the trouble. She had to argue or cajole or insult or fight her way out. All men wanted the same thing from her, and that was just the way it was. She took it for granted and it was true.

When she'd been young she'd suffered from it. There had been a sense of guilt and of nastiness. But now she was older she just accepted it and developed her techniques. Sometimes she gave in and sometimes she got money or clothes. She knew most of the approaches. She could probably have foretold everything Louie would do or say in the next half hour. By anticipating, she could sometimes stave off unpleasantness. Older men wanted to help her, put her in school or on the stage. Some young men wanted to marry her or protect her. And a few, a very few, openly and honestly simply wanted to go to bed with her and told her so.

These were the easiest because she could say yes or no and get it over with. What she hated most about her gift, or her failing, was the fighting that went on. Men fought each other viciously when she was about. They fought like terriers, and she sometimes wished that women could like her, but they didn't. And she was intelligent. She knew why, but there wasn't anything she could do about it. What she really wanted was a nice house in a nice town, two children, and a stairway to stand on. She would be nicely dressed and people would be coming to dinner. She'd have a husband; of course, but she couldn't see him in her picture because the advertising in the women's magazines from which her dream came never included a man. Just a lovely woman in nice clothes coming down the stairs and guests in the dining room and candles and a dark wood dining table and clean children to kiss good night. That's what she really wanted. And she knew as well as anything that that was not what she would ever get.

There was a great deal of sadness in her. She wondered about other women. Were they different in bed than she was? She knew from watching that men didn't react to most women the way they did to her. Her sexual impulses were not terribly strong nor very constant, but she didn't know about other women. They never discussed this kind of thing with her. They didn't like her. Once the young doctor to whom she had gone to try to have the pain of her periods relaxed had made a pass at her, and when she had talked him out of that he had told her, "You just put it out in the air. I don't know how, but you do it. Some women are like that," he said. "Thank God there aren't many of them or a man would go nuts."

She tried wearing severe clothes, but that didn't help much. She couldn't keep an ordinary job. She learned to type, but offices went to pieces when she was hired. And now she had a racket. It paid well and it didn't get her in much trouble. She took off her clothes at stags. A regular agency handled her. She didn't understand stags or what satisfaction the men got out of them, but there they were, and she made fifty dollars for taking off her clothes and that was better than having them torn off in an office. She'd even read up on nymphomania, enough, anyway, to know that she didn't have it. She almost wished she had. Sometimes she thought she'd just go into a house and make a pile of dough and retire to the country—that, or marry an elderly man she could control. It would be the easiest way. Young men who were attractive to her had a way of turning nasty. They always suspected her of cheating them. They either sulked or tried to beat her up or they got furious and threw her out.

She'd tried being kept and that was the way it ended. But an old man with some money—that might be the way. And she would be good to him. She'd really make it worth his money and his time. She had only two girl friends, and both of them were house girls. They seemed to be the only kind who weren't jealous of her and who didn't resent her. But one was out of the country now. She didn't know where. She followed troops somewhere. And the other was living with an advertising man and didn't want her around.

That was Loraine. They had had an apartment together. Loraine didn't care much about men; still, she didn't go for women. But then Loraine got caught short with this advertising man and asked her to move out. Loraine explained everything when she told her not to come around.

Loraine was working in a house and this advertising man fell for her. Well, Loraine had got gonorrhea, and before she even had a symptom she gave it to this advertising man. He was a nervous type and he blew his top and lost his job and came bellyaching to Loraine. She felt responsible in a way so she took him in and fed him while they both got cured. That was before the new treatment, and it had been pretty rough.

And then this advertising man went on a sleeping-pill pitch. She'd find him passed out and he was pretty vague, and his temper was bad unless he had his pills, and he took more and more of them. Twice Loraine had to have him pumped out.

Loraine was a really good girl and things were hard because she couldn't work in the house until she was cleared up. She didn't want to infect anybody she knew, and still she had to have money for doctor's bills and rent and food. She had to work the streets in Glendale to make it, and she wasn't feeling good herself. And then, with everything else, the advertising man turned jealous and didn't want her to work at all in spite of the fact that he didn't have a job. It would be nice if the whole thing had blown over by now and she and Loraine could have the apartment together. They had been a good pair together. They had had fun, good, quiet fun.

There had been a whole series of conventions in Chicago and she had saved some money from the stags. She was taking busses back to Los Angeles to save money. She wanted to live quietly a while. She hadn't heard from Loraine for a long time. The last letter said this advertising man was reading her mail so not to write.

The last passengers were coming through the doors and getting into the bus.

Louie had his legs crossed. He was a little timid with this girl. "I see you're going to L.A.," he said. "Do you live there?"

"Part of the time."

"I like to try and figure people out," he said. "A guy like me sees so many people."

The motor of the bus breathed softly. The old woman was glaring at Louie. He could see her in the mirror. She would probably write a letter to the company.

"Well," Louie said to himself, "the hell with the company." He could always get a job. The company didn't pay much attention to old ladies' letters anyway. He glanced back down the bus. It looked like the two Hindus were holding hands. The Chinese had both *Time* and *Newsweek* open on his lap and he was comparing stories. His head swung from one magazine to the other, and a puzzled wrinkle marked his nose between his brows. The dispatcher waved at Louie.

Louie swung the lever that closed the door. He eased his gear into compound-reverse and crept out of the concrete slip, then swung delicately and wide so that his front fender cleared the north wall by a part of an inch. He swung wide again in compound-low and cleared the other side of the alley by a fraction of an inch. At the entrance to the street from the alley he stopped and saw that the street was clear for him. He turned the bus and it took him over to the other side of the street. Louie was a good driver with a perfect record. The bus moved down the main street of San Ysidro and came to the outskirts and to the open highway.

The sky and the sun were washed and clean. The colors were sharp. The ditches ran full of water; and in some places, where the ditches were clogged, the water extended out onto the highway. The bus hit this water with a great swish, and Louie could feel the tug at the wheel. The grass was matted down from the force of the rain, but now the warmth of the sun was putting strength into the rich grass and it was beginning to rise up again on the high places.

Louie glanced in the rear-view mirror at the girl again. She was looking at the back of his head. But something made her look up at the mirror and right into Louie's eyes, and the eyes with their dark lines and the straight, pretty nose and the mouth painted on square photographed permanently in Louie's brain. When she looked into his eyes she smiled as though she felt good.

Louie knew that his throat was closing, and a rising pressure was in his chest. He thought he must be nuts. He knew he was shy, but mostly he convinced himself that he was not, and he was going through all the symptoms of a sixteen-year-old. His eyes flicked from road to mirror, back and forth. He could see that his cheeks were red. "What the hell is this?" he said to himself. "Am I going to go ga-ga over a chippie?" He looked at her more closely to find some thought to save himself, and then he saw deep forceps marks along her jaws. That made him feel more comfortable. She wouldn't be so god-damned confident if she knew he saw the forceps marks. Forty-two miles. Louie would have to make time. He couldn't waste a minute if he wanted to throw a line over this little hustler. And when he tried to speak his voice was hoarse.

She leaned close behind him. "I couldn't hear you," she said.

Louie coughed. "I said the country looks nice after the rain."

"Yes, it does."

He tried to get back to his usual opening. He noticed in the mirror that she was still leaning forward to listen.

"Like I said," he began, "I try to figure people out. I'd say you was in the movies or on the stage."

"No," said the girl. "You'd be wrong."

"Aren't you in show business?"

"No."

"Well, do you work?"

She laughed, and her face was very charming when she laughed. But Louie noticed that one of her upper front teeth was crooked. It leaned over and interfered with its neighbor. Her laughter stopped and her upper lip covered the tooth. "Conscious of it," Louie thought.

She was ahead of him. She knew what he was going to say. It had happened so many times before. He was going to try to find out where she lived. He wanted her telephone number. It was simple. She didn't live anywhere. She had a trunk stored with Loraine with some books in it—*Captain Hornblower,* and a *Life of Beethoven,* and some paper books of the short stories of Saroyan, and some old evening dresses to be made over. She knew Louie was having trouble. She knew that blush that rose out of a man's collar and the thickness of labored speech. She saw Louie glance apprehensively in the mirror at the rear of the bus.

The Hindus were smiling a little at each other. The Chinese was staring up in the air, trying to work up in his mind some discrepancy in the stories he had been reading. A Greek in the rear seat was cutting an Italian cigar in two with a pocketknife. He put one piece in his mouth and thoughtfully placed the other half in his breast pocket. The old woman was working herself up into a rage at Louie. She directed an iron look at the back of his head, and her chin quivered with fury and her lips were white with the tension of their compression.

The girl leaned forward again. "I'll save you time," she said. "I'm a dental nurse. You know, I do all those things in a dentist's office." She often used this. She didn't know why. Perhaps because it stopped speculation and there were never any more questions after she said it. People didn't want to talk much about dentistry.

Louie digested this. The bus came to a railroad crossing. Automatically Louie set his air brakes and stopped. The brakes hissed as he released them and went through the gears to cruising speed again. He sensed that things were closing in on him. The old bitch was going to start trouble any minute now. He didn't have forty-two miles at all. Once the old bitch put in her oar the thing would be over. He wanted to make time while he could, but it was too soon according to Louie's methods. He shouldn't make a play for a good half hour, but the old bitch was going to force his hand.

"Sometimes I get into L. A.," he said. "Is there someplace I could call you and maybe we could—have dinner and go to a show?"

She was friendly about it. There wasn't anything mean or

bitchy about her. She said, "I don't know. You see, I haven't any place to live now. I've been away. I want to get an apartment as soon as I can."

"But you work someplace," said Louie. "Maybe I could call you there."

The old woman was squirming and twitching in her seat. She was mad because Louie had kicked her out of the front seat.

"Well, no," said the girl. "You see, I haven't got a job. Of course, I'll get one right away because you can always get a job in my profession."

"This isn't a brush-off?" Louie asked.

"No."

"Well, maybe you could drop me a line when you get settled."

"Maybe."

"Because I'd like to know someone to take out in L. A."

And now here it came, the voice as shrill as a whetstone. "There's a state law about talking to passengers. You watch the road." The old woman addressed the whole bus. "This driver's putting our lives in danger. I'm going to ask to get off if he can't keep his attention on his driving."

Louie closed up. This was serious. She really could make trouble. He looked in the mirror and found the girl's eyes. With his lips he said, "The god-damned dried-up old bitch!"

The girl smiled and put her fingers to her lips. In a way she was relieved and in another she was sorry. She knew that sooner or later she would have trouble with Louie. But she also knew that in many ways he was a nice guy and one she could handle up to a certain point. She knew from his blush that she could probably stop him by hurting his feelings.

But it was over and Louie knew it. The girl wasn't going to get herself in a mess. He had to make time while the bus was rolling. He knew that. Once you got to a station the passengers wanted out as quick as possible. Now he'd lost out. At Rebel Corners he would stop only long enough to let her off and unload that god-damned crate of pies. He hunched over the wheel. The girl had folded her hands in her lap and her eyes would not raise to meet his in the mirror. There were lots of girls prettier than this one. Those forceps scars were damned ugly. They'd give a guy the shivers. Of course, she wore her hair long and forward to cover them. A girl like that couldn't wear her hair up. Louie liked hair up and, Jesus! suppose you woke up in bed and saw those scars. There were plenty of pigs in the world and Louie could get along. But in his chest and his stomach there was a weight of sorrow. He fought at it and picked at it but it wouldn't move. He wanted this girl more than he had ever wanted anyone, and in a different way. He felt a dry and grainy sense of loss. He didn't even know her name, and now he wouldn't get to know her. He could see Edgar's eager eyes questioning him when he came back to San Ysidro. Louie wondered if he would lie to Edgar.

The great tires sang on the road, a high, twanging song, and the motor throbbed with a heavy beat. There were big, wet, floppy clouds in the sky, dark as soot in the middle and white and shining on the edges. One of them was creeping up on the sun now. Already, ahead on the highway, Louie could see the shadow of it rushing toward the bus, and far ahead on the highway he could see the towering green mound of the oaks that grew about the lunchroom at Rebel Corners. He was filled with disappointment.

Juan Chicoy came to the side of the bus as it pulled in.

"What you got for me?" he asked as the door opened.

"One passenger and a flock of pies," said Louie. He got up from his seat, reached around, and lifted the girl's suitcase. He climbed down to the ground and held up his hands, and the girl put her hands on his arms and stepped down. They walked toward the lunchroom.

"Good-by," she said.

"Good-by," said Louie. He watched her go through the door, her little behind bobbing up and down.

Juan and Pimples had the crate of pies off the top of the bus. Louie climbed back into the bus.

"So long," said Juan.

The old woman had moved up into the front seat. Louie levered the door shut. He went into gear and moved away. When he was in cruising speed and the tires were ringing on the highway, he looked in the mirror. The old woman wore a look of mean triumph.

"You killed it," Louie said to himself. "Oh, you murdered it."

The woman looked up and caught his eyes in the mirror. Deliberately Louie made silent words with his lips. "You god-damned old bitch!" He saw her lips grow tight and white. She knew what he meant.

The highway sang along ahead of the bus.

Chapter 8

JUAN and Pimples carried the crate of Mother Mahoney's Home-Baked Pies near to the door of the lunchroom and set it down on the ground. Both of them watched the blonde go through the door. Pimples whistled a low gurgling note. The palms of his hands turned suddenly sweaty. Juan's eyes had lowered until only a little glint of light shone between his lashes. He licked his lips quickly and nervously.

"I know what you mean," said Juan. "Want to take time out and go over and lift your leg on a tree?"

"God Almighty," said Pimples. "Whew!"

"Yeah," said Juan. He bent over, turned the latch on the crate, and raised the hinged side. "I'll take a small bet, Kit."

"What's that?" Pimples asked.

"I bet," said Juan, "I bet two to one you already got in your mind the idea that you didn't have a day off for two weeks and you'd like to take today and ride over to San Juan with me. Maybe it would even help if the bus breaks down again."

Pimples started to blush around his eruptions. He raised his eyes uneasily and looked at Juan, and there was so much humor without poison in Juan's eyes that Pimples felt better. "God damn!" he thought, "there is a man. "Why'd I ever work for anybody else?"

"Well," Pimples said aloud, and he felt he was talking to a man. Juan understood how a guy looked at things. When a cookie went by, Juan knew how a guy felt. "Well," he said again.

"Well," Juan mimicked him, "and who's gonna take care of the gas pumps and fix the flats?"

"Who done it before?" Pimples asked.

"Nobody," said Juan. "We used to just put a sign on the

garage—Closed For Repairs. Alice can pump gas." He slapped Pimples on the shoulder.

"What a guy," Pimples thought. "What a guy!"

The pies were held by little traylike slots which gripped the edges of the pans and left each pie separate from all the others. There were four stacks of twelve pies—forty-eight pies.

"Let's see," said Juan, "we get six raspberry, four lemon cream, four raisin, and two caramel custard cream." He pulled out the pies as he spoke and laid them on top of the crate. "Take them in, Pim—Kit, I mean."

Pimples took a pie in each hand and went into the lunchroom. The blonde was sitting on a stool drinking a cup of coffee. He couldn't see her face but he felt the electricity or whatever it was she had. He put the pies on the counter.

As he turned to go out again he felt the silence in the room.

Mr. Pritchard and the crabby old guy and the young fellow, Horton, were entranced. Their eyes rose and washed the blonde and fell away. Miss Pritchard and her mother looked pointedly at the piles of bran in back of the counter. Alice was not there, but Norma was in front of the blonde, wiping the counter with her rag.

"Like to have a snail?" Norma asked.

Pimples paused. He had to hear the tone of the blonde's voice.

"Yes, I guess so," she said. A quick spasm kinked Pimples' stomach at the throaty tone. He hurried outside and gathered up more pies.

"Get moving," Juan said. "You can look at her all the way over to San Juan, unless you'd rather drive."

Pimples rushed the pies in. Sixteen pies out. That left thirty-two. Juan closed the side of the crate and turned the catch. When Pimples came out the last time he helped Juan put the pie crate in the big black trunk of "Sweetheart," the bus. She was ready now. Ready to go. Juan stood back and looked at her. She was no Greyhound but she wasn't bad. Around the windows a little rust showed through the aluminum paint. He would have to touch that up. And the hub caps could take a new coat too.

"Let's get going," he said to Pimples. "Lock the garage doors. Right between the benches under the radiator hose connections

you'll find the sign to put on the door. Jump now if you want
to get your clothes changed."

Pimples leaped for the garage door. Juan straightened up
and stretched his arms from his sides and moved toward the
lunchroom.

Mr. Pritchard's right leg was crossed over his left and his
suspended toe made little convulsive jumps. He had glanced
into the blonde's face when she came in and now there was a
pleasant excitement in him. But he was puzzled. Somewhere, he
had seen this girl. Maybe she'd worked in one of his plants,
maybe a secretary, maybe in some friend's office. But he'd seen
her. He felt sure he had. He truly believed that he never forgot
a face, when the truth was that he rarely remembered one. He
didn't look closely at any face unless he planned to do business
with its owner. He wondered about the sense of sin he got out
of the recognition. Where could he have seen this girl?

His wife was looking secretly at his swinging foot. Ernest
Horton was frankly gazing at the blonde's legs. Norma liked
the girl. In one respect Norma was like Loraine. She didn't
love anyone—well, except one—so she had nothing to be taken
away, nothing to lose. And this girl was nice. She was pleasant-
spoken and polite. Actually the girl felt good toward Norma
too, sensing that this girl could like her.

Just before the Greyhound came in Alice had said to Norma,
"Watch the counter, will you? I'll be right back." And then the
bus and the blonde and getting the coffee had taken up Norma's
thoughts. But now a certain knowledge struck her, made her
turn cold and nauseous inside. She knew what was happening
as though she could see it. She knew, and knowing, many cal-
culations came into her head around her sick anger. The little
roll of money in small bills. That could be used until she could
get a job. And why couldn't she go now? She was going to
sometime. She opened the cabinets beneath the shelves in back
of the lunch counter and shoved the pies in, all except one of
each kind. One raspberry, one raisin, one lemon cream, and one
caramel custard cream she lined up on the counter, and the
smell of them made her sicker. She still didn't quite know what
to do.

Juan came through the front door and stood looking at the
back of the blonde's head.

Norma said, "Will you watch the counter a minute, Mr. Chicoy?"

"Where's Alice?" Juan asked.

"I don't know," said Norma. She could see Alice in her mind. Alice's eyes weren't so good. She would take the letter to the window and hold it up to the light. She wasn't really interested. It was a casual, vague kind of curiosity. She would lean sideways to the light and her hair would fall in her eyes so she would blow it, and her fingers would scrabble through the pages. Norma shivered. She saw herself hurtling into the room. She saw herself snatch the letter, and her fingers flexed. She felt Alice's skin against her fingernails and her nails striking and clawing for Alice's eyes, those horrible, wet, juicy eyes. Alice would fall on her back and Norma would come down on that great, soft stomach with her knees, and she'd scratch and tear at Alice's face and the blood would run in the scratches.

Juan, looking at Norma, said, "What's the matter? Are you sick?"

"Yes," said Norma.

"Go ahead before you get sick here."

Norma edged down the counter and opened the bedroom door softly. The door to her own room was open just a crack. She closed the door into the lunchroom and moved silently toward her own door. She was cold now and shivering. Cold as ice. Noiselessly she pushed her door open. And there it was— Alice, by the window, holding the letter to Clark Gable up to her eyes and blowing her hair sideways.

Alice blew her hair and looked up and saw Norma standing in the doorway. Her mouth was open, her face avid. She couldn't change her expression. Norma took a step into the room. Her chin was set so hard that the lines receded from her mouth. Alice stupidly held her letter out to her. Norma took it, folded it carefully, and tucked it in her bodice. And then Norma went to her bureau. She drew her suitcase from underneath. She unpinned the key from the inside of her dress and unlocked the suitcase. Heavily she began to pack. She emptied the bureau drawers into the suitcase and pressed the mound of clothes down with her fist. From the closet she dragged out her three dresses and her coat with the rabbit collar and she laid the coat on the bed and rolled the dresses up around the hangers and poked them in the suitcase too.

Alice couldn't move. She watched Norma, her head swinging as the girl passed back and forth. In Norma's brain there was a silent scream of triumph. She was on top. After a life of being pushed around, she was on top and she was silent. She felt good about that. Not one word did she say and not one word would she say. She threw two pairs of shoes into the suitcase and put the lid firmly down and locked it.

"You going right now?" Alice asked.

Norma didn't answer. She wouldn't break her triumph. Nothing could force her.

"I didn't mean to do anything wrong," Alice said.

Norma didn't look up.

"You'd better not tell or I'll fix you," Alice suggested uneasily. Still Norma did not speak. She went to the bed and got her black coat with the rabbit collar. Then she picked up her suitcase and walked out of the room. Her breath was whistling in her nose. She went in back of the lunch counter and pushed the "No Sale" button on the cash register. Norma took out ten dollars, a five and four ones and a half and two quarters. She shoved the money in the side pocket of her black coat. Her weak mouth was set in a hard line.

Juan said, "What's going on here?"

"I'm going to San Juan with you," said Norma.

"You've got to help Alice," said Juan. "She can't stay here alone."

"I've quit," said Norma. She saw that the blonde watched her as she came around the edge of the counter. Norma went out the screen door. She carried her suitcase to the bus and she climbed in and took a seat toward the rear. She stood her suitcase up on its end beside her. She sat very straight.

Juan watched her go out of the door. He shrugged his shoulders. "What do you suppose that was?" he asked of no one in particular.

Ernest Horton was scowling. He hated Alice Chicoy. He said, "What time you think we'll get started?"

"Ten-thirty," said Juan. "It's ten-ten now." He glanced at the Pritchards. "Look, I've got to change my clothes. If you folks want coffee or anything, just come back here and get it."

He went into the bedroom. He slipped the shoulder straps of his overalls and let the pants fall down around his shoes. He had on shorts with narrow blue stripes. He peeled his blue chambray shirt over his head and kicked off his moccasins and stepped out of the overalls, leaving shoes and socks and overalls in a pile on the floor. His body was hard and brown, colored not by the sun but by brown ancestry. He moved over to the bathroom and knocked on the door. Alice flushed the toilet and opened the door. She had been washing her face again and a wet strand of hair was plastered to her cheek. Her mouth was lax and her eyes were swollen and red.

"What's going on?" Juan asked. "You're having one hell of a time for yourself, aren't you?"

"I've got a toothache," Alice said. "I can't help it. I've got a jumping pain right here."

"What's the matter with Norma?" Juan asked.

"Let her go," Alice said. "I knew I'd catch up with her sometimes."

"Well, what did she do?"

"She's just a little light-fingered," said Alice.

"What did she take?"

"Just thought I'd see. Remember that bottle of Bellodgia you gave me for Christmas? Well, it was gone and I found it in her suitcase. She came in when I found it and she got huffy and I told her she could go."

Juan's eyes veiled. He knew it was a lie, but he didn't much care what the truth was. Women fights didn't interest him at all. He got in the tub and pulled the shower curtain about him.

"You've been a mess all morning," he said. "What's the matter with you?"

"Well, it's my time," said Alice, "and then this toothache."

Juan knew the first was not true. But he only suspected the second could be false. "Take yourself a slug of liquor when we go. That'll be good for both ends," he said.

Alice was pleased. She wanted him to suggest it.

"You've got to take care of everything," Juan went on. "Pimples is going along with me today."

Excitement surged in Alice. She would be alone, all by herself. But she couldn't let Juan know that was what she wanted. "What's Pimples going for?" she asked.

"He wants to get some things over in San Juan. Say, why don't we close up the place? You can go to the dentist in San Juan."

"No," Alice said. "It's not a good idea. I'll go in to San Ysidro tomorrow or the next day. It's not a good idea to close the lunchroom."

"O.K. It's your tooth," said Juan, and he turned on the water. He poked his head out of the curtain. "Go on out there and take care of the passengers."

Ernest Horton had moved in on the blonde when Alice came into the lunchroom.

"Now, let's have a couple of cups of coffee," he said. And to the blonde, "You rather have a coke?"

"No. Coffee. Cokes make me fat."

Ernest had been making time. He had asked her name and the blonde had said it was Camille Oaks. It wasn't, of course. It was a quick grouping of a Camel advertisement on the wall —another blonde on a poster with balloon-like breasts—and a tree she could see through the window. But Camille Oaks she was from now on, for this trip at least.

"I heard that name recently some place," Ernest said. He passed the sugar dispenser politely to her.

Mr. Pritchard's foot was swinging in little jerks and Mrs. Pritchard was watching. She knew Mr. Pritchard was getting irritable at something, but she didn't know why. She had no experience with this kind of thing. Her women friends were not of a kind to put Mr. Pritchard's foot swinging. And she knew nothing about his life outside of her own social movements.

He uncrossed his legs, stood up, and went to the counter. "You're thinking of the Oakes murder trial," he said to Ernest. "I'm sure this young lady wasn't murdered or vice versa," he chuckled. "A little more coffee," he said gallantly to Alice.

His daughter pulled her right eye sideways to look at him. There was a quality in his voice she had never heard before. And there was a little grandeur in his tone. He was broadening his "a" and putting an unnatural formality into his speech. It shocked his daughter. She peered at the girl and suddenly she knew what it was. Mr. Pritchard was reacting to Camille Oaks. He was making a play—a kind of fatherly play. His daughter didn't like it.

Mr. Pritchard said, "I have an impression I have met you. Could that be?"

In her head Mildred paraphrased it, "Ain't I seen you somewheres?"

Camille looked at Mr. Pritchard's face and her eyes flicked to the club button on his lapel. She knew where he had seen her. When she took off her clothes and sat in the bowl of wine she very carefully didn't look at the men's faces. There was something in their wet, bulging eyes and limp, half-smiling mouths that frightened her. She had a feeling that if she looked directly at one he might leap on her. To her, her audiences were blobs of pink faces and hundreds of white collars and neat four-in-hand ties. The Two Fifty—Three Thousand Clubs usually wore tuxedos.

She said, "I don't remember."

"Ever been in the Middle West?" Mr. Pritchard insisted.

"I've been working in Chicago," said Camille.

"Where?" Mr. Pritchard asked. "The impression is very strong."

"I'm a dental nurse," said Camille.

Mr. Pritchard's eyes brightened behind his glasses. "Say, I'll bet that's it. Dr. Horace Liebholtz, he's my dentist in Chicago."

"No," said Camille, "no, I never worked for him. Dr. T. S. Chesterfield, that was my last job." She got that from a poster too and it wasn't clever. She hoped he wouldn't notice right over his shoulder the sign, "Chesterfields—They Satisfy."

Mr. Pritchard said gaily, to his daughter's disgust, "Well, I'll remember sooner or later. I never forget a face."

Mrs. Pritchard had caught her daughter's eyes and she saw the distaste in Mildred's expression. She glanced at her husband again. He was acting queerly. "Elliott," she said, "will you bring me a little coffee?"

Mr. Pritchard seemed to shake himself into reality. "Oh, yes —sure," he said, and his voice returned to normal. But he was irritated again.

The screen door opened and banged shut. Pimples Carson entered, but a Pimples transformed. His face was heavily powdered in an attempt to cover up the eruptions, and this succeeded in turning their redness to a rich purple. His hair was slicked back and stuck with pomade. He wore a shirt with a very tight collar, a green tie with a small knot, and the shirt collar was pinned under the knot with a gold collar pin. Pimples seemed to be strangling a little, so tight was his collar. Shirt and tie rose and fell slightly when he swallowed. His suit was a chocolate brown, a hairy material, and on the sides of the trousers were the almost indistinguishable prints of bedsprings. He wore white shoes with brown saddles and woolen socks of red and green plaid.

Alice looked up at him in astonishment. "Well, will you look what just come in!" she said.

Pimples hated her. He sat on a stool in the place Mr. Pritchard had only just vacated to take coffee to his wife. "I'd like to have a piece of that new raspberry pie," he said. He glanced nervously at Camille and his voice strangled a little. "Miss, you ought to have a piece of that pie."

Camille looked at him and her eyes grew warm. She knew when a man was having trouble. "No, thanks," she said kindly. "I had breakfast in San Ysidro."

"It's on me," said Pimples frantically.

"No, really, thanks. I couldn't."

"Well, he could," said Alice. "He could eat pies standing on his head in a washtub of flat beer on Palm Sunday." She whirled a pie and got out a knife.

"Double, please," said Pimples.

"I don't think you got any pay coming," said Alice cruelly. "You've eaten yourself right through your salary this week."

Pimples winced. God, how he hated Alice! Alice was watching the blonde. She'd caught it. Every man in the room was alert, his senses feeling toward this girl. Alice was nervous about it. She would know when Juan came in. A moment ago she had wanted the bus to be on its way so she could have a good big drunk. But now, now she was getting nervous.

Ernest Horton said, "If I can get to my sample case I'll show you some cute gadgets I'm selling. New stuff. Very cute."

Camille said, "How long you been out of the Army?"

"Five months," said Ernest.

She dropped her eyes to his lapel with the blue bar and white stars. "That's a nice one," she said. "That's the real big one, isn't it?"

"That's what they tell me," said Ernest. "It don't buy any groceries, though." They laughed together.

"Did the big boss pin it on you?"

"Yeah," said Ernest.

Mr. Pritchard leaned forward. It bothered him that he didn't know what was happening.

Pimples said, "You ought to try some of this raspberry pie."

"I couldn't," said Camille.

Alice said, "You find a fly in that and I'll let you have the rest of the pie right in the kisser."

Camille knew the symptoms. This woman was getting ready to hate her. She glanced uneasily at the other two women in the room. Mrs. Pritchard wouldn't bother her. But the girl, there, who was trying to go without her glasses. Camille just hoped she didn't cross with her. That could be a tough babe. She cried in her mind, "Oh, Jesus, Loraine, get rid of that jerk and let's live in the apartment again." She had a dreadful sense of loneliness and weariness. She wondered how it would be to be married to Mr. Pritchard. He was something like the man she had in mind. It was probably not very hard being married to him. His wife didn't look as though he gave her much trouble.

Bernice Pritchard was in the dark. She didn't hate Camille. Vaguely she knew that some change had come over the room, but she didn't know what it was. "I guess we'd better get our things together," she said brightly to Mildred. And this in spite of the fact that their things were together.

Now Juan came out of the bedroom. He was dressed in clean corduroy trousers, a clean blue shirt, and a leather windbreaker. His thick hair was combed straight back and his face was shiny from shaving.

"All ready, folks?" he said.

Alice watched him as he walked around the end of the lunch counter. He didn't look at Camille at all. Alice felt a stir of alarm. Juan looked at all girls. If he didn't there was something wrong. Alice didn't like it.

Mr. Van Brunt, the old gentleman with the stiff neck, came in from outside and held the screen door open a little. "Looks like more rain," he said.

Juan addressed him shortly. "You'll get on the next Greyhound north," he said.

"I changed my mind," said Van Brunt. "I'm going along with you. I want to see that bridge. But it's going to rain more, I tell you that."

"I thought you didn't want to go."

"I can change my mind, can't I? Why don't you call up again about that bridge?"

"They said it was all right."

"That was some time ago," said Van Brunt. "You're a stranger here. You don't know how fast the San Ysidro can rise. I've seen it come up a foot an hour when the hills dump into her. You better call up."

Juan was exasperated. "Look," he said, "I drive the bus. I've been doing it for some time. Would you mind? You just ride and take a chance on me, or don't, but let me drive it."

Van Brunt turned his face up sideways and stared at Juan coldly. "I don't know whether I'll go with you or not. I might even write a note to the railroad commission. You're a common carrier, you know. Don't forget that."

"Let's go, folks," said Juan.

Alice kept secret eyes on him, and he didn't look at Camille, didn't offer to carry her suitcase. That was bad. Alice didn't like it. It wasn't like Juan.

Camille picked up her suitcase and scuttled out of the door. She didn't want to sit with any of the men. She was tired. Quickly her mind had gone over the possibilities. Mildred Pritchard was unattached and already Mildred didn't like her. But the girl who had quit was out there in the bus. Camille hurried out the door and climbed in. As quickly as they could, Ernest Horton and Mr. Pritchard followed, but Camille was in the bus. Norma sat quite still. Her eyes were hostile and her nose red and shiny. Norma was very much frightened at what she had done.

Camille said, "Would you mind if I sit with you, honey?"

Norma turned her head stiffly and regarded the blonde. "There's plenty of seats," she said.

"Would you mind? I'll tell you why later."

"Suit your own convenience," said Norma grandly. She could tell that this girl was expensively dressed. It didn't make sense. People didn't want to sit with Norma. But there was a reason. Maybe a mysterious reason. Norma knew her movies. Things like this could turn into nine reels of pure delight. She moved over near the window and made room.

"How far are you going?" Norma asked.

"To L. A."

"Why, I'm going there too! Do you live there?"

"Off and on," said Camille. She noticed that the men who had come piling out of the lunchroom had seen her sit down with

Norma. Their drive slowed down. There was going to be no competition. They clustered around the rear end of the bus to have the bags put in the luggage compartment.

Juan lingered at the lunchroom door with Alice looking through the screen at him. "Take it easy," he said. "Had a goddamn mess all morning. Try to get it cleared up before I get home."

A sharpness came on Alice's face. She was about to answer.

Juan went on, "Or one of these days I won't get home."

Her breath caught. "I just don't feel good," she whined.

"Well, start feeling good, then, and don't run it into the ground. Nobody likes sick people very long. Nobody. Get that straight." His eyes were not looking at her but around her and through her, and panic came over Alice. Juan turned away and walked toward the bus.

Alice leaned her elbows on the cross piece of the screen door. Big soft tears filled her eyes. "I'm fat," she said quietly, "and I'm old. Oh, Jesus, I'm old!" The tears ran into her nose. She snorted them back. She said, "You can get young girls, but what can I get? Nothing. An old slob." She sniffled quietly behind the screen.

Mr. Pritchard would have liked to have sat behind the blonde to watch her, but Mrs. Pritchard took a seat near the front and he had to sit down beside her. Mildred sat alone on the other side and behind them. Pimples climbed on and he got the seat Mr. Pritchard wanted, and Ernest Horton sat with him.

Juan noticed with dismay that Van Brunt took the seat directly behind the driver's seat. Juan was nervous. He hadn't had much sleep and some kind of hell had been popping since early morning. He got the bags neatly stacked in the rear trunk, pulled the canvas cover down, and closed the door of the trunk. He waved his hand at Alice leaning inside the screen door. He knew from her posture that she was crying and he intended that she should. She'd got out of hand. He wondered why he stayed with her. Just pure laziness, he guessed. He didn't want to go through the emotional turmoil of leaving her. In spite of himself he'd worry about her and it was too much trouble. He'd need another woman right away and that took a lot of talking and arguing and persuading. It was different just to lay a girl but he would need a woman around, and that was the difference. You got used to one and it was less trouble. Besides, Alice was the only woman he had ever found outside of Mexico who could cook beans. A funny thing. Every little Indian in Mexico could cook beans properly and no one up here except Alice—just enough juice, just the right flavor of the bean without another flavor mixed up with it. Here they put tomatoes and chili and garlic and such things in the beans, and a bean should be cooked for itself, with itself, alone. Juan chuckled. "Because she can cook beans," he said to himself.

But there was another reason too. She loved him. She really did. And he knew it. And you can't leave a thing like that. It's a structure and it has an architecture, and you can't leave it without tearing off a piece of yourself. So if you want to remain whole you stay no matter how much you may dislike staying. Juan was not a man who fooled himself very much.

He was almost to the bus when he turned back and walked quickly to the screen door. "Take care of yourself," he said. His eyes were warm. "Get a slug of liquor for that tooth." He turned away and walked back to the bus. She'd be drunker than a skunk when he got back, but maybe that would blow out her tubes and she'd feel better. He would sleep in Norma's bed if Alice passed out. He couldn't stand the smell of her when she was drunk. She had an acid, bitter smell.

Juan glanced up at the sky. The air was still but up high a wind was blowing, bringing legions of new clouds over the mountains, and these clouds were flat and they were joining together and moving in on one another as they hurried across the sky. The big oaks still dripped water from the morning rain and the geranium leaves held shining drops in the centers. There was a hush on the land and a great activity.

Much as he hated to give Van Brunt any credit, Juan was afraid it was going to rain some more, and soon. He climbed up the steps of the bus. Van Brunt caught him before he even sat down.

"Know where that wind's coming from? Southwest. Know where those clouds are coming from? Southwest. You know where our rain comes from?" he demanded triumphantly. "Southwest."

"O.K., and we're all gonna die sometime," said Juan. "Some of us pretty horribly. You might get run over by a tractor. Ever seen a man run over by a tractor?"

"How do you figure that?" Van Brunt demanded.

"Let it rain," said Juan.

"I don't own a tractor," said Van Brunt. "I got four pair of the best horses in this state. How do you figure that tractor?"

Juan stepped on the starter. It had a high, thin, scratchy sound, but almost immediately his motor started and it sounded good. It sounded smooth and nice. Juan turned in his seat.

"Kit," he called, "keep listening to that rear end."

"O.K.," said Pimples. He felt good about Juan's confidence.

Juan waved his hand to Alice and closed the bus door with his lever. He couldn't see what she was doing through the screen. She would let him get out of sight before she brought out a bottle. He hoped she wouldn't get into any trouble.

Juan drove around the front of the lunchroom and turned right into the black-top road that led to San Juan de la Cruz. It wasn't a very wide road but it was fairly smooth and the crown had a high arch so that it shed the water nicely. The valley and the hills were splashed with gouts of sunlight, and they were fenced with the moving shadows of clouds rushing across the sky. The sun spots and the shadows were somber gray, threatening and sad.

"Sweetheart" bumped along at forty. She was a good bus and the rear end sounded good too.

"I never liked tractors," said Mr. Van Brunt.

"I don't either," Juan agreed. He felt fine all of a sudden.

Van Brunt couldn't let it alone. Juan had succeeded beyond his hopes. Van Brunt turned his head sideways on his stiff neck. "Say, you're not one of these fortunetellers or anything like that?"

"No," said Juan.

"Because I don't believe any stuff like that," said Van Brunt.

"Neither do I," said Juan.

"I wouldn't have a tractor on the place."

Juan was about to say "I had a brother who was kicked to death by a horse," but he thought, "Aw, nuts, the guy's a pushover. I wonder what he's scared of."

Chapter 9

THE highway to San Juan de la Cruz was a black-top road. In the twenties hundreds of miles of concrete highway had been laid down in California, and people had sat back and said, "There, that's permanent. That will last as long as the Roman roads and longer, because no grass can grow up through the concrete to break it." But it wasn't so. The rubber-shod trucks, the pounding automobiles, beat the concrete, and after a while the life went out of it and it began to crumble. Then a side broke off and a hole crushed through and a crack developed and a little ice in the winter spread the crack, so the resisting concrete could not stand the beating of rubber and broke down.

Then the county maintenance crews poured tar in the cracks to keep the water out, and that didn't work, and finally they capped the roads with an asphalt and gravel mixture. That did survive, because it offered no stern face to the pounding tires. It gave a little and came back a little. It softened in the summer and hardened in the winter. And gradually all the roads were capped with shining black that looked silver in the distance.

The San Juan road ran straight for a long way through level fields, and the fields were not fenced because cattle didn't wander any more. The land was too valuable for grazing. The fields were open to the highway. They terminated in ditches beside the road. And in the ditches the wild mustard grew rankly and the wild turnip with its little purple flowers. The ditches were lined with blue lupines. The poppies were tightly rolled, for the open flowers had been beaten off by the rain.

The road ran straight toward the little foothills of the first range—rounded, woman-like hills, soft and sexual as flesh. And the green clinging grass had the bloom of young skin. The hills were rich and lovely with water, and along the smooth and beautiful road "Sweetheart" rolled. Her washed and shining sides reflected in the water of the ditches. The little tokens swung against the windshield—the tiny boxing gloves, the

95

baby's shoes. The Virgin of Guadalupe on her crescent moon on top of the instrument board looked benignly back at the passengers.

There was no rough or ill sound from the rear end, just the curious whine of the transmission. Juan settled back in his seat prepared to enjoy the trip. He had a big mirror in front of him so that he could watch the passengers, and he had a long mirror out the window in which he could see the road behind. The road was deserted. Only a few cars passed, and none came from the direction of San Juan. At first this puzzled him unconsciously, and then he began to worry actively. Perhaps the bridge was out. Well, if it was he would have to come back. He'd take the whole crowd of passengers into San Ysidro and turn them loose there. If the bridge was out, there would be no bus line until it was in again. He noticed in his mirror that Ernest Horton had got his sample case open and was showing Pimples some kind of gadget that whirled and flashed and disappeared. And he noticed that Norma and the blonde had their heads together and were talking. He increased his speed a little.

He didn't think he was going to do anything about the blonde. There wasn't any possible way to get at her. And Juan was old enough not to suffer from something that was out of possibility. Given the opportunity there wasn't any question about what he would do. He had felt a wrench in the pit of his stomach when he first saw the blonde.

Norma had been stiff with Camille so far. She was so frozen up it took her some time to thaw. But Camille needed Norma as a kind of shield, and they had their destination in common.

"I've never been in L. A. or Hollywood," Norma confided softly so that Ernest could not hear. "I won't know where to go or anything."

"What are you going to do?" Camille asked.

"Get a job, I guess. Waitress or something. I'd like to get in pictures."

Camille's mouth tightened in a smile. "You get a job waitressing first," she said. "Pictures are a very tough racket."

"Are you an actress?" Norma asked. "You look like you might be an actress."

"No," said Camille. "I work for dentists. I'm a dental nurse."

"Well, do you live in a hotel, or a room, or a house?"

"I don't have any place to live," said Camille. "I used to have an apartment with a girl friend before I went to Chicago to work."

Norma's eyes grew eager. "I've got a little money put away," she said. "Maybe we could get an apartment together. Say, if I got a job in a restaurant it wouldn't cost hardly anything for food. I could bring stuff home." A hunger was growing in Norma's eyes. "Why, maybe sharing the rent it wouldn't be much. I could make good tips, maybe."

Camille felt warmth for the girl. She looked at the red nose and the dull complexion, the small pale eyes. "We'll see how it goes," she said.

Norma leaned close. "I know your hair's natural," she said. "But maybe you could show me how to kind of touch mine up. My hair's mousy. Just mousy."

Camille laughed. "You'd be surprised if you knew what color my hair is," she said. "Hold still a minute." She studied Norma's face, trying to visualize what cold cream and powder and mascara could do for her, and she thought of the hair shining and waved, and the eyes made a little larger with eyeshadow, and the mouth reshaped with lipstick. Camille hadn't any illusions about beauty. Loraine was a washed-out little rat without make-up but Loraine did all right. It would be fun and company to make this girl over and to give her some confidence. It might even be better than Loraine.

"Let's think about it," she said. "This is pretty country. I'd like to live in the country some time." A picture had projected itself on her mind, the pattern of what would happen. She would fix Norma up. She could be kind of pretty if she was careful. And then Norma would meet a boy and naturally she'd bring him home to show him off and the boy would make passes at Camille and Norma would hate her. That's the way it would happen. That's the way it had happened. But what the hell! it would be fun before it happened. And maybe she could anticipate it and never be in when Norma brought a boy home.

She felt warm and friendly. "Let's think about it," she said.

On the highway ahead Juan saw a crushed jackrabbit. Lots of people like to run over things like that, but Juan didn't. He moved his steering wheel so that the flattened carcass passed between the wheels and there was no crunching under the tires. He had the bus at forty-five. The big highway busses sometimes went sixty miles an hour, but Juan had plenty of time. The road was straight for another two miles before it began wandering into the soft foothills. Juan took one hand off the wheel and stretched.

Mildred Pritchard felt the telegraph poles whipping by as little blows on her eyes. She had her glasses on again. She watched Juan's face in the mirror. She could see little more than a profile from her angle. She noticed that he raised his head to look back at the blonde every minute or so, and she felt a bitter anger. She was confused about what had happened that morning. No one knew, of course, unless Juan Chicoy had guessed. She was still a little swollen and itchy from the thing. A sentence kept repeating itself in her mind. She's not a blonde and she's not a nurse and her name is not Camille Oaks. The sentence went on, over and over. And then she chuckled at herself inwardly. "I'm trying to destroy her," she thought. "I'm doing a stupid thing. Why not admit I'm jealous? I'm jealous. All right. Does admitting it make me any less jealous? No, it does not. But she forced my father to make a fool of himself. All right. Do I care whether my father is a fool? No, I do not—if I'm not with him. I don't want people to think I'm his daughter, that's all. No, that's not true either. I don't want to go to Mexico with him. I can hear everything he'll say." She was uncomfortable and the movement of the bus was not helping. "Basketball," she thought, "that's the stuff." She flexed the muscles of her thighs and thought about the engineering student with the crew-cut hair. She pictured her affair with him.

Mr. Pritchard was bored and tired. He could be very irritating when he was bored. He twitched. "This looks like rich country," he said to his wife. "California raises most of the vegetables for the United States, you know."

Mrs. Pritchard could hear herself talking after she got home. "Then we drove through miles and miles of green fields with poppies and lupines, just like a garden. There was a blond girl got on at a funny little place and the men made fools of themselves, even Elliott. I joshed him about it for a week afterward." She'd write it in a letter. "And I'm pretty sure the poor little painted thing was just as nice and sweet as could be. She said she was a nurse, but I think she was probably an actress—little parts, you know. There are so many of them in Hollywood. Thirty-eight thousand listed. They've got a big casting agency.

Thirty-eight thousand." Her head nodded a little. Bernice was sleepy and hungry. "I wonder what adventures we'll have now," she thought.

When his wife slipped into her daydream Mr. Pritchard knew it. He had been married to her long enough to know when she wasn't listening to him, and ordinarily he went right on talking. He often clarified his thinking about business or politics by telling his thoughts to Bernice when she wasn't listening. He had a trained memory for figures and for bits of information. He knew approximately how many tons of sugar beets were produced in the Salinas valley. He had read it and retained it in spite of the fact that he had no use whatever for the information. He felt that such information was good to know and he had never questioned its value or why it might be good to know. But now he had no inclination toward knowledge. A powerful influence was battering at him from the rear of the bus. He wanted to turn around and look at the blonde. He wanted to sit where he could watch her. Horton and Pimples were behind him. He couldn't just sit opposite and look at her.

Mrs. Pritchard asked, "How old do you think she is?" And the question shocked him because he had been wondering the same thing.

"How old who is?" he asked.

"The young woman. The blond young woman."

"Oh, her. How should I know?" His answer was so rough that his wife looked a little bewildered and hurt. He saw it and tried to cover his mistake. "Little girls know more about little girls," he said. "You could tell better than I could."

"Why? I don't know. Well, with that make-up and the hair tint it's hard to tell. I just wondered. Somewhere between twenty-five and thirty, I guess."

"I wouldn't know about that," said Mr. Pritchard. He looked out the window at the approaching foothills. His palms were a little damp and the magnet drew at him from the rear of the bus. He wanted to look around. "I don't know about that," said Mr. Pritchard. "But I'm interested in that young Horton. He's young, and he's got lots of get-up, and he's got ideas. He really caught my fancy. You know, I might find a place for a man like that in the organization." This was business.

Bernice too could draw a magic circle around herself, with

motherhood, or say, menstruation, a subject like that, and no man could or would try to get in. Business was her husband's magic circle. She had no right to go near him when it was business. She had no knowledge nor interest in business. It was his privacy and she respected it.

"He seems a nice young man," she said. "His grammar and his background—"

"My God, Bernice!" he cried irritably. "Business isn't background and grammar. It's what you can produce. Business is the most democratic thing in the world. It's what you can do that counts."

He was trying to remember what the blonde's lips looked like. He believed that full-lipped women were voluptuous. "I'd like to have a little talk with Horton before he gets away," Mr. Pritchard said.

Bernice knew that he was restless.

"Why don't you talk to him now?" she suggested.

"Oh, I don't know. He's sitting with that boy."

"Well, I'm sure that boy will move if you ask him nicely." She was convinced that anyone would do anything if nicely asked. And in her case she was right. She claimed and got the most outrageous favors from strangers simply by asking nicely. She would ask a bellboy to carry her bags four blocks to the station because it was too close, really, to get a cab, and then thank him nicely and give him a dime.

Now she knew she was helping her husband to do something he wanted to do. What it was she didn't quite know. She wanted to get back to writing the imaginary letter about their trip. "Elliott is so interested in everything. He had long talks with everyone. I guess that's why he's so successful. He takes such an interest. And he's so thoughtful. There was a boy with big pimples and Elliott didn't want to disturb him, but I told him just to ask nicely. People do love nice manners."

Mr. Pritchard was cleaning his nails again with the gold appliance he wore on his watch chain.

Pimples' eyes were on the back of Camille's head. But first when he had sat down he made sure that he couldn't see her legs under the seat, not even her ankles. Now and then she turned to look out of the window, and he could see her profile, the long, darkened eyelashes which curled upward, the straight, powdered nose, nostrils a little coated with tobacco smoke and the dust of traveling. Her upper lip curved upward to a sharp line before it pillowed out in its heavy red petal, and Pimples could see the downy hair on her upper lip. For some reason this aroused him agonizingly. When her head was turned straight ahead he could see one of her ears where the hair parted a little and exposed it. He could see the heavy lobe and the crease behind her ear where it fitted so close to her head. The edge of her ear was fluted. As he stared at the ear she almost seemed to be conscious of his look, for she raised her chin and shook her head from side to side so that the part in her hair fell together and concealed the ear. She got a comb from her purse because the backward shake had uncovered the deep forceps scars along her jaw. Now Pimples saw the ugly scars for the first time. He had to lean sideways to see them, and a stab of pain entered his chest. He felt a deep and unreasoning sorrow, but the sorrow was sexual too. He imagined himself holding her head in his arms and stroking the poor scars with his finger. He swallowed several times.

Camille was saying softly to Norma, "Then there's this Wee Kirk i' the Heather. I guess that's the prettiest cemetery in the world. You know, you have to get a ticket to get in. I like just to walk around in there. It's so beautiful and the organ plays nearly all the time and you find people buried there that you've seen in pictures. I always said I'd like to be buried there."

"I don't like to talk about things like that," said Norma. "It's bad luck."

Pimples had been vaguely discussing the Army with Ernest Horton. "They say you can learn a trade and travel all over. I don't know. I'm taking a course in radar engineering. It starts next week by mail. I guess radar is going to be pretty hot stuff. But you can get a real good course in radar in the Army."

Ernest said, "I don't know how it would be in peacetime. You can have it when there's a war."

"Did you get to do some real fighting?"

"I didn't ask for it but I got it."

"Where were you?" Pimples asked.

"All over hell," said Ernest.

"Maybe I could get a good line and get in selling, like you," Pimples suggested.

"Oh, that's just plain starvation till you get your contacts," Ernest said. "It took me five years to build up my contacts and then I got drafted. I'm just getting back on my feet now. You can't just step into it and you've got to work at it. It doesn't look like work but it is. If I was to start over again I'd learn a trade so I could have a home. Pretty nice to have a wife and a couple of kids." Ernest always said this. When he was drunk he believed it. He didn't want a home. He loved moving around and seeing different people. He would run away from home immediately. Once he had been married, and the second day he had walked out, leaving a thoroughly frightened and angry wife, and he never saw her again, nor wrote to her. But he saw her picture once. She was picked up for marrying five men and drawing Army allotments from each one. What a dame. A real hustler. Ernest almost admired her. There was hustling that paid dividends.

"Why don't you go back to school?" he asked Pimples.

"I don't want no fancy stuff," said Pimples. "Them college boys are just a bunch of nances. I want a man's life."

Camille had leaned close to Norma and was whispering in her ear. The two girls were shaking with laughter. The bus surged around the bend and entered the hill country. The road cut between high banks, and the soil of the cuts was dark and dripping with water. Little goldy-backed ferns clung to the gravel and dripped with rain. Juan put his right hand on the wheel and let his elbows hang free. There would be fifteen minutes of twisting hill road now with no straight stretches at all. He glanced in his rear-view mirror at the blonde. Her eyes were puckered with laughter and she'd covered her mouth with spread fingers the way little girls do.

Mr. Pritchard, going back, was not careful, and when the bus took a curve he was flung sideways. He clutched at the seat-back, missed it, and fell sprawling on Camille's lap. His right hand reaching to break his fall whipped her short skirt up and his arm went between her knees. Her skirt was slightly torn. She helped him disengage himself and she pulled down her skirt. Mr. Pritchard was blushing violently.

"I'm very sorry," he said.

"Oh, it's all right."

"But I've torn your skirt."

"I can mend it."

"But I must pay to have it mended."

"I'll just patch it up myself. It isn't bad." She looked at his face and knew that he was prolonging the affair as much as he could. "He'll want to know what address to send the money to," she thought.

Mrs. Pritchard called, "Elliott, are you trying to sit in that lady's lap?"

Even Juan laughed then. Everyone laughed. And suddenly the bus was not full of strangers. Some chemical association was formed. Norma laughed hysterically. All the tension of the morning came out in her laughter.

Mr. Pritchard said. "I must say, you take it very well. I didn't come back here to sit in your lap. I wanted to have a few words with this gentleman. Son," he said to Pimples, "would you mind moving for just a little while. I have some business I'd like to talk over with Mr.—I don't think I heard your name."

"Horton," said Ernest, "Ernest Horton."

Mr. Pritchard had a whole series of tactics for getting on with people. He never forgot the name of a man richer or more powerful than he, and he never knew the name of a man less powerful. He had found that to make a man mention his own name would put that man at a slight disadvantage. For a man to speak his own name made him a little naked and unprotected.

Camille was looking at her torn skirt and talking softly to Norma. "I always wanted to live on a hill," she said. "I love hills. I love to walk in hills."

"It's all right after you're rich and famous," Norma said firmly. "I know people in pictures that every chance they get, why, they go hunting and fishing and wear old clothes and smoke a pipe."

Camille was bringing Norma out. She had never in her whole life felt so excited and free. She could say anything she wanted. She giggled a little.

"It's nicer to wear old dirty clothes if you've got a closet full of nice fresh clean ones," she said. "Old clothes are the only kind I've got and I'm god-damned sick of it." She glanced at Camille to see how she'd react to such candor.

Camille nodded. "You aren't kidding, sister." Something very strong and sympathetic was growing up between these two. Mr. Pritchard tried to hear the conversation but he couldn't.

The ditches beside the highway ran full with water descending toward the valley. The heavy clouds were massing for a new attack.

"It's coming on to rain," Van Brunt said happily.

Juan grunted. "I had a brother-in-law kicked to death by a horse," he observed.

"Couldn't have used any sense," said Van Brunt. "Horse kicks a man, it's usually the man's fault."

"Killed him anyway," said Juan, and he settled into silence.

The bus was nearing the top of the grade and the turns were becoming tighter all the time.

"I was very much interested in our little talk this morning, Mr. Horton. It's a pleasure to talk with a man with some get-up and go. I'm always on the look-out for men like that for my organization."

"Thanks," said Ernest.

"We're having trouble right now with these returning veterans," said Mr. Pritchard. "Good men, you understand. And I think everything should be done for them—everything. But they've been out of the run. They're rusty. In business you've got to keep up every minute. A man that has kept up is twice as valuable as a man that has been out of the mill, so to speak." He looked at Ernest for approval. Instead he saw a kind of hard, satiric look come into Ernest's eyes.

"I see your point," Ernest said. "I was four years in the Army."

"Oh!" said Mr. Pritchard. "Oh, yes—you're not wearing your discharge button, I see."

"I've *got* a job," Ernest said.

Mr. Pritchard fumbled with his thoughts. He had made a bad mistake. He wondered what the thing was in Ernest's lapel button. It looked familiar. He should know. "Well, they're a fine bunch of boys," he said, "and I only hope we can put in an administration that will take care of them."

"Like after the last war?" Ernest asked. It was a double brush, and Mr. Pritchard began to wonder if he'd been right about Horton. There was a kind of brutality about Horton. He had a kind of swagger and a headlong quality so many ex-soldiers had. The doctors said they would get over it just as soon as they lived a good normal life for a while. They were out of line. Something would have to be done.

"I'm the first one to come to the defense of our veterans," Mr.

Pritchard said. He wished to God he could get off the subject. Ernest was looking at him with a slightly crooked smile that he was beginning to recognize in applicants for jobs. "I just thought I'd like to interview a man with your get-up and go," Mr. Pritchard said uneasily. "When I get back from my vacation I'd be very glad to have you call on me. We can always make room for a man who's got it."

"Well, sir," said Ernest, "I get very sick of running around the country all the time. I often thought I'd like to have a home and a wife and a couple of kids. That's the real way to live. Come home at night and lock the whole world outside, and a boy and a girl, maybe. This sleeping in hotels isn't living."

Mr. Pritchard nodded. "You're four-square right," he said, and he was very much relieved. "I'm just the right man to say that to. Twenty-one years married and I wouldn't have it any other way."

"You've been lucky," said Ernest. "You're wife's a fine-looking woman."

"And she's a fine woman," said Mr. Pritchard. "The most thoughtful person in the world. I often wonder what I'd do without her."

"I was married once," said Ernest. "My wife died." His face was sad.

"I'm sorry," said Mr. Pritchard. "And this may sound silly. Time does heal wounds. And maybe some day—well, I wouldn't give up hope."

"Oh, I don't."

"I didn't mean to pry into your affairs," said Mr. Pritchard, "but I've been thinking about your idea for those lapel slipcovers for a dark suit to convert into a tuxedo. If you're not tied up with anyone I thought we might—well, talk about doing a little business."

"Well," said Ernest, "it's like I told you. Clothes manufacturers won't want something that will rule out some of their business. I just don't see the angle right now."

Mr. Pritchard said, "I forget whether you said you had applied for a patent."

"Well, no. I told you. I just registered the idea."

"How do you mean, registered?"

"Well, I wrote out a description and made some drawings and put it in an envelope and mailed it to myself, registered mail. That proves when I did it because that envelope is sealed."

"I see," said Mr. Pritchard, and he wondered whether such a method would have any standing in court. He didn't know. But it was always better to take the inventor in on a percentage. Only the really big fellows could afford to lift an invention whole. The big fellows could afford a long fight. They figured it was cheaper than cutting in an inventor and the figures proved they were right. But Mr. Pritchard's firm wasn't big enough and, besides, he always thought that generosity paid off.

"I've got an idea or two that might work out," he said. "Course, it'll take some organization. Now, suppose you and I could make a deal. This is just a supposition, you understand. I'd handle the organization and we would take a percentage of profit after expenses."

"But they don't want it," Ernest said. "I've asked around."

Mr. Pritchard laid a hand on Ernest's knee. He had a hollow feeling that he ought to shut up, but he remembered the satiric look in Ernest's eyes and he wanted Ernest to admire him and to like him. He couldn't shut up.

"Suppose we formed a company and we protected the idea?" he said. "Patent it, I mean. Now we organize to manufacture this product, a national advertising campaign—"

"Just a moment," Ernest broke in.

But Mr. Pritchard was carried away. "Now suppose these layouts just happened to fall into the hands of, say, oh, Hart, Schaffner and Marx or some big manufacturer like that, or maybe the association. They'd get ahold of it by accident, of course. Well, maybe they'd like to buy us out."

Ernest began to look interested. "Buy the patent?"

"Buy not only the patent but the whole company."

"But if they bought the patent then they could kill it," Ernest said.

Mr. Pritchard's eyes were slitted and his pupils shone through his glasses and a little smile lay on the corners of his mouth. For the first time since she had got off the bus from San Ysidro he had forgotten Camille. "Look ahead a little further," he said. "When we sell and dissolve the company we only pay a capital gain tax on the profits."

"That's smart," said Ernest excitedly. "Yes, sir, that's very smart. That's blackmail and a very high-class blackmail. Yes, sir, nobody could touch us."

The smile vanished from Mr. Pritchard's mouth. "What do you mean, blackmail? We would intend to go ahead and manufacture. We could even order machinery."

"That's what I mean," said Ernest. "It's very high class. It's all wrapped up. You're a smart man."

Mr. Pritchard said, "I hope you don't think it's dishonest. I've been in business thirty-five years and I've climbed to the head of my company. I can be proud of my record."

"I'm not criticizing you," Ernest said. "I think you've got a very sound idea there. I'm for it, only—"

"Only what?" said Mr. Pritchard.

"I'm kind of low on dough," said Ernest, "and I'm gonna need a quick buck. Oh, well, I can borrow it, I guess."

"What do you need money for? Maybe I could advance—"

"No," said Ernest, "I'll get it myself."

"Is it some new wrinkle you figured out?" Mr. Pritchard asked.

"Yes," said Ernest. "I gotta get this idea into the patent office by carrier pigeon."

"You don't think for one minute—"

"Of course not," said Ernest. "Certainly not. But I'm gonna be happier when that envelope gets to Washington alone."

Mr. Pritchard leaned back in his seat and smiled. The highway whirled and twisted ahead, and between two great abutments was the pass into the next valley.

"You'll be all right, son. I think we can do business. I don't want you to think I'd take advantage though. My record speaks for itself."

"Oh, I don't," said Ernest. "I don't." He looked secretly at Mr. Pritchard. "It's just that I've got a couple of very luscious dames in L. A. and I don't want to get in that apartment and forget everything." He saw the reaction he wanted.

"I'm going to be two days in Hollywood," Mr. Pritchard said. "Maybe we could talk a little business."

"Like in these dames' apartment?"

"Well, a man needs some kind of relaxation. I'm going to be at the Beverly Wilshire. You could call me there."

"I sure will," said Ernest. "What color dame you like best?"

"Don't misunderstand me," said Mr. Pritchard. "I like to sit and have a scotch and soda but I've got a position, you know. I don't want you to misunderstand."

"Oh, I don't," said Ernest. "I could maybe pick up the blonde ahead here, if you want."

"Don't be silly," said Mr. Pritchard.

Pimples had moved forward in the bus. On the underside of his jaw he felt an itching burn and he knew an eruption was forming. He sat down in the seat across from Mildred Pritchard. He didn't want to touch the new place but he was powerless over his hands. His right hand moved upward and his forefinger rubbed the lump under the chin. It was a very sore lump. This one was going to be a devil. He knew already what it would look like. He wanted to squeeze it, to scratch it, to rip it out. His nerves were on edge. He forced his hand into his coat pocket and clenched his fist there.

Mildred was staring vacantly out of the window.

"I wish I could go to Mexico," Pimples said.

Mildred looked around at him in surprise. Her glasses caught the light from his window and glared blindly at him.

Pimples swallowed. "I never been there," he said weakly.

"Neither have I," said Mildred.

"Yeah, but you're going."

She nodded. She didn't want to look at him because she couldn't keep her eyes from his eczema and that embarrassed him. "Maybe you can go soon," she said uneasily.

"Oh, I'll go," said Pimples. "I'll go everywhere. I'm a great traveler. I'd rather travel than anything. You get experience that way."

She nodded again and took off her glasses in protection against him. Now she couldn't see him so clearly.

"I thought maybe I'd be a missionary like Spencer Tracy and go to China and cure them of all those diseases. You ever been to China?"

"No," said Mildred. She was fascinated by his thinking.

Pimples took most of his ideas from moving pictures and the rest from radio. "It's very poor people there in China," he said, "some of them so poor they just starve to death right outside your window if some missionary don't come along and help them. And if you help them, why, they love you, and let any Jap come around and make trouble and they stick a knife right in him." He nodded solemnly. "I think they're just as good as you and me," he said. "Spencer Tracy just came along and he cured them up and they loved him—and you know what he done? He found his own soul. And there was this girl and he didn't know whether he ought to marry her because she had a past. Of course, it came out it wasn't her fault and it wasn't even true, but this old dame told lies about her." Pimples' eyes glowed with pity and enthusiasm. "But Spencer Tracy didn't believe those lies and he lived in an old palace that had secret passages and tunnels and—well, then the Japs come."

"I saw the picture," Mildred said.

The bus went into second gear for the last climb. Now it was in the gap at the top and then it emerged and turned sharp left, and below was the valley gloomy with gray clouds, and the great loop of the San Ysidro River gleamed like dark steel under the glowering light. Juan eased the bus into high gear and began the descent.

Chapter 10

THE San Ysidro River runs through the San Juan valley, turning and twisting until it discharges sluggishly into Black Rock Bay under the protection of Bat Point. The valley itself is long and not very wide, and the San Ysidro River, having not very far to run, makes the most of what distance it has by moving from one side of the level stretch to the other. Here it cuts under a cliff, against a mountain, and then it spreads thinly out on sandbanks. During a good part of the year there is no surface water at all, and the sandy bed grows full of willows which stretch their roots down toward underground water.

Rabbits and raccoons and small foxes and coyotes make their homes in the willows of the river bottom when the water is down. At the head of the valley to the north and east the river rises, not as one head, but in many little branches, so that the source on a map looks like a tree with small, leafless branches. The dry and stony hills with shoulders and gullies and canyons do not supply water to the river during all the year, but when the rains fall in the late winter and spring the rocky shoulders absorb a little of the water and cast the rest in black torrents to the little streams that tumble out of the creases, and the streamlets combine and join larger creeks and the creeks come together at the northern end of the valley.

So it is that in the late spring, when the hills have digested as much rain as they can, a heavy storm may swell the San Ysidro River to a raging flood in a very few hours. Then the foamy yellow water cuts at the banks and great hunks of farmland cave into the river. Then the bodies of cows and sheep go tumbling and rolling in the yellow flood. It is an unstable and precocious river; dead during part of the year and deadly during another part.

In the middle of the valley, which is on a direct line between Rebel Corners and San Juan de la Cruz, the river makes a great loop, ranging from side to side of the level valley, casting its coil against the mountain on the eastern edge and moving away to cross the fields and farmlands. In the old times the road followed the loop of the river and crawled up the side of the hill to avoid crossing. But with the coming of engineers and steel and concrete, two bridges had been thrown over the river, and these cut out twelve miles of the San Ysidro's playfulness.

They were wooden bridges, backed and suspended by steel rods, and each one was supported in the middle and at the ends by concrete piers. The wood was painted dark red and the iron was dark with rust. On the river side of each bridge backwaters of piles and braided, mattressed willow deflected the water toward the spans and kept the gnawing current from undermining the bridgeheads.

These bridges were not very old, but they had been built at a time when the tax rate was not only low, but much of it uncollectable because of what was called "hard times." The county engineer had found it necessary to build within a budget that allowed only the simplest construction. His timber should have been heavier and his struts more numerous, but he had to build a bridge within a certain cost and he did. And every year the farmers of the middle valley watched the river with cynical apprehension. They knew that some time there would be a quick and overwhelming flood that would take the bridges out. Every year they petitioned the county to replace the wooden bridges, but there weren't enough votes in the rural section to make the petitions mandatory. The large towns, which had not only the votes but the taxable assets, got the improvements. People were not moving to the medium-rich farmlands. A good service-station corner in San Juan had a higher assessed valuation than a hundred acres of grainland in the valley. The farmers knew that it was only a question of time before the bridges were destroyed and then, they said, the county would god-damned well come to its senses.

A hundred yards from the first bridge toward Rebel Corners there was a little general store on the highway. It stocked the groceries, the tires, the hardware a man bought on Saturday afternoon or when he didn't have time to drive either to San Juan de la Cruz or to San Ysidro over the range. This was Breed's General Store. And of late years it had, as did all country stores, added gas pumps and a stock of automobile accessories.

Mr. and Mrs. Breed were unofficial custodians of the bridge, and at flood time their phone rang constantly and they supplied information about the river's rise. They were used to this. Their one great fear was that some day the bridge would go out and the new one might be quarter of a mile down the river, and then they would have to move their store or build a new one near the new bridge.

At least half of their trade nowadays was in soft drinks, sandwiches, gasoline, and candy bought by travelers on the highway. Even the bus between Rebel Corners and San Juan invariably stopped there. It brought express packages, and the passengers drank soft drinks. Juan Chicoy and the Breeds were old and good friends.

And now the river was up, and not only up, but, as Mr. Breed said to his wife, "there's a backwash cutting in under the piles above the bridge, and if it cuts a channel in back, there goes your ball game." He had made half a dozen trips to the bridgehead since daylight. This was a bad one and Mr. Breed knew it. Thin-lipped and unshaven, he had stood on the bridge at eight o'clock this morning and watched the tumbling yellow water laced with yellow foam and dotted with uprooted scrub oak and cotton-wood. And he had seen a few planks of planed lumber come twisting down, and then a piece of roof with shingles still on, and then the drowned, bobbing body of McElroy's black Angus bull, square and short-legged. As it went under the bridge it rolled over on its back, and Breed could see the wild upturned eyes and the flapping tongue. It made Breed sick to his stomach.

Everyone knew McElroy's barn was too close to the bank and that bull cost eighteen hundred dollars. McElroy didn't have that kind of money to throw away. He didn't see any of the rest of the herd come down, but the bull would be enough. Mac had put a lot of faith in that bull.

Breed walked farther out on the bridge. The water was only three feet below the timbers now and Breed could feel the plunging water plaguing the caissons to protest under his feet. He rubbed his unshaven chin with his fingers and walked back to the store. He didn't tell his wife about McElroy's black Angus. It would only make her sad.

When Juan Chicoy called up about the bridge Breed told him the truth. The bridge was still in, but God knew for how long. The water was still rising. The bare, stony hills were still emptying their freshets into into the river, and it was clouding up again.

At nine o'clock the lower timbers cleared the flood only by eighteen inches. Once the pressure came on those struts and braces and a few uprooted trees banged into the bridge, it was only a question of time. Breed stood inside his screen door and drummed his fingers on the wire.

"Let me fix you some breakfast," his wife said. "You'd think you owned the bridge."

"I guess I do in a way," said Breed. "If it went out they'd say it was my fault. I've called the supervisor's office and I've called the county engineer. They're both closed. If that channel gets back of the pier, there goes your ball game."

"You'd better eat some breakfast. I'll make you some wheat cakes."

"All right," Breed said. "Don't make them too thick."

"I never make them thick," said Mrs. Breed. "Want an egg on top?"

"Sure," said Breed. "I don't know whether Juan is going to make it or not. He's not due for more than an hour yet and, Jesus! how the water is coming up!"

"No reason to swear," said Mrs. Breed.

Her husband looked around at her. "I'd say this was one of the times when there's every reason to swear. I'm going to take a drink."

"Before breakfast?"

"Before anything."

She didn't know about the black bull, of course. He went to the wall phone and rang McElroy's, a three-two ring, and he kept it up until Pinedale, two miles this side of McElroy's, answered.

"I've been trying to get him too," Pinedale said. "His line's dead. I'm going to ride up and see if he's all right."

"I wish you would," said Breed. "His new bull went under the bridge this morning."

Mrs. Breed raised frightened eyes. "Walter!" she cried.

"Well, it's true. I didn't want you to fret."

"Walter! Oh, my God!" said Mrs. Breed.

Chapter 11

ALICE CHICOY stood inside the screen door and watched the bus pull away. She let the tears dry on her cheeks.

When the bus passed beyond her view from the door she went to the side window from which she could see the county road. The bus ran into a patch of sunlight and gleamed for a moment, and then she couldn't see it any more. Alice drew a great breath and released it in a luxurious sigh. It was her day! She was alone. She felt happy and secret, and she felt sinful too. Slowly she smoothed her dress down over her hips and caressed her thighs. She looked at her nails. No, later for that.

She looked slowly around the lunchroom. She could still smell cigarette smoke. There were things to be done, yet it was her day and she went about them slowly. First she got from the cupboard a cardboard sign that said "Closed" in large letters. She went outside and hung the sign on a nail on the edge of the screen door. Then she went inside and closed and latched the screen door. And she pulled the inner door and turned the key in it. Next she went from window to window and let down the Venetian blinds and pulled the slats downward so no one could see in.

The lunchroom was dusky and very quiet. Alice worked deliberately. She washed and put away the dirty coffee cups and she washed the lunch counter and the tabletops. The pies she put out of sight under the counter. Then she brought a broom from the bedroom and swept the floor and put the dust and the mud and the cigarette butts in the garbage can. The counter gleamed a little in the dusky light and the tabletops looked white and clean.

Alice came around the counter and sat on one of the stools. It was her day! She felt silly and giddy. "Well, why not?" she said aloud. "I don't have much fun. Bring me," she said, "bring me a double whisky and hurry it up."

She put her hands on the counter and looked at them carefully. "Poor work-ruined hands," she whispered, "dear hands." Then in a shout, "Where the hell is that whisky?" And she answered herself, "Yes, ma'am, it's coming right up, ma'am."

"Well, that's better," said Alice. "I just want you to know who you're talking to. Don't put on any lip because you can't get away with it. I've got my eye on you."

"Yes, ma'am," she answered herself. And she got up and went in back of the counter.

At the far end and low to the floor there was a small cabinet. Alice bent over, opened the door, and reached blindly in and brought out a fifth of Old Grandad bourbon. She picked a water glass from the rack and carried the bottle and the glass to the counter in front of the stool where she had been sitting.

"Here you are, ma'am."

"Take it over to that table. Do you think I look like someone that stands up at bars?"

"No, ma'am."

"And bring another glass. And a bottle of cold beer."

"Yes, ma'am."

She carried all these things to the table beside the door and laid them out. "You can go now," she said, and answered, "Yes, ma'am."

"But don't go far, I might want something."

As she poured out the beer she giggled to herself. If anybody heard me they'd think I was crazy. Well, maybe I am. She poured out a fine shot in the other glass. "Alice," she said, "ready, set, go!" She waved the glass and drank slowly. She did not toss it. She let the hot, straight whisky ease and burn and flow over her tongue and in back of her tongue, and she swallowed slowly and felt the bite on her palate, and the warmth of the whisky went into her chest and into her stomach. Even after she had emptied the glass she still held it to her lips. She put down the glass and she said, "Ah!" and breathed outward harshly.

She could taste the sweet whisky again on her returning breath. Now she reached for the tumbler of beer. She crossed her legs and drank very slowly until the glass was empty.

"God!" she said.

It seemed to Alice she had never realized how utterly comfortable and charming the lunchroom was, the light glimmering down between the slanting blinds. She heard a truck go by on the highway and it disturbed her. Suppose something happened to interfere with her day? Well, they'd have to break the door down. She wouldn't let anyone in. She poured two fingers of whisky in one glass and four fingers of beer in the other glass.

"There's more than one way to skin a drink," she said, and she tossed the whisky in and tossed the beer right in after it. Now, there's an idea. It doesn't taste the same. The way you drink changes the taste. Why had no one else ever found that out, only Alice. Somebody should write that down—"The way you drink makes the taste." There was a little tension in her right eyelid, and a curious but pleasant pain ran down the veins of her arms.

"Nobody has time to find out things," she said solemnly. "No time." She poured half a glass of beer and filled the glass with whisky. "I wonder if anybody ever tried this before?"

The metal paper-napkin holder was in front of her and she could see her face in it. "Hello, kid," she said. She waved the glass, and it was as distorted in the shining metal as her face. "Here's a go, kid. Your health, kid." And she drank the beer and the whisky the way a thirsty man drinks milk. "Ah," she said, "that's not so god-damned bad. No sir. I think I've got something there. That's good."

She adjusted the paper-napkin holder so that she could see herself better. But a bend in the metal surface made her nose look broken at the top and fat and bulbous at the bottom. She got up and went around the counter and into the bedroom, and she brought a round hand mirror back to the table and propped it against the sugar dispenser. She settled herself and crossed her legs. "Now there! I'd like to invite you for a drink." She poured whisky in each glass. "No beer," she said. "All out of beer. Well, we'll fix that."

She went to the icebox and brought another bottle of beer. "Now, you see," she said to the mirror, "we first put a little whisky—not too much—not too little—and we add just the right amount of beer. And there you are." She pushed one glass toward the mirror and drained the other one. "Some people are afraid to take a drink," she said. "They can't handle it."

"Oh, you don't want it? Well, that's your privilege. I'm not going to make you take it. I'm not going to let it go to waste, either." And she drank off the other glass. Her cheeks were tingling now as though a frost were stinging the surface. She brought the mirror close and inspected herself. Her eyes were damp and shiny. She whipped back a strand of loose hair.

"No reason to let yourself run down just because you're having a good time." And without warning a vision flipped into place in her head and she turned the mirror face down. The vision struck so hard and so quickly that it was like a blow. Perhaps it was the darkened room. Alice cried, "I don't want to think about that. I hate to think about that."

But the thought and vision were in. A darkened room and a white bed and her mother paralyzed, rigid, unmoving, the eyes staring straight up, and then the white hand rising from the counterpane in a gesture of despair, a gesture for help. Alice could creep in, no matter how stealthily, and that hand would rise in frightful helplessness, and Alice would hold it for a moment and then put it gently down and go out. Every time she came into that room she would beg the hand not to rise, to lie still, to be dead, like the rest of the body.

"I don't want to think about that," she cried. "How did that get in?" Her hand shook and the bottle rattled against the glass. She poured an enormous drink and drained it and it caught in her throat so that she coughed, and she just saved herself from being sick. "That'll fix you," she said. "I want to think about something else."

She imagined herself in bed with Juàn, but her mind slipped on past that. "I could have had any man I wanted," she boasted. "Enough made passes at me, God knows, and I didn't give in much." Her lips writhed away from her teeth a little salaciously. "Maybe I should of while I could. I'm getting along—That's a god-damned lie," she shouted, "I'm as good as I ever was. I'm better! Who the hell wants a skinny bitch that don't know what to do? No real man wants stuff like that. I could go right out now and pick them off like flies."

The bottle was a little less than half full now. She spilled some in pouring and giggled at herself. "I do believe I'm getting a little drunk," she said.

There came a great knocking at the screen door and Alice froze and sat silent. The knocking came again. A man's voice called, "Nobody here. I thought I heard talking."

"Well, try it again. They might be in back," a woman's voice answered.

Alice picked up the hand mirror gently and looked at herself. She nodded her head and closed one eye in a large wink. The knocking came again.

"I tell you there's nobody here."

"Well, try the door."

Alice heard the rattling of the screen door.

"It's locked up," the man said, and the woman replied, "It's locked on the inside. They must be in there."

The man laughed and his feet scraped on gravel. "Well, if they're in there they want to be alone. Don't you ever want to be alone, baby? With me, I mean."

"Oh, shut up," said the woman. "I want a sandwich."

"For that you'll have to wait."

Alice wondered why she hadn't heard the car or the footsteps on the gravel before the knock. "I'll bet I'm plastered," she thought. She could hear the car drive away all right.

"Can't take 'no' for an answer," Alice said aloud. "Just because a person wants to take a day to rest and get pulled together, why, they've got to have a god-damned sandwich."

She held up the bottle and squinted judiciously through the glass. "Not a lot left." She became frightened. Suppose she should run out before she was ready? And then she nodded and smiled to herself. There were two bottles of port wine right in the back of that cabinet. They gave her a sense of security and she poured herself a big drink and sipped at it. Juan didn't like to be around women when they were drinking. He said their faces got crooked and he hated that. Well, Alice would just show him. She drank half the whisky in her glass and stood up heavily.

"Now, you just stay here and wait for me," she said politely to the glass. Turning the edge of the counter she swayed a little, and the corner bit into her side just above the hip. "That's going to be black and blue," she said. She crossed the bedroom and went into the bathroom.

She dampened the washcloth and rubbed soap into it till she had a thick paste and then she scrubbed her face. She scrubbed hard beside her nose and in the little crease that crossed her chin. She put the cloth over her little finger and twisted it into her nostrils and she washed her ears. Then, with her eyes squinted shut, she rinsed the soap off and looked at herself in the mirror over the basin. Her face seemed very red and her eyes were a little bloodshot. For a long time she worked on her face. Cream, and then that rubbed off on a towel. She inspected the towel for dirt and found it. She worked at her eyebrows with a brown eyebrow pencil. The lipstick gave her some trouble. She got a blob of carmine red too low on her under lip and had to wipe it all off on the towel and start again. She made her lips very full and then put them together and rolled one against the other, and she looked at her teeth and rubbed some lipstick off with her towel. She should have washed her teeth before she put on the lipstick. Now powder. That would take the redness out of her face. Then she brushed her hair. She had never liked her hair. Holding it this way and that for effect, she began to lose interest.

In the bedroom she dug out a close-fitting black felt hat with a kind of a visor. She pushed her hair up inside the hat and angled the brim rakishly.

"Now," she said, "now we'll see how a woman's face gets crooked. I wish Juan would come home right now. He'd change his tune."

In the bedroom she got the bottle of Bellodgia from her dresser drawer and put perfume on her bosom and on the lobes of her ears and at her hair line. And she patted a little on her upper lip. "I like to smell it too," she said.

She walked back to the lunchroom, carefully avoiding the corner that had struck her before. It was even darker than it had been, for the clouds were getting thick and very little light was coming through. Alice sat down at her table and adjusted her hand mirror. "Pretty," she said, "you're kind of pretty. What are you doing this evening? Would you like to go dancing?"

She poured off the drink in her glass. Suppose that driver for

the Red Arrow Line should come by and knock on the door.
She'd let him in. He was a great kidder. She'd give him a drink
or two and then she'd show him a thing or two.

"Red," she'd say, "you set yourself up as a great kidder but
I'm going to show you something. There's some kidding on the
level." She let her mind dwell on his narrow waist and heavy
muscled forearms. He wore a broad belt around his blue jeans,
and the jeans—well, the guy was O.K. Something about thinking of those jeans. There was a copper rivet at the bottom where
the fly started. And something about that rivet brought sorrow
to Alice. Bud had had one. A copper rivet just there. She tried
to evade this vision too, and failing, gathered it—gathered it to
her mind. He had begged her over and over again. And finally
they walked four miles out to the picnic grounds. Bud carried
the lunch—hard-boiled eggs and ham sandwiches and an apple
pie. Alice bought the pie but she told Bud she made it. And he
didn't even wait for the lunch.

He hurt her. And after, she said, "Where are you going?"

"I've got work to do," Bud said.

"You said you love me."

"Did I?"

"You aren't going to leave me, Bud?"

"Listen, sister, you got laid, that's all. I didn't sign no long-
term contract."

"But it's the first time, Bud."

"There's got to be a first time for everybody," he said.

Alice was crying over herself now. "It's no damn good!" she
shouted at herself in the mirror. "None of it's any damn good."
She blubbered while she drank off another whisky and poured
the last of the bottle into her glass.

All the others were no damn good, either, and what had she
now? A stinking job with bed privileges and no pay. That's
what. And married to a stinking louse, that's what. Married to
him! Too far out in the country to go to the movies. Got to sit
in a stinking lunchroom.

She put her head down on her arms and cried broken-heart-
edly. And a second Alice could hear her crying. A second Alice
stood at her shoulder and watched her. Got to walk on eggs all
the time to keep him happy. She raised her head and looked in
the mirror. The lipstick was smeared all over her upper lip. Her

eyes were red and her nose was running. She reached for the napkin container, pulled out two paper napkins, and blew her nose. She balled up the paper and threw it on the floor.

What did she want to keep this joint clean for? Who cared? Who gave a damn about her? Nobody! But she could take care of herself. Nobody was going to kick Alice around and get away with it. She emptied the last of the whisky.

Getting out the port wine was a job. She staggered and fell against the sink. There was hot pressure against the inside of her nose and her breath whistled in her nostrils. She stood the bottle of port wine on the counter and got a corkscrew. The bottle fell over when she tried to get the corkscrew into it, and the second time the cork broke into small pieces. She pushed the rest of it into the bottle with her thumb and lunged back to the table.

"Soda pop," she said. She filled her glass full of the dark red wine. "Wish there was some more whisky." Her mouth was dry. She drank half the tumbler of wine thirstily. "Why, that's good," she giggled. Maybe she'd always have whisky first to give flavor to the wine.

She drew the mirror close to her. "You're an old bag," she said bitterly. "You're a dirty drunken old bag. No wonder nobody wants you. I wouldn't have you myself."

The image in the mirror was not double but it had double outlines, and at the outside of her range of vision Alice could feel the room begin to rock and sway. She drank the rest of the glass and choked and sputtered and the red wine ran out of the corners of her mouth. She missed the glass and poured wine over the tabletop before she got her glass filled. Her heart was pounding. She could hear it, and she could feel it beat in her arms and shoulders and in the veins on her breasts. She drank solemnly.

I'm gonna pass out, and a damn good thing. I wish I would never come to. I wish that would be the end of it—the end of it—the end of it—Show these bastards I don't have to live if I don't want to. I'll show 'em.

And then she saw the fly. He wasn't an ordinary housefly but a newborn bluebottle, and his body shone with an iridescent blue sheen. He had come to the table and was standing on the edge of the pool of wine. He dipped his proboscis and went back to cleaning himself.

Alice sat perfectly still. Her flesh crawled with hatred. All her unhappiness, all her resentments, centered in the fly. With an effort of will she forced the two images of the fly to be one image. "You son of a bitch," she said softly. "You think I'm drunk. I'll show you."

Her eyes were wary and smart. Slowly, slowly, she slipped sideways from the table and crouched low to the floor, supporting herself with her hand. She kept her eyes on the fly. He had not moved. She crept over to the counter and went behind it. A dish towel was lying on the stainless steel sink. She took it in her right hand and folded it carefully. It was too light. She dampened it under the tap and squeezed out the excess water. "I'll show the son of a bitch," she said, and she moved catlike along the counter. The fly was still there, still shining.

Alice raised her hand and let the towel fall back on her shoulder. Step by careful step she moved close, her hand raised and flexed. She struck. Bottle and glasses and sugar dispenser and napkin holder all crashed to the floor. The fly zoomed and circled. Alice stood still, following him with her eyes. He landed on the lunch counter. She lunged, striking at him, and when he rose again she flailed the air with the towel.

"That's not the way," she said to herself. "Creep up on him. Creep up on him." The floor tilted under her feet. She put out her hand and supported herself on the stool. Where was he now? She could hear the buzz. The angry, sickening whine of his wings. He's got to land sometime, somewhere. She felt sickness rising in her throat.

The fly made a series of loops and eights and circles and then settled down to low, swooping flights from one end of the room to the other. Alice waited. There was darkness crowding in on the edges of her vision. The fly landed with a little plop on the box of cornflakes on the top of the great pyramid of dry cereals on the shelf behind the counter. He landed on the "C" of "corn" and moved restlessly over to the "O." He stood very still. Alice snuffled.

The room was rocking and whirling but with will power the fly and the area around him were unblurred. Her left hand reached back to the counter and her fingers crept across it. She moved silently, slowly, around the end of the counter. She raised her right hand very, very carefully. The fly sprang forward a step and paused again. He was ready to take off. Alice sensed it.

She sensed his rise before he rose. She swung with all the weight of her body. The wet towel smashed against the pyramid of cardboard boxes and followed through. Boxes and a row of glasses and a bowl of oranges crashed to the floor behind the counter and Alice fell on top.

The room rushed in on her with red and blue lights. Under her cheek a broken box spilled out its cornflakes. She raised her head once and then put it down again and a rolling darkness dropped over her.

The lunchroom was dusky and very quiet. The fly moved to the edge of the drying pool of wine on the white tabletop. For a moment he sensed in all directions for danger, and then deliberately he dipped his flat proboscis into the sweet, sticky wine.

Chapter 12

THE clouds piled in gray threat on threat and a blue darkness settled on the land. In the San Juan valley the darker greens seemed black and the lighter green of grass, a chilling wet blue. "Sweetheart" came rolling heavily along the highway and the aluminum paint on her gleamed with the evil of a gun. Away to the south a bank of dark cloud fringed off into rain and the curtain of it descended slowly.

The bus pulled in close to the gas pumps in front of Breed's store and stopped. The little boxing gloves, the baby's shoe, swung back and forth in little pendulum jerks. Juan sat in the seat after the bus had stopped. He raced the motor for a moment, listening to it, and then he sighed and turned the key and the engine stopped.

"How long are you going to wait here?" Van Brunt asked.

"I'm going to take a look at the bridge," said Juan.

"It's still there," Van Brunt said.

"So are we," said Juan. He pulled the lever to open the door.

Breed came out of his screen door and walked toward the bus. He shook hands with Juan. "Aren't you a little late?"

"I don't think so," said Juan, "unless my watch is off."

Pimples climbed down and stood beside them. He wanted to be ahead so he could see the blonde get off the bus.

"Got any coke?" he asked.

"No," said Breed. "Few bottles of Pepsi-Cola. Haven't had any coke for a month. It's the same stuff. You can't tell them apart."

"How's the bridge?" Juan asked.

Mr. Breek shook his head. "I think here goes your ball game. Take a look for yourself. I don't like it."

"There's no break yet?" Juan asked.

"She could go like that," said Breed, and he sideswiped the palms of his hands together. "She's got a strain on her that makes her cry like a baby. Let's take a look."

Mr. Pritchard and Ernest climbed down from the bus and then Mildred and Camille, with Norma behind her. Camille was expert. Pimples didn't see anything.

"They got some Pepsi-Cola," Pimples said. "You like to have one?"

Camille turned to Norma. She was beginning to see how Norma could be valuable. "Like a drink?" she asked.

"Well, I wouldn't mind," said Norma.

Pimples tried not to show his disappointment. Breed and Juan strolled down the highway toward the river. "Going to look at the bridge," Juan called over his shoulder.

Mrs. Pritchard called from the step, "Dear, do you think you could get me a cold drink? Just water if there isn't anything else. And ask where the 'you-know-what' is."

"It's around back," said Norma.

Breed fell into step beside Juan as they strode toward the bridge. "I've been expecting her to go out every year," he said. "I wish we'd get a bridge so when a big rain came I could sleep at night. I just lay in bed and hear the rain on the roof, but I'm listening for the bridge to go out. And I don't even know what kinda sound she'll make when she goes."

Juan grinned at him. "I know how that is. I remember in Torreón when I was a little kid. We used to listen at night for the popping that meant fighting. We kinda liked the fighting, but it always meant my old man would go away for a while. And at last he went away and he didn't come back. I guess we always knew that would happen."

"What became of him?" Breed asked.

"I don't know. Somebody got him, I guess. He couldn't stay home when there was any fighting. He had to get in it. I don't think he much cared what they were fighting about. When he came home he was full of stories every time." Juan chuckled. "He used to tell one about Pancho Villa. He said a poor woman came to Villa and said, 'You have shot my husband and now I and the little ones will starve.' Well, Villa had plenty of money then. He had the presses and he was printing his own. He turned to his treasurer and said, 'Roll out five kilos of twenty-peso bills for this poor woman.' He wasn't even counting it, he had so much. So they did and they tied the bills together with wire and that woman went out. Well, then a sergeant said to Villa, 'There was a mistake, my general. We did not shoot that woman's husband. He got drunk and we put him in jail.' Then Pancho said, 'Go immediately and shoot him. We cannot disappoint that poor woman.' "

Breed said, "It don't make any sense."

Juan laughed. "I know, that's what I like about it. God, that river is eating around the back of the breakwater."

"I know. I tried to phone and tell them," said Breed. "I can't get anybody on the phone."

They walked together out on the wooden bridge. And the moment Juan stepped on the flooring he could feel the thrumming virbration of the water. The bridge shivered and trembled. And there was a deep hum in the timbers that was louder than the rush of the water. Juan looked over the side of the bridge. The supporting timbers were under water and the river foamed and bubbled under it. And the whole bridge trembled and panted, and there were little strained cries from the timbers where the iron turnbolts went through. As they watched, a great old live oak tree came rolling heavily down the stream. When it struck the bridge and turned, the whole structure cried out and seemed to brace itself. The tree caught in the submerged underpinning and there came a shrill, ripping sound from under the bridge. The two men moved quickly back off the bridgehead."

"How fast is she coming up?" Juan asked.

"Ten inches in the last hour. Of course, she might start to go down now. Might have reached flood."

Juan looked at the side of the supporting streamers. His eye found a brown bolthead on the edge of the water and he kept his eyes on it. "I guess I could make it all right," he said. "I could make a run for it. Or I could get the passengers to walk across and I could drive over and pick them up on the other side. How's the other bridge?"

"I don't know," said Breed. "I tried to phone and find out but I can't get anybody. And suppose you cross this one and the other one's out, and you come back and this one's out? You'd be trapped in the bend. You'd have some mighty sore passengers."

"I'm going to have some mighty sore passengers anyway," said Juan. "I've got one—no, two—that are going to raise hell no matter what happens. I know the signs. You know a man named Van Brunt?"

"Oh, that old fart! Yes, I know him. He owes me thirty-seven dollars. I sold him some alfalfa seed and he claimed it was no good. Wouldn't pay for it. He's got bills all over the county. Nothing he buys is any good. I wouldn't sell him a candy bar on credit. He'd claim it wasn't sweet. So you got him along?"

"I got him," said Juan. "And I got a man from Chicago. Big business bug. He's going to be pretty sore if things don't come out the way he wants them to."

"Well," said Breed, "you got to make up your own mind."

Juan looked at the threatening sky. "I guess it's going to rain, all right. And with the hills full up it'll dump right into the river. I could get over all right, but about what chance have I got to get back?"

"About ten per cent," said Breed. "How's your wife?"

"Not too good," said Juan. "She's got a toothache."

"It pays to keep your teeth up," said Breed. "Should go to the dentist every six months."

Juan laughed. "I know. Are you acquainted with anybody that does?"

"No," said Breed. He liked Juan. He didn't even consider him a foreigner.

"I don't either," said Juan. "Well, there's one other way to stay out of trouble with the passengers."

"What's that?"

"Let them decide. This is a democracy, isn't it?"

"They'll just get to fighting."

"Well, what's wrong with that if they fight each other?" said Juan.

"You've got something there," Breed said. "But I'll tell you one thing. Whatever side everybody else is on, Van Brunt is gonna be on the other side. There's a fellow wouldn't vote for the second coming of Christ if it was a popular measure."

"He's all right," said Juan. "You just gotta know how to handle him. I had a horse once that was so ornery that if you reined left he'd turn right. I fooled him. I did everything opposite and he thought he was getting his own way. You could get Van Brunt to do almost anything by disagreeing with him."

"I'm going to forbid him to pay that thirty-seven dollars," said Breed.

"It might work at that," Juan said. "Well, the river isn't at flood. That bolthead is covered. I'm going to see what the passengers want to do."

Back in the store Pimples felt a little cheated. He had been maneuvered into buying both Norma and Camille a Pepsi-Cola. Try as he would, he couldn't separate Camille from Norma. And it wasn't Norma's fault. Camille was using her.

Norma was flushed with pleasure. She had never been so happy in her life. This beautiful creature was nice to her. They were friends. And she didn't say they'd live together. She said she'd see how things worked out. For some reason this gave Norma a great deal of confidence. People had not been nice to Norma. They had said "yes" to things and then wormed out of them. But this girl, who looked like everything Norma wanted to be, said "she'd see." In her mind Norma could see the apartment they would get. It would have a velvet davenport and a coffee table in front of it. And the drapes would be wine-colored velvet. They'd have a radio and phonograph combination, of course, and plenty of records. She didn't like to think past that. It was almost like spoiling her luck to think past that. There was a kind of an electric blue for the davenport.

She raised her glass of Pepsi-Cola and let the sweet, biting drink run down her throat, and in the middle of the swallow despair settled down on her like a heavy gas. "It won't ever happen," her mind cried. "It'll get away! It'll be just like always and I'll be alone again." She squeezed her eyes shut and wiped the back of her hand across them. When she opened her eyes again she was all right. "I'll save it," she thought. "Little by little I'll make the apartment, and then if it doesn't happen I'll still have it." A hardness came over her and an acceptance. "If any of it comes through it'll just be gravy. But I can't expect it, I can't let myself expect it. That will take it away from me."

Pimples said, "I've got plenty of plans. I'm studying radar. That's going to be a very important job. Fellow that knows radar is going to be fixed pretty nice. I think a person's got to look ahead, don't you? You take some people, they don't look ahead into the future and they end up right where they started." A little smile was fixed on Camille's lips.

"You got something there," she said. She wished she could get away from this kid. He was a nice kid, but she just wished she could get away from him. She could practically smell him. "Thank you very much for the drink," she said. "I think I'll just go and freshen up a little. You want to come, Norma?"

A look of devotion came on Norma's face. "Oh, yes," she said. "I guess I ought to freshen up too." Everything Camille said was right, was dainty and fine. "Oh, Jesus Christ, let it happen!" Norma cried in her mind.

Mrs. Pritchard was sipping a lemonade. It had taken a little time to get it because they didn't serve lemonade. But when Mrs. Pritchard had pointed out the lemons in the grocery section and had even offered to squeeze them herself—well, there was nothing Mrs. Breed could do, and she'd made it.

"I just can't drink old bottled things," Mrs. Pritchard explained. "I like just the pure fruit juice." Mrs. Breed resentfully went down under this wave of sweetness. Mrs. Pritchard sipped her lemonade and looked through a rack of postcards on the novelty counter. There were pictures of the courthouse in San Juan de la Cruz and of the hotel in San Ysidro which was built over a hot spring of Epsom salts. A fine old hotel much frequented by rheumatic people who bathed in the strong waters. The hotel was called a spa on the postcards. There were other items on the novelty counter. Painted plaster dogs and glass pistols full of colored candy and bright kewpie dolls and fancy redwood boxes of glacé California fruits. And there were lamps whose shades turned when the lights were on so that the forest fires and ships under full sail moved and shone in a very lifelike manner.

Ernest Horton stood at the counter too and looked at the display with a certain amount of contempt. He said to Mr. Pritchard, "Sometimes I think I ought to open a novelty store with all new stuff. Some of this old stuff's been on the market

for years and nobody buys it. Now my company has nothing
but up-and-coming stock, all new."

Mr. Pritchard nodded. "Gives a man confidence to work for
a firm he knows is on its toes," he said. "That's why I think you
might like to work for us. You could be sure we're on our toes
every hour of the day."

Ernest said, "Excuse me, I'm going to get my case. I've got
an item that really isn't before the public yet but it's gone like
hot cakes to the trade already, just to the trade. I'd like to place
a few here, maybe."

He went out quickly and lugged his sample case in. He
opened it and brought out a cardboard box. "Plain wrapping,
you see. That's for the surprise." He opened the box and took
out a perfect little high-tank toilet twelve inches high. There
was the box and a little chain with a brass knob on the bottom,
and the toilet bowl was white. And it even had a little seat cover
colored to look like wood.

Mrs. Breed had moved down in back of the counter. "My
husband does all the buying," she said. "You'll have to see him."

"I know," said Ernest. "I just want you to look at this item.
It sells itself."

"What's it for?" Mr. Pritchard asked.

"You just watch," said Ernest. He pulled the little chain and
immediately the toilet bowl flushed with a brown fluid. Ernest
lifted the toilet seat right out of the bowl and it was a small
glass. "That's one ounce," he said triumphantly. "If you want a
double shot, say for a highball, you pull the chain twice."

"Whisky!" cried Mr. Pritchard.

"Or brandy, or rum," said Ernest. "Anything you want. See,
here in the tank is the place you fill it, and the tank is guaranteed plastic. It knocks 'em cold. I've got orders for eighteen
hundred of this little item already. It's a knockout. It gets a
laugh every time."

"By George, that's clever," Mr. Pritchard said. "Who thinks
these things up?"

"Well," Ernest explained, "we've got an idea department.
Everybody puts ideas in. This item was suggested by our salesman in the Great Lakes area. He'll make himself a nice bonus.
Our company gives two per cent of the profits to any employee
who sends in a workable idea."

"It's clever," Mr. Pritchard repeated. In his mind he could

see Charlie Johnson when he first saw it. Charlie would want to rush right out and get one for himself. "What do you get for them?" Mr. Pritchard asked.

"Well, this one retails for five dollars. But if you don't mind my making the suggestion, we have a model that sells for twenty-seven fifty."

Mr. Pritchard pursed his lips.

"But look what you get," Ernest went on. "This one is plastic. The better item is—well, the box is oak and is made of old whisky barrels so that it'll take the liquor fine. The chain is real silver and it has a Brazilian diamond for a knob. The bowl is porcelain, real toilet quality porcelain, and the seat is hand-carved mahogany. And on the box there's a little silver plate for, if, like you wanted to present it to a lodge or a club, your name goes on that."

"It sounds like a good value," Mr. Pritchard said. His mind was made up. He knew how he would get the better of Charlie Johnson now. He would give one of the toilets to Charlie. But on the plate he would put "Presented to Charlie Johnson, the all-American soandso, by Elliott Pritchard," and then let Charlie show off all he wanted to. Everybody would know who had the idea first.

"You haven't got one with you, have you?" he asked.

"No, you have to order."

Mrs. Pritchard spoke up. She had moved close, quietly. "Elliott, you're not going to get one of those. Elliott, they're vulgar."

"I wouldn't have it around if there were ladies, of course," said Mr. Pritchard. "No, little girl. Know what I'm going to do? I'm gonna send one of them to Charlie Johnson. That'll get back at him for sending me that stuffed skunk. Yes, sir, I'll fix him."

Mrs. Pritchard explained. "Charlie Johnson was Mr. Pritchard's roommate in college. They have the wildest jokes. They're like little boys when they get together."

"Now," said Mr. Pritchard seriously, "if I ordered one, could you have it sent to an address I'll give you? And could you have it engraved? I'll write what I want you to put on the plate."

"What are you going to say?" Bernice asked.

"Little girls keep their noses out of big man's business," said Mr. Pritchard.

"I'll bet it'll be awful," said Bernice.

Mildred was in the dumps. She felt heavy and tired and she wasn't interested in anything. She was sitting in a twisted wire candy-store chair all by herself at the end of the counter. Cynically she had watched Pimples trying to get the blonde alone. The trip had let her down. She was disgusted with herself and what had happened. What kind of a girl was she if a bus driver could set her off? She shivered a little with distaste. Where was he now? Why didn't he come back? She smothered her impulse to get up and go look for him. Van Brunt's voice sounded beside her so that she jumped.

"Young lady," he said, "your skirt shows. I thought you'd like to know."

"Oh, yes. Thank you very much."

"You might have gone all day thinking you were all fixed up if somebody didn't tell you," he said.

"Oh, yes, thank you." She stood up and, leaning backward, pushed her skirt against her legs so that she could see. There was an inch of slip showing behind.

"I think it's better to be told things like that," Van Brunt said.

"Oh, it is. I guess I broke a shoulder strap."

"I don't care to hear about your underwear," he said coldly. "My only remark is—and I repeat it—your skirt shows. I don't want you to think I had any other motive."

"I don't," said Mildred helplessly.

Van Brunt went on, "Too many young girls get self-conscious of their legs. They think everybody is looking at them."

Suddenly Mildred was laughing wildly like a sick woman.

"What's so funny?" Van Brunt demanded angrily.

"Nothing," said Mildred. "I just thought of a joke." She had remembered that Van Brunt had never missed any show of legs all morning.

"Well, if it's that funny, tell it," he said.

"Oh, no. It's a personal joke. I'll go out and fix my strap." She looked at him and then, deliberately, she said, "You see, there are two straps on each shoulder. One is for the slip and the other supports the brassière and the brassière holds the breasts up firmly." She saw Van Brunt's color come up out of his collar. "There isn't anything below that until the panties, if I wore panties, which I don't."

Van Brunt turned and walked away quickly and Mildred felt better. Now the old fool wouldn't have a comfortable moment. She could watch him and maybe later trick him and catch him in the act. She got up, laughing to herself, and went out around the back of the store to the lean-to marked "Ladies."

A lattice covered the door and the morning glory was beginning to climb up. Mildred stood in front of the closed door. She could hear Norma talking to the blonde inside. She listened. Maybe this would make the trip worth while, just listening to people talk. Mildred liked to eavesdrop on people. Sometimes her liking to bothered her. She could listen to inanities with interest. But of all the listening, the best was in women's rest rooms. The freedom of women in any room where there was a toilet, a mirror, and a washbowl had interested her for a long time. She had once written a paper in college, which had been considered daring, in which she had maintained that women lost their inhibitions when their skirts were up.

It must be either that, she thought, or the certainty that man, the enemy, could never invade this territory. It was the one place in the world where women could be certain there would be no men. And so they relaxed and became outwardly the people they were inwardly. She had thought a great deal about it. Women were more friendly or more vicious to one another in public toilets, but on personal terms. Perhaps that was because there were no men. Because, where there were no men, there was no competition, and their poses dropped from them.

Mildred wondered whether it was the same in men's toilets. She just didn't think it was likely, because men had many competitions besides women, while most of women's insecurities had to do with men. Her paper on the subject had been returned marked "Not carefully thought out." She planned to do it over again.

Out in the store she had not been friendly toward Camille. She just didn't like her. But she knew her dislike would not carry into the rest room. She thought, "Isn't it strange that women will compete for men they don't even want?"

Norma and Camille were talking on and on. Mildred put her hand on the door and pushed it open. In the small room were a toilet stall and a washbowl with a square mirror over it. A dispenser of paper seatcovers was on one wall, and paper towels beside the basin. A slot machine for sanitary pads was on the wall beside the frosted glass window. The concrete floor was painted dark red and the walls were thick with layers of white paint. There was a sharp smell of perfumed disinfectant in the air.

Camille was seated on the toilet and Norma stood in front of the mirror. They both looked at Mildred as she came in.

"Want to get in here?" Camille asked.

"No," said Mildred. "I've got a drooping strap on my slip."

Camille looked down at the skirt. "You have, all right. No, not that way," she said to Norma. "You see the way your hair line goes? Well, make the eyebrows go up a little on the outside, just a little. Wait, honey. Wait a minute and I'll show you."

She stood up and moved to Norma. "Turn around so I can see you. There, now. And there, now look at yourself. See how it kind of brings down your hairline a little bit? Your forehead's high so you try to bring it down. Now look, close your eyes." She took the eyebrow pencil from Norma and rubbed it gently on the lower lids just below the lashes, making the line a little darker as it passed the outside corners.

"You've got the mascara on too thick, honey," she said. "See how the lashes stick together? Use more water and take a little more time. Wait a minute." She brought out of her purse a little plastic case of eyeshadow. "Now you go careful with this stuff." She dipped her finger into the blue paste, rubbed a little on each of Norma's upper eyelids, making it heavier toward the outside corners. "Now, let me see." She inspected her work. "Look, honey, you keep your eyes too wide, like a rabbit. Let your upper lids down a little bit. No, and don't squint. Just let your upper lids droop down a little bit. There, like that. Now look at yourself. See the difference?"

"My God, I look different," Norma said. Her voice was awed.

"Sure you do. Now, you've got the lipstick on all wrong. Look, honey, your lower lip is too thin. So is mine. Bring the lipstick down a little bit here, and a little here."

Norma stood still like a good child and let her work.

"See? Heavier in the corners," Camille said. "Now your lower lip looks fuller."

Mildred said, "You're good. I could use some advice too."

"Oh, well," said Camille. "It's pretty simple."

"That's theatrical make-up," Mildred said. "I mean it's a kind of theatrical type make-up."

"Well, you know, dealing with the public—dentists use their nurses almost like receptionists."

"Oh, damn it!" Mildred exclaimed. "This strap isn't loose, it's broken." She peeled her dress off her shoulder and she had a little silken string in her hand.

"You'll have to pin it," Camille said.

"But I haven't got a pin and my needle and thread's in one of the suitcases!"

Camille opened her purse again, and in the lining were half a dozen tiny safety pins. "Here," said Camille, "I always go heeled." She unfastened one of the pins. "You want me to fix it for you?"

"If you don't mind. My damned eyes. I can't see anything."

Camille pulled the loose slip up, folded the end of the strap, and pinned it firmly to the edge of the slip. "That's hardly all right, but at least it doesn't show. It's still a pin job. You always been shortsighted, honey?"

"No," said Mildred. "I was all right until—well, right when I was about fourteen. One doctor said it had to do with puberty. He said some girls get their eyesight back when they have their first baby."

"That's tough," said Camille.

"It's a damn nuisance," Mildred said. "I don't care how much they make new shapes of glasses. They still aren't very good-looking."

"Ever heard of that kind that fit right down against the eyes?"

"I've thought about it and I haven't done anything about it. I guess I'm scared to have anything touch my eyes."

Norma was still regarding herself with wonder in the mirror. Her eyes had suddenly become larger and her lips fuller and softer and the wet-rat look had gone from her face.

"Isn't she wonderful?" Norma said to no one. "Isn't she just wonderful?"

Camille said, "She's gonna be a pretty kid when she learns a few tricks and gets some confidence. We'll touch up that hair, honey, as soon as we get in."

"You mean you've thought it over?" Norma cried. "You mean we'll get the apartment?" She whirled on Mildred. "We're going to have an apartment," she said breathlessly. "We're going to have a davenport and Sunday morning we'll wash and set our hair—"

"We'll see," Camille broke in. "We'll just have to see how things work out. Here's the two of us without jobs and already she's got a duplex rented. Hold your horses, honey."

"It's a funny trip," Mildred said. "We're on our way to Mexico. Everything's gone wrong from the start. My father wanted to see the country. He thinks we might settle in California some time. So he wanted to take the bus to Los Angeles. He thought he could see the country better."

"Well, he can," said Camille.

"He can see too much of it maybe," Mildred said. "But did you ever see such a collection of people as we've got?"

"They're all about the same," said Camille.

"I like Mr. Chicoy," said Mildred. "He's part Mexican, you know. But that boy! I've got a feeling he'd climb all over you if you weren't careful."

"Oh, he's all right," Camille said. "He's just a little goaty. Most kids are like that. He'll probably get over it."

"Or maybe he won't," said Mildred. "Did you take a good look at that old fellow, Van Brunt? He didn't get over it. It just ingrew. That's a pretty filthy man in his mind."

Camille smiled. "He's pretty old," she said.

Mildred went into the little cubicle and sat down. "There's something I wanted to ask you," she said. "My father thinks he's seen you somewhere. He's got a pretty good memory. Did you ever see him?"

For a second Mildred saw the hostility in Camille's eyes, saw the tightened mouth, and she knew she'd touched something sore. And instantly Camille's face was placid again.

"I think I must look like somebody else," she said. "This time he's made a mistake unless he saw me in the street somewhere."

"On the level?" Mildred asked. "I'm not trying to catch you now. I just wondered."

The friendliness, the companionship, the relaxation, slipped from the room. It was as though a man had entered. Camille's eyes stabbed at Mildred. "He made a mistake," she said coldly. "You can take that any way you want."

The door opened and Mrs. Pritchard came in. "Oh, there you are," she said to Mildred. "I thought you'd wandered off."

"Oh, I broke a strap on my slip," said Mildred.

"Well, hurry up. Mr. Chicoy's back and there's quite an argument going on— Thank you, dear," she said to Norma, who had moved away from the basin to make room for her. "I'll just moisten my handkerchief and take a little of the dust off— Why don't you have a lemonade?" she said to Mildred. "That nice woman doesn't mind making them at all. I told her she'd be quite famous if she just served pure fruit juices."

Suddenly Camille said, "I wish we could get something to eat. I'm getting hungry. I'd like something good."

"So would I," said Mrs. Pritchard.

"I'd like a cold cracked crab with mayonnaise and a bottle of beer," Camille said.

"Well, I've never had crab that way," said Mrs. Pritchard, "but I wish you could have tasted the way my mother fried butterfish. She used to take an old-fashioned cast-iron skillet— and the fish, it had to be very fresh and very carefully trimmed. She'd make a batter with brown toasted crumbs—bread crumbs, not cracker crumbs—and she'd put a whole tablespoon —no, two tablespoonfuls—of Worcestershire sauce in a beaten egg. I think that was the secret."

"Mother," said Mildred, "don't start on the butterfish recipe."

"You'd better have a lemonade," said Mrs. Pritchard. "It'd clean up your skin. A good long trip makes a person blotchy."

"I wish we'd get moving," Mildred said. "We can get lunch in the next town. What's its name?"

"San Juan de la Cruz," said Norma.

"San Juan de la Cruz," Mrs. Pritchard repeated softly. "I think the Spanish names are so pretty."

Norma took a long, astonished look at herself in the mirror before they went out. She dropped her eyes. It was going to take practice to remember to do that all the time, but it changed her whole appearance and she liked it.

Chapter 13

JUAN sat on a stool drinking a Pepsi-Cola and rubbing the shiny end of his amputated finger over the corduroy ridges of his trousers. When the women came around from the back and entered the store he looked up at them and the rubbing of his finger became a tapping.

"Is everybody here?" he asked. "No, there's one missing. Where's Mr. Van Brunt?"

"I'm over here." He spoke from behind the counter on the grocery side, where, concealed by a stacked wall of canned coffee, he was inspecting the shelves idly.

Mr. Pritchard said, "I want to know when we can get started. I have connections to make."

"I know," Juan said gently, "and that's what I want to talk about. The bridge is not safe. I can probably get across it. But there's another bridge and it may be out, or it may go out. We can't get any news about it. If we get into the bend of the river with both bridges out, we'd be caught, and nobody could make any connections. Now, I'm willing to take a vote and do anything the majority of the passengers want to do. I'll make a run for it and take a chance, or I'll take you back and you can make other plans. It's up to you. But when you make up your minds I want you to stick to the verdict."

He raised the bottle and drank the Pepsi-Cola.

"I haven't the time," Mr. Pritchard said loudly. "Look, my friend. I've had no vacation since the war started. I've been making the implements of war that gave us the victory, and this is my first vacation. I just haven't the time to go gallivanting all over the country. I need a rest. I only have a few weeks and this is eating them up."

Juan said, "I'm sorry. I'm not doing it on purpose, you know, and if you got caught in the bend of the river you might lose a lot more time and I might lose the bus getting it across. The bridge is strained to the breaking point. It may come down any minute. The only other choice is to go back."

Van Brunt came from behind the stack of coffee. He had a two-and-a-half pound can of sliced peaches in his hand. He crossed the store to Mrs. Breed. "How much?" he asked.

"Forty-seven cents."

"My God! For a can of peaches?"

"The profit hasn't changed," she said. "We've just got to pay more for them."

Van Brunt threw a half-dollar violently down on the counter. "Open 'em up," he said. "Forty-seven cents for a mean little can of peaches!"

Mrs. Breed put the can in a wall opener, turned the crank, and stopped just as the edge raised. She passed the can over the counter to Van Brunt. He drank off part of the juice first, then reached in and picked out a yellow slice with his fingers. He held it over the open can to drip.

"Now I heard what you said," he observed. "You think you can waste our time. I've got to get in to the courthouse and I've got to get in this afternoon. And it's up to you to get me through. You're a common carrier, subject to the rules of the railroad commission."

"That's what I'm trying to do," said Juan. "And one of the rules of the commission is don't kill the passengers."

"It comes of not knowing the country," Van Brunt went on. "There ought to be a strict law that you've got to know the country before you can drive a bus." He waved a slice of peach and flipped it into his mouth and picked up another slice between his thumb and forefinger. He was enjoying himself.

"You said there was only two things to do. Well, there's three. You don't know about the old road that was there before they put in those damn-fool bridges. It goes right around the outside of the bend. The stagecoaches used to use it."

Juan looked questioningly at Mr. Breed. "I heard about it, but what condition is it in?"

"Stages used it for over a hundred years," said Van Brunt.

Mr. Breed said, "I know it's all right for a couple of miles, but I don't know it beyond that. It goes up the side of the mountain to the east, there. It might be washed out. I haven't been over it since way before the rains."

"You've got your choice," Van Brunt said. He waved his

piece of peach, flung it into his mouth, and talked around it. "I told you it was going to rain. I told you the river would be up, and now, when you're stuck, I tell you how to get out of it. Do I have to drive your god-damned bus too?"

Juan bawled, "Keep your pants on and watch your language. There's ladies here."

Van Brunt tilted the can and drank the rest of the juice, straining the peaches out with his teeth. The thick juice ran down his chin and he wiped it off with his sleeve. "God, what a trip!" he said. "Right from the beginning."

Juan turned and faced the other passengers. "Well, there it is. My franchise says I'm supposed to go on the highway. I don't know the old road. I don't know if I could get through or not. It's up to you to decide what you want to do. If we get hung up I don't want to be to blame."

Mr. Pritchard said, "I like to see things get done. Now, I've got to get to Los Angeles, man. I've got airplane tickets for Mexico City. Do you know what they cost? And the planes are booked solid. We've got to get through. Let's get some action on this. You think the bridge is dangerous?"

"I know it's dangerous," said Juan.

"Well," said Mr. Pritchard, "you say you don't know whether you can get through on the old road?"

"That's right," said Juan.

"So you've got two gambles and one sure thing. And the sure thing don't get you through either. Hmmmm," said Mr. Pritchard.

"What do you think, dear?" Mrs. Pritchard said. "We've got to do something. I haven't had a good bath for three days. Dear, we've got to do something."

Mildred said, "Let's try the old road. It might be interesting." She glanced at Juan to see how he would take this attitude, but already his eyes had moved from her to Camille.

Something about the recent association made Camille say, "I vote for the old road. I'm so tired and dirty now, nothing would make much difference to me."

Juan looked down and his eyes sharpened when he saw Norma's face. She didn't look like the same girl. And Norma knew he had noticed. "I say the old road," she said breathlessly.

Ernest Horton found a chair, the one Mrs. Breed ordinarily

used when her legs swelled up in the afternoons. He had been watching the counting of noses.

"I don't much care," he said. "Of course, I'd like to get to L. A., but it don't make much difference. I'll stick with the others, whatever they say."

Van Brunt put the can down loudly on the counter. "It's going to rain," he said. "That back road can get awful slippery. You might not make it up over the hill, to the eastward. It's steep and slick. If you mired down there I don't know how you'd ever get out."

"But you're the one that suggested it," Mildred said.

"I'm just getting all the objections down," Van Brunt said. "Just getting them in order."

"How would you vote?" Juan asked.

"Oh, I won't vote. That's the silliest thing I ever heard of. Seems to me the driver ought to make the decisions, like a captain of a ship."

Pimples went to the candy counter. He laid down a dime and picked up two Baby Ruths. He put one in his side pocket to give to Camille when he could get her alone, and the other he unwrapped slowly. A wild, exciting thought had just popped into his mind. Suppose they went over the bridge and right in the middle the span broke and the bus fell into the river? Pimples would be thrown clear, but the blonde would be trapped in the bus. And Pimples dived and dived and he was nearly dead, but at last he broke a window and pulled Camille out and he swam ashore and laid her, unconscious, on the green grass and he rubbed her legs to get the circulation started. But better, he turned her over and he put his hands under her breasts and gave her artificial respiration.

But suppose they took the old road and the bus mired down? Then they'd be there all night, with maybe a fire going, and they'd be together and sit together in front of the fire with a light on their faces and maybe a blanket thrown over the two of them.

Pimples said, "I think we'd better try the old road." Juan looked at him and grinned.

"You've got real Kit Carson blood in you, haven't you, Kit?" And Pimples knew it was a joke, but it wasn't a mean joke.

"Well, I guess that's everybody but one, and he won't vote. What's the matter? Do you want to be able to sue?"

Van Brunt swung around to the others. "You're all being crazy," he said. "Know what he's doing? He's pulling out from under. If anything should happen he won't get the blame because he could say he only did what you told him to. No, he's not going to trap me that way."

Mr. Pritchard cleaned his glasses on his white linen handkerchief. "It's an idea," he said. "I hadn't thought of it quite that way. We're really giving up our rights."

Juan's eyes glowed with rage. His mouth grew thin and tight. "Get in the bus," he said. "I'm taking you back to San Ysidro and dumping you. I'm trying to get you through and you act as though I were trying to murder you. Come on, get in the bus. I'm sick of it. Since last night I've had my life turned upside down for your comfort and I'm tired of it. So come on. We're going back."

Mr. Pritchard walked over to him. "No, I didn't mean that," he said. "I appreciate what you've done. We all do. I was just trying to think clearly on all sides of the subject. That's what I do in business. Don't do anything until you've thought it through."

"I'm sick of it," Juan said again. "You had my bed last night. I just want to get rid of you."

Van Brunt said, "Don't forget, it was your bus that broke down. It wasn't our fault."

Juan said evenly, "Mostly, I think, I want to get rid of you."

"Watch yourself," Van Brunt said. "Don't forget, you're a common carrier with a franchise. After this example it wouldn't be hard to get the franchise removed."

Juan changed suddenly. He laughed. "Boy, that would be a relief. I'd be free of people like you, and I can think where I would put that franchise, rolled up and tied with barbed wire."

Camille laughed aloud and Ernest Horton giggled happily. "I've got to remember that," he said, "yes, sir. Look, Mr. Chicoy, these two men have been talking. The rest of us want to go. We'll take our chance. Why don't you just draw a line and anybody over the line wants to go, the rest stay here. That's fair enough."

Mildred said, "Mr. Chicoy, I want to go."

"O.K.," said Juan. "That big crack there in the floor. Everybody that don't want me to take the back road get over on the other side with the vegetables."

Nobody moved. Juan looked carefully into each face.

"It isn't legal," Van Brunt said. "It won't hold in any court."

"What won't hold?"

"What you're doing."

"It isn't in any court."

"It may be," said Van Brunt.

"You can't come even if you want to," said Juan.

"You just try to keep me off. I've got a ticket and I've got a right to go on the bus. You just try to keep me off and I'll have you up so fast it'll make your head spin."

Juan hunched his shoulders. "And you would too," he said. "O.K., let's get started." He turned to Mr. Breed. "Could you lend me a few tools? I'll bring them right back."

"What kind of tools?"

"Oh, a pick and shovel."

"Oh, sure. You mean in case you get stuck?"

"Yeah, and have you got a block and tackle?"

"Not a very good one. The blocks are all right, but there's just some old half-inch line on them. I don't know how much strain it would take. That's a pretty heavy bus."

"Well, it would be better than nothing," Juan said. "Haven't got any new line I could buy here, have you?"

"I haven't had a new piece of Manila line since the war started," said Breed. "But you're welcome to what I have got. Come along. Pick up what you want."

Juan said, "Come along, Kit, and give me a hand, will you?" The three went out of the store and around to the back.

Ernest said to Camille, "I wouldn't have missed this. I wouldn't for anything."

"I just wish I wasn't so tired," she said. "I've been riding busses for five days. I want to get out of my clothes and get some real sleep for a couple of days."

"Why didn't you take the train? Chicago, you said?"

"Yes, Chicago."

"Well, you coulda got on the Super Chief and slept all the way to L.A. That's a nice train."

"Saving pennies," said Camille. "I've got a little piece of change and I want to lay around for a few weeks before I got to work. And I'd rather do it in a double bed than a berth."

"Did I catch you right?" he asked.

"You did not," said Camille.

"O.K., you're the boss."

"Look, let's not play," Camille said. "I'm too damn tired to play guessing games with you."

"O.K., sister, O.K. I'll play any way you want."

"Well, then, let's just sit this one out. Do you mind?"

"You know? I like you," Ernest said. "I'd like to take you out when you get rested up."

"Well, we'll see how it goes," Camille said. She liked him. She could talk to him. He knew a few answers and that was a relief.

Norma had been watching them, listening. She was full of admiration for Camille. She wanted to learn just how it was done. Suddenly she realized that her eyes were wide open as a rabbit's and she dropped the upper lids.

Mrs. Pritchard said, "I hope I'm not going to get a headache. Elliott, see if they have any aspirins, will you?"

Mrs. Breed tore a cellophane bag off a big cardboard display. "You want one of them? That's a nickel."

"We better have half a dozen," Mr. Pritchard said.

"That'll be twenty-six cents with tax."

"You needn't have got so many, Elliott," Mrs. Pritchard said. "I have a bottle of five hundred in my bag."

"It's best to be prepared," he answered. He knew her headaches and they were dreadful. They twisted her face and reduced her to a panting, sweating, grinning, quivering blob of pain. They filled a room and a house. They got into everyone around her. Mr. Pritchard could feel one of her headaches through walls. He could feel it all over his body, and the doctor said there was nothing to do about it. They injected calcium and they gave her sedatives. The headaches usually came when she was nervous and when things, through no fault of her own, were not going well.

Her husband would have liked to protect her. They seemed to be selfish, these headaches, and yet they were not. The pain was real. No one could simulate such agonizing pain. Mr. Pritchard dreaded them more than anything in the world. A good one could make the whole house vibrate with horror. And they were a little like conscience. Try as he would, Mr. Pritchard could never lose the feeling that they were in some way his fault. Not that Mrs. Pritchard ever said anything or indicated

that this might be so. In fact she was very brave. She tried
to muffle her screams with a pillow.

Mr. Pritchard didn't bother her much in bed—very seldom,
in fact. But in a curious way he tied up his occasional lust and
his loss of self-control with her headaches. It was planted deep
in his mind that this was so, and he didn't know how it had
got planted. But he did have a conscience about it. His bestial-
ity, his lust, his lack of self-control, were the cause. And he
didn't have any means of saving himself. Sometimes he found
himself hating his wife very deeply because he was unhappy.
He stayed in his office overtime when she had a headache, and
sometimes he just sat at his desk for hours, staring at the brown
paneling, his body throbbing with his wife's pain.

In the middle of one of her worst spells she would try to
save him. "Go to a movie," she would moan. "Go over to
Charlie Johnson's. Take some whisky. Get drunk. Don't stay
here. Go to a movie." But it was impossible. He couldn't.

He put the six little transparent bags into his coat pocket.
"Would you like to take a couple now, just in case?" he asked.

"No," she said. "I think I'm going to be all right." She
smiled her brave, sweet smile.

Mildred, when she heard the first mention of aspirin, went to
the grocery side and studied the OPA price-ceiling chart on
the wall. Her mouth pinched tight and her throat was con-
vulsed. "Oh, Jesus Christ," she said softly under her breath.
"Oh, Christ, is she going to start that already?" Mildred didn't
quite believe the headaches. She'd never had a bad headache
herself, only mild periodic ones and a few hangover headaches at school. She called her mother's psychosomatic and psy-
chotic, and she dreaded them even more than her father did.
As a little girl she had run from them and gone to earth in the
cellar or in the space behind the cabinet in the sewing room.
And usually she was pulled out and taken in to her mother
because when mother had a headache she needed love and she
needed to be petted. Mildred thought of the headaches as a
curse. She hated them. And she hated her mother when she had
them.

For a time Mildred had thought them pure sham, and even
now, when through reading she knew the pain was real, Mildred still considered the headaches a weapon her mother used

with complete cunning, with complete brutality. The headaches were pain to her mother, truly, but they governed and punished the family too. They brought the family to heel. Certain things her mother didn't like were never done because they brought on a headache. And when she was at home, Mildred knew that her fear about getting into the house not later than one in the morning was caused by the almost certainty that her mother would get a headache if she didn't.

Between headaches you forgot how devastating they were. Mildred thought that a psychiatrist was what her mother needed. And Bernice would have done anything. She wanted to do anything. It was Mr. Pritchard who put his foot down. He didn't believe in psychiatrists, he said. But actually he did believe in them, so much that he was afraid of them. For Mr. Pritchard had gradually come to depend on the headaches. They were in a way a justification to him. They were a punishment on him and they gave him sins to be atoned for. Mr. Pritchard needed sins. There were none in his business life, for the cruelties there were defined and pigeonholed as necessity and responsibility to the stockholders. And Mr. Pritchard needed personal sins and personal atonement. He denounced the idea of a psychiatrist angrily.

Mildred forced herself to turn around and go back to her mother. "Are you all right, dear?"

"Yes," Bernice said brightly.

"No headache?"

Bernice was apologetic. "I just had a twinge and it frightened me," she said. "I could never forgive myself if I had one of those horrible things and ruined papa's trip."

Mildred felt a little shiver of fear at this woman who was her mother—at her power and her ruthlessness. It must be unconscious. It had to be. Mildred had seen and heard the engineering of this trip to Mexico. Her father hadn't wanted to go. He would have liked to take a vacation by just staying home from the office, which would mean that he would go to the office every day; but by going at odd hours and returning, not by the clock but by his feeling, he would have had a sense of vacation and rest.

But the trip to Mexico had been planted. When and how? Mildred didn't know and her father didn't know. But gradually he became convinced not only that it was his idea, but that he was forcing his family with him. And this gave him a fine sense of being boss in his own home. He had walked through closing door after closing door in the maze. It was rather like a trap nest. A hen finds a hole, looks in, sees there is a bit of grain, steps through the door—the door closes. Well, here is a nest. It's dark and quiet. Why not lay an egg? It'd be a good joke on whoever left that door open.

Her father had almost forgotten that he didn't want to go to Mexico. Both Mr. and Mrs. Pritchard were doing it for Mildred. That was really the safe thing. She was studying Spanish in college, a language she was incapable of understanding, just as her instructors were. Mexico would be just the place to practice up. Her mother said there was no way of learning a language like having to use it.

Mildred, looking at her mother's sweet, relaxed face, simply could not believe that this woman could engineer a thing and then destroy it. Why? And she would do it. She had planted the idea. Sure as hell she was going to have a headache. But she would wait until she was out of touch with doctors, until her headache would cause the greatest possible impression. It was hard to believe. Mildred didn't think her mother really knew what she was doing. But there was a doughy lump in Mildred's chest and it weighed down on her stomach. The headache was coming. She knew it.

She envied Camille. Camille was a tramp, Mildred thought. And things were so much easier for a tramp. There was no conscience, no sense of loss, nothing but a wonderful, relaxed, stretching-cat selfishness. She could go to bed with anyone she wanted to and never see him again and have no feeling of loss or insecurity about it. That was the way Mildred thought it was with Camille. She wished she could be that way, and she knew she couldn't. Couldn't because of her mother. And the unbidden thought entered her mind—if her mother were only dead Mildred's life would be so much simpler. She could have a secret little place to live somewhere. Almost fiercely, she brushed the thought away. "What a foul thing to think," she said to herself ceremoniously. But it was a dream she often had.

She looked out the front window. Pimples had helped to put the block and tackle into the bus, and the Manila line had grease on it and the grease had got on Pimples' chocolate brown trousers. He was trying to rub out the spot with a handkerchief.

"Poor kid," Mildred thought, "that's probably his only suit." She was going to tell him not to touch it when she saw him go to the gasoline pump and put a little of the gas on his handkerchief and go to work expertly on the spot.

And there was Juan calling, "Come on, you folks."

Chapter 14

THE back road around the San Ysidro River bend was a very old road, no one knew how old. It was true that the stage coaches had used it, and men on horseback. In the dry seasons the cattle had been driven over it to the river, where they could lie in the willows during the heat of the day and drink from holes dug in the river bed. The old road was simply a slice of country, uncultivated to start, marked only by wheel ruts and pounded by horses' hoofs. In the summer a heavy cloud of dust arose from its surface when a wagon went by, and in winter, pastelike mud spurted from under horses' feet. Gradually the road became scooped out so that it was lower than the fields through which it traveled, and this made it a long lake of standing water in the winter, sometimes very deep.

Then it was that men with plows made ditches on either side, with the embankments toward the road. And then cultivation came in and the cattle became so valuable that the owners of the property along the road put up fences to keep their cattle in and other people's cattle out.

The fences were split redwood posts set in the ground with one-by-six planks nailed halfway up connecting them. And along the top of the posts was old-fashioned barbed wire, a strip of twisted metal with sharpened spikes. The fences weathered in the sun and rain, the redwood planks and the posts turned light gray and gray-green, and lichens grew on the wood and moss formed on the shady sides of the posts.

Walking men burning with messages came by and painted their messages on the planks. "Repent, for the Kingdom of Heaven is at hand"—"Sinner, come to God"—"It is late"—

"Wherefore shall it profit a man . . ."—"Come to Jesus." And other men put other signs on the fence with stencils. "Jay's Drugs"—"Cyrus Noble—The Doctors' Whisky"—"San Ysidro Bicycle Shop." These signs were all weathered and dimmed now.

As the fields were used less for grazing and more for wheat and oats and barley, the farmers began to remove from their fields the weeds, the field turnip, the yellow mustard, the poppies and thistles and milkweeds, and these refugees found a haven in the ditches beside the road. The mustard stood seven feet high in the late spring, and red-winged blackbirds built their nests under the yellow flowers. And in the damp ditches the water cress grew.

The ditches beside the road under the high growth of weeds became the home of weasels and bright-colored water snakes, and the drinking places for birds in the evening. The meadow larks sat all morning on the old fences in the spring and whistled their yodeling song. And the wild doves sat on the barbed wire in the evening in the fall, shoulder to shoulder for miles, and their call rang down the miles in a sustained note. At evening the night hawks coursed along the ditches, looking for meat, and in the dark the barn owls searched for rabbits. And when a cow was sick the great ugly turkey buzzards sat on the old fence waiting for death.

The road was well-nigh abandoned. Only a few families who had farms that could not be reached in any other way ever used it any more. Once there had been many little holdings here, with a man living close to his acres and his farm behind him and his vegetable patch under the parlor window. But now the land stretched away, untenanted, and the little houses and the old barns stood windowless and gray and unpainted.

As noon came on the clouds hurried in from the southwest and bunched together. It is the rule that the longer the clouds prepare, the longer the rain will continue. But it was not ready yet. There was still some patches of blue sky and now and then a blinding flash of sun struck the ground. Once a tall cloud cut sun streaks into long, straight ribbons.

Juan had to drive back a little along the highway to reach the entrance to the old road. Before he turned into it he stopped the bus and got down and walked ahead. He felt the greaselike mud under his feet. And Juan knew a sense of joy. He had been trying to push his carload of cattle bodily about their business in which he had no interest. There was almost a feeling of malice in him now. They had elected this road, and it might be all right. He had a happy vacation-feeling. They wanted it, now let them take it. He would see what they would do if the bus stalled. He dug his toe into the mixed mud and gravel before he turned back. He wondered what Alice was doing. He knew damn well what Alice was doing. And if he wrecked the bus—well, he might just walk away from it, just walk away and never come back. It was a very happy vacation-feeling he had. His face was glowing with pleasure when he climbed into the bus.

"I don't know whether we'll make it or not," he said happily. And the passengers were a little nervous at his exuberance.

The passengers were seated in a bunch, as far forward as they could get. Every one of them felt that Juan was their only contact with the normal, and if they had known what was in his mind they would have been very much frightened. There was a high glee in Juan. He closed the door of the bus and he put his foot twice on the throttle to race his engine before he set the bus in low gear and turned it into the muddy country road.

The clouds were almost prepared for the stroke now. He knew that. In the west he could see one cloud fraying down. There it was starting, and it would move over the valley in another spring downpour. The light had turned metallic again with a washed, telescopic quality that meant only violent rain.

Van Brunt said brightly, "The rain's coming."

"Looks like," said Juan, and he turned his bus into the road. He had good tread on his tires, but as he left the blacktop he could feel the rubber slip a little on the greasy mud and the rear end swing in a small arc. But there was a bottom to it, and the bus lumbered over the road. Juan put it in second gear. He would keep it there probably for the whole distance.

Mr. Pritchard called above the beat of the motor, "How long is this detour?"

"I don't know," said Juan. "I've never been over it. They say thirteen or fifteen miles—something like that." He hunched over the wheel and his eyes lifted from the road and glanced at the Virgin of Guadalupe in her little shrine on top of his instrument board.

Juan was not a deeply religious man. He believed in the Virgin's power as little children believe in the power of their uncles. She was a doll and a goddess and a good-luck piece and a relative. His mother—that Irish woman—had married into the Virgin's family and had accepted her as she had accepted her husband's mother and grandmother. The Guadalupana became her family and her goddess.

Juan had grown up with this Lady of the wide skirts standing on the new moon. She had been everywhere when he was little—over his bed to supervise his dreams, in the kitchen to watch over the cooking, in the hall to check him in and out of the house, and on the *zaguán* door to hear him playing in the street. She was in her own fine chapel in the church, in the classroom in school, and, as if that wasn't ubiquitous enough, he wore her on a little gold medal on a golden chain about his neck. He could get away from the eyes of his mother or his father or his brothers, but the dark Virgin was always with him. While his other relatives could be fooled or misled and tricked and lied to, the Guadalupana knew everything anyway. He confessed things to her, but that was only a form because she knew them anyway. It was more a recounting of your motives in doing a certain thing than a breaking of the news that you had done it. And that was silly too, because she knew the motives. Then, too, there was an expression on her face, a half smile, as though she were about to break out into laughter. She not only understood, she was also a little amused. The awful crimes of childhood didn't seem to merit hell, if her expression meant anything.

Thus Juan as a child had loved her very deeply and had trusted her, and his father had told him that she was the one set aside especially to watch over Mexicans. When he saw German or American children in the streets he knew that his Virgin didn't give a damn about them because they were not Mexicans.

When you add to this the fact that Juan did not believe in her with his mind and did with every sense, you have his attitude toward Our Lady of Guadalupe.

The bus slithered along the muddy road, moving very slowly and leaving deep ruts behind. Juan flicked his eyes to the Vir-

gin and he said in his mind, "You know that I have not been
happy and also that out of a sense of duty that is not natural to
me I have stayed in the traps that have been set for me. And now
I am about to put a decision in your hands. I cannot take the
responsibility for running away from my wife and my little
business. When I was younger I could have done it, but I am
soft now and weak in my decisions. And I am putting this in
your hands. I am on this road not of my own volition. I have
been forced here by the wills of these people who do not care
anything for me or for my safety or happiness, but only for
their own plans. I think they have not even seen me. I'm an
engine to get them where they are going. I offered to take them
back. You heard me. So I am leaving it to you, and I will know
your will. If the bus mires down so that ordinary work will let
me get it out and proceed, I will get it out. If ordinary precaution will keep the bus safe and on the road, I will take that
precaution. But if you, in your wisdom, wish to give me a sign
by dropping the bus into the mud up to the axles, or sliding it
off the road into a ditch where I couldn't do anything about it,
I will know you approve of what I want to do. Then I will
walk away. Then these people can take care of themselves. I
will walk away and disappear. I will never go back to Alice. I
will take off my old life like a suit of underwear. It is up to
you."

He nodded and smiled at the Virgin, and she had the little
smile on her face too. She knew what was going to happen,
but, of course, there was no way of finding that out. He couldn't
run away without sanction. He had to have the approval of
the Virgin. It was directly up to her. If she felt strongly about
his going back to Alice, she would smooth the road and get the
bus through, and he would know that he was set for life with
what he had.

He breathed high in his lungs with excitement and his eyes
shone. Mildred could see his face in the rear-view mirror. She
wondered what terrible joy there was in his mind to make his
face light up. This was a man, she thought, a man of complete
manness. This was the kind of a man that a pure woman would
want to have because he wouldn't even want to be part woman.
He would be content with his own sex. He wouldn't ever try
to understand women and that would be a relief. He would

just take what he wanted from them. Her disgust for herself passed, and she felt pretty good again.

Her mother was writing another letter in her mind. "There we were on that muddy road, miles from any place. And even the driver didn't know the road. Well, just anything could happen. Anything. There wasn't a house in sight and the rain was starting."

The rain was starting. Not like the gusts and spurts of the morning, but a heavy, driving, drumming, businesslike rain that delivered so many gallons an hour in a given area. And there was no wind. This was downpour, pure, straight rainfall. The bus hissed and splashed over the level road, and Juan, when he turned the front wheels a little, could feel the rear end slide.

"You got any chains?" Van Brunt called.

"No," said Juan happily. "Haven't been able to get chains since before the war."

"I don't think you're going to make it," said Van Brunt. "You're all right on the level but you've got to start going up-hill pretty soon." He motioned to the east and the mountains toward which they were crawling. "The river cuts right up against a bluff," he shouted to the other passengers. "The road goes up over that bluff. I don't think we're going to make it."

To Pimples it had been a morning of conflicts and stresses. There weren't many relaxed moments in his life anyway, but this day had been particularly tearing. His body burned with excitement. Pimples was loaded with the concupiscent juices of adolescence. His waking and his sleeping hours were pre-occupied with the one goal. But so variable was the reaction to the single stimulus that he found himself one moment as lustful as a puppy on a curtain, the next floundering in thick and idealistic sentiment, and the next howling with self-condemnation. He felt then that he was alone, that he, alone, was the great sinner of the world. He looked with fawning adoration at the self-control of Juan and other men he knew.

Since she had come into his sight all of his body and his brain yearned toward Camille, and his yearning went from lustful pictures of himself and her to visions of himself married to her and settled down with her. One moment he felt almost forward enough to just out and out ask her, and the next, her glance in his direction forced a quivering embarrassment on him.

Again he had tried to get a seat where he could watch her without being noticed, and again he had failed. He could see the back of her head, but he could see Norma's profile. So it was that only at this late time did Pimples notice the change in Norma and, noticing, he drew a deep breath. She was not the same. He knew that it was only make-up, for he could see the eyebrow pencil and the lipstick from where he sat, but that wasn't what sent his blood coursing hotly in his stomach. She was changed. There was a conscious girlness about her that had not been there before, and Pimples' wild juices whispered to him. If, as he really knew deep in his heart, he couldn't have Camille, he might maybe get Norma. He wasn't as frightened of her as he was of the goddess Camille. Unconsciously he began to make plans for trapping Norma, overwhelming her. A new pustule was forming right in front of his left ear. Automatically he scratched it, and the angry red of his tainted flesh spread outward on his cheek. He looked secretly at the fingernail that had done the business and put it in his pocket and cleaned it. He had made his cheek bleed. He took out his handkerchief and held it to his face.

Mr. Pritchard was worried about getting through and making his connection. There was a gnawing in him that would not let him rest or relax. He had tried to laugh it off to himself. He had used all the ordinary methods for throwing out unpleasant thoughts, and they didn't work.

Ernest Horton had said Mr. Pritchard's plan was blackmail, and Ernest had almost indicated that he thought Elliott Pritchard would steal his slipcover for a dark suit if he wasn't watched. This had at first outraged Mr. Pritchard—a man of his reputation and standing. And then he had thought, "Yes, I have standing and reputation in my own community, but here I have nothing. I am alone. This man thinks I am a crook. I can't send him to Charlie Johnson so he can get an idea of how wrong he is." This bothered Mr. Pritchard very much. Ernest had gone even further. He had indicated that he thought Mr. Pritchard was the kind of man who would go to an apartment with blondes. He had never done that in his life. He had to prove to Ernest Horton that his judgment had been wrong. But how could he do it?

Mr. Pritchard's arm was over the back of the seat, and Ernest was sitting alone in the seat behind him. The engine of the bus, traveling in second gear, was loud, and the old body vibrated noisily. There was only one way—to offer Ernest Horton something, something open and honest, so that he would see that Mr. Pritchard was not a crook.

A vague thought came back to him. He turned in his seat. "I was interested in what you said about what your company does with ideas that come in."

Ernest looked at him with amusement. The guy wanted something. He suspected the old boy wanted to get in on a party or two. Ernest's boss was that way. He wanted conferences at night and always ended up in a whorehouse and was always surprised at how he got there.

"We've got a very nice relationship," Ernest said.

"This idea is nothing much that I had," Mr. Pritchard said. "It's just something that came to me. You can have it if you want it and if it'll do you any good."

Ernest waited without comment.

"You take cuff links," Mr. Pritchard said. "Now, I always wear French cuffs and cuff links, and once you get the links in—well, you've got to take them out before you can take off the shirt. And if you want to push up your sleeves to wash your hands you've got to take out the cuff links. It's easy to put in cuff links before you put on the shirt, but you can't get your hands through. When you've got the shirt on it's hard to get the cuff links in. See what I mean?"

"There's that kind that clicks together," Ernest said.

"Yes, but they aren't popular. You're always mislaying or losing part."

The bus stopped. Juan put the car in low gear and moved quickly on. There was a jar as he hit a hole and a second jar as the rear wheels went through it, and the bus moved slowly on. The rain drummed heavily on the roof. The windshield wiper squeaked on the glass.

Mr. Pritchard leaned back farther in his seat and pulled up his sleeve so that his plain gold cuff links showed. "Now, suppose," he said, "instead of links or a bar, there was a spring. When you put the cuff on over your hand the spring would give and you could push the cuff up your arm to wash, and then the spring would go right back into place." He watched Ernest's face closely.

Ernest's eyes were half closed in thought. "But how would it look? It would have to be a steel spring or it wouldn't last."

Mr. Pritchard said eagerly, "I thought that through. On the cheaper ones you could gold-plate the spring or silver-plate it. But on the expensive ones, like pure gold or platinum—the quality ones—why, instead of a bar it's a tube, and when the cuff is at your wrist, why, the little spring has disappeared right into the tube."

Ernest nodded slowly. "Yes," he said. "Yes, sir. Sounds pretty good."

"You can have it," said Mr. Pritchard. "It's yours to make anything you want out of it."

Ernest said, "My company goes in for a different kind of novelties, but maybe—maybe I could talk them into it. The best-selling things in the world—for men, that is—are razors or razor gadgets, pens and pencils, and personal jewelry. The fellow that don't write five lines a year will buy a tricky fountain pen for fifteen dollars any day. And jewelry? Yes, sir, it might work out. What would you want out of it if they thought it was a good idea?"

"Nothing," Mr. Pritchard said. "Absolutely nothing. It's yours. I like to help an up-and-coming young fellow." He was beginning to feel good again. But suppose the thing worked out, this idea he'd cooked up. Suppose it made a million dollars. Suppose—but he had said it and his word was good. His word was his bond. If Ernest wanted to show appreciation, that was up to him. "I don't want a single thing," he repeated.

"Well, that's mighty nice of you." Ernest took a notebook from his pocket, made an entry, and tore out the page. "Of course, in a thing like that I'd have to get an assignment," he said. "If you've got a moment while you're in Hollywood, maybe you could give me a call and we'll talk some business. We might be able to do business." His left eye dropped a little as he said it, and then his eyes turned and rested a moment on Mrs. Pritchard. He passed the slip to Mr. Pritchard and said, "Aloha Arms, Hempstead 3255, apartment 12B."

Mr. Pritchard colored a little, took out his wallet and put the paper in it, and he pushed the paper down in the back of the slot. He didn't really need to keep it. He could throw it away the first chance he got, for his memory was good. It would be years before he would forget that phone number. The system had clicked in his head, his old system. Three and two are five and repeat. And Hempstead. Hemp is rope. Yellow hemp, and you can't use anything instead of hemp. He used hundreds of memory tricks like that. Yellow hemp, blond hemp. His fingers itched to throw the paper away. Sometimes Bernice looked in his wallet for some change. He told her to. But he felt danger in his stomach—the miserable feeling of having been called a thief.

He said to his wife, "You feel all right, little girl?"

"Yes," she said. "I think I fought it off. I just said to myself, 'I won't let it come. I won't let it interfere with my darling's vacation.'"

"I'm glad," said Mr. Pritchard.

"And, dear," she went on, "how do you men get such ideas?"

"Oh, they just come to you," he said. "That new shirt with the small buttonholes is the cause of this one. I got caught in it a few days ago and nearly had to call for help."

She smiled. "I think you're very nice," she said. And he reached over and put his hand on her knee and squeezed her leg. She slapped his hand playfully and in a moment he took it away.

Norma had her head turned so that her mouth was close to Camille's ear. She spoke as softly as she could because she knew that Pimples was trying to listen. She was conscious of his gaze, and in a way she was gratified. She had never been so confident in her life as she was now.

"I haven't really got any family, like you'd call a family," she said. She was tumbling herself out in front of Camille. She was explaining and pouring out her life. She wanted Camille to know all about her, the way she was before this morning and the way she was now, and that would make Camille her family and would tie this beautiful and sure creature to her.

"When you're alone you do such funny things," she said. "I used to lie to people. I'd pretend things to myself. I would—well, do things like the things I was pretending were true. You know what I'd do? I'd picture like a certain movie star was—well, was my husband."

It had jumped out. She hadn't intended to go so far. She blushed. She shouldn't have told that. It was kind of like letting Mr. Gable down. But she inspected this and found it wasn't so. She didn't feel quite the same about Mr. Gable as she had. Her feeling had moved on to Camille. It was a shock to realize it. She wondered if she were being inconstant.

"It's when you don't have any family and no friends," she explained. "I guess you just make them up if you haven't got them. But now, well, if we could get an apartment I wouldn't have to make up anything."

Camille turned her face away so she couldn't see the nakedness in Norma's eyes, the complete defenselessness. "Oh, brother!" Camille thought. "What have I let myself in for now? I've got a baby. I've gone and got caught in something. How did this happen? I'm going to have to make her over and live her life and in a little while it'll probably bore the hell out of me and I'll be in too deep to get out of it. If Loraine's shucked off that advertising man and we can go back together, what am I going to do with this? How did it start? How the hell did I get into it?"

She turned to Norma. "Listen, honey," she said crisply. "I didn't say we could do it. I said we'd have to see how it worked out. There's a lot you don't know about me. For one thing, I'm engaged to be married, and my boy friend, he thinks it might be pretty soon. So you see, if he wants to now, why I couldn't go along with you."

Camille saw the despair come into Norma's eyes, like a cold horror, and the sagging of her cheeks and mouth and how the muscles of her shoulders and arms collapsed. Camille said to herself, "I can get a room in the next town and hide out till she gets lost. I can run out on her. I can—oh, Jesus, how did I let myself in for this? I'm too tired. I need a hot bath."

Aloud she said, "Don't take it so hard, honey. Maybe he isn't ready. Maybe—oh, look, honey, maybe it will work out. Maybe it will. Really. We'll just see how it goes."

Norma compressed her lips tightly and squinted her eyes. Her head jiggled with the vibration of the bus. Camille didn't want to look at her. After a time Norma got herself under control. She said quietly, "Maybe you're ashamed of me, and I wouldn't blame you. I can only be a waitress, but if you'd show me I could maybe get to be a dental nurse like you. I'd study nights and I'd work as a waitress in the daytime. But I'd do it, and then you wouldn't have to be ashamed of me. It wouldn't be so hard with you to help me."

Camille felt a rolling wave of nausea in her stomach. "Oh, God Almighty! Now I'm really trapped. What do I say? Tell her another lie? Would it be better to tell this girl exactly what I do for a living? Or would that make it worse? That might shock her so she wouldn't want me for a friend. Maybe that'd be the best thing. No, it would be best just to lose her in a crowd, I guess."

Norma was saying, "I'd like to have what you'd call a profession that had some dignity to it, like you."

Camille said in despair, "Look, honey, I'm awful tired. I'm too tired to think. I've been traveling for days. I'm too worn out to think about anything. Let's just let it lay for a while. We'll just see how it goes then."

"I'm sorry," Norma said. "I got excited and I forgot. I won't talk about it any more. We'll just see how it goes, huh?"

"Yes, we'll see how it goes," said Camille.

The bus jerked to a stop. They were coming near to the foothills now and the green billows of land were dimly visible through the rain. Juan half stood up to look down at the roadbed. There was a hole in the road, a hole full of water, no telling how deep. It might drop the bus clear out of sight. He glanced quickly at the Virgin. "Shall I take a chance?" he said under his breath. His front wheels were on the edge of the pool. He grinned, put the bus in reverse, and backed up twenty feet.

Van Brunt said, "You going to try a run for it? You'll get stuck."

Juan's lips moved silently. "My dear little friend, if you only knew," he whispered. "If all of the rest of you only knew." He put the bus in first gear and ran at the hole. The water splashed away with a rushing hiss. The rear wheels went into the hole. The bus slipped and floundered. The rear wheels spun and the motor roared and the spinning wheels edged the bumping body slowly across and slithered it out on the other side. Juan slipped the gears to second and crawled on.

"Must have been a little gravel mixed in with that," he said over his shoulder to Van Brunt.

"Well, you wait till you start up the hill," Van Brunt said ominously.

"You know, for a man that wants to get through you put more things in the way," Juan said.

The road began to climb and the water did not stand any more. The ditches along the side were running full. The driving wheels of the bus slipped and churned in the ruts. Juan suddenly knew what he was going to do if the bus piled up. He hadn't known. He had thought he might go to Los Angeles and get a job driving a truck, but he wouldn't do that. He had fifty dollars in his pocket. He always carried that much for repair emergencies, and that would be enough too. He would walk away, but not far. He'd get under cover and wait until the rain stopped. He might even sleep some place. For food he would grab one of those pies. Then, when he was rested, he would walk over to the highway, bum a ride, just wait at a service station until someone picked him up. He would thumb his way to San Diego and then he'd go across the border to Tijuana. It would be nice there, and he might just lie on the beach for two or three days. The border wouldn't bother him. On this side he'd say he was American. On the other side he'd be Mexican. Then, when he was ready, he'd go out of town, maybe catch a ride or maybe just walk over the hills and by the little streams, perhaps as far as Santo Tomás, and there he'd wait for the mail carrier. He would buy a lot of wine in Santo Tomás, and he'd pay the mail carrier, and then down the peninsula he would go, through San Quintin, past Ballenas Bay. It might take two weeks through the rocks and the prickly desert and then across to La Paz. He would see that he had some money left. At La Paz he would catch a boat across the gulf to Guaymas or Mazatlán, maybe even to Acapulco, and in any of those places he would find tourists. More at Acapulco than at Guaymas or Mazatlán. And where there were tourists floundering around with the Spanish language in a strange country Juan would be all right. Gradually he'd work his way up to Mexico City and there were really tourists. He could conduct tours, and there were plenty of ways of getting money. He wouldn't need much.

He chuckled to himself. Why in God's name had he stuck to this as long as he had? He was free. He could do whatever he wanted to. Let them look for him. He might even see a note about it in the L. A. papers. They'd think he was dead and they'd look for his body. Alice would raise hell for a while. It would give her a great sense of importance. Plenty of people could cook beans in Mexico. He might lay up with one of those American women in Mexico City who lived down there to beat the taxes. With a few good suits of clothes Juan knew he was presentable enough. Why in hell hadn't he gone back before?

He could smell Mexico in his nose. He couldn't think why he hadn't done it before. And the passengers? Let them take care of themselves. They weren't very far out. They'd got so used to throwing their troubles on other people they had forgotten how to take care of themselves. It would be good for them. Juan could take care of himself and he was going to start doing it too. He'd been living a silly kind of life, worrying about getting pies from one town to the next. Well, that was over.

He glanced up with secret eyes at the Guadalupana. "Oh, I'll keep my word," he said under his breath. "I'll get them through if you want me to. But even then I'm not so sure I won't walk away."

His mind plunged with pictures of the sun-beaten hills of Lower California and the biting heat of Sonora, the chill morning air on the plateau of Mexico with the smell of pine knots in the huts and the popcorn smell of toasting tortillas. And a homesickness fell on him like a sweet excitement. The taste of fresh oranges and the bite of chili. What was he doing in this country anyway? He didn't belong here.

The curtain of the years rolled back, and superimposed on the muddy country road he saw and heard and smelled Mexico, the chattering voices of the market, the squawking parrot in the garden, the quarreling pigs in the street, the flowers and fish and the little modest dark girls in blue *rebozos*. How strange that he had forgotten for so long. He yearned toward the south. He wondered what crazy trap could have kept him here. Suddenly he was impatient to be away. Why couldn't he just slam on the brakes and open the door and walk away through the rain? He could see their stupid faces looking after him and hear their outraged comments.

He glanced again at the Virgin. "I'll keep my word," he whispered. "I'll get through if I can." He felt the wheels slip in the mud and he grinned at the Virgin of Guadalupe.

The river cut in close to the hills now, bringing its border of willows with it. And the road dodged sideways, away from it. The rain was thinning out, and from the road they could see the light yellow water whirling in the broad basin of the river and dragging lines of dirty foam in twisting streaks. Ahead the road climbed up the hill, and at the top there was a yellow cut, a kind of cliff, and the road ran in front of it. At the very top of the yellow cliff, in great faint letters, was the single word REPENT. It must have been a long and dangerous job for some wild creature to put it there with black paint, and it was nearly gone now.

In the cliff of sandstone there was erosion caves cut by the wind and dug out by animals. The caves looked like dark eyes peering out of the yellow cliff.

The fences were fairly strong here, and in the upland grass red cows stood dark and wet and some of them had already borne their spring calves. The red cows turned their heads slowly and watched the bus as it ground by, and one old fool of a cow became panic-stricken and ran away, kicking and bucking as though that would remove the bus.

The roadbed had changed. The gravel gave the bus better footing. The body bumped and jarred over the rain-rutted gravel, but the wheels did not slip. Juan looked suspiciously at the Virgin. Was she tricking him? Would she get him through and force him to make his own decision? That would be a dirty trick. With no sign from Heaven Juan didn't know what he would do. The road took a long loop around an old farm and then climbed toward the cliff in earnest.

Juan had the bus in low gear again and a wisp of steam came out of the overflow pipe and curled up in front of the radiator. The high point of the road was right in front of the cliff with its dark caves. Almost angrily Juan speeded his motor. The wheels threw gravel. There was a place where the ditch was plugged and water and topsoil flowed across the road. Juan raced at the dark streak. The front wheels crossed it and the back wheels spun in the greasy mud. The rear end swung around and the wheels spun and the hind end of the bus settled heavily into the ditch.

Juan's face had a fierce grin. He raced his motor and the wheels dug deeper and deeper. He reversed his direction and spun his wheels, and the spinning tires dug holes for themselves and settled into the holes, and the differential rested on the ground. Juan idled his motor. In the rear-view mirror he could see Pimples looking at him in amazement.

Juan had forgotten that Pimples would know. Pimples' mouth was open. Juan knew better than that. When you come to a soft place you don't spin the wheels. Juan could see the questions in Pimples' eyes. Why had he done it? He wasn't that stupid. He caught Pimples' eye in the mirror and all he could think to do was to wink secretly. But he saw relief come over Pimples' face. If it was a plan it was O.K. If there was something in back of it Pimples would go along. And then a horrible thought crossed Pimples' mind. Suppose it was Camille. If Juan wanted her Pimples wouldn't have a chance. He couldn't compete with Juan.

The angle of the bus was sharp. The rear wheels were buried and the front end stood high up on the road. "Sweetheart" looked like a crippled bug. Now Van Brunt's face cut out Pimples' reflection in the mirror. Van Brunt was red and angry and his bony finger cut the air under Juan's nose.

"So you did it," he cried. "So you tied us up. I knew you'd do it. By God, I knew you would! How am I going to get into the courthouse now? How are you going to get us out of this?"

Juan knocked the finger aside with the back of his hand. "Take your finger out of my face," he said. "I'm sick of you. Now get back to your seat."

Van Brunt's angry eyes wavered. He suddenly realized that this man was out of control. He wasn't afraid of the railroad commission or anybody. Van Brunt backed up a little and sat down on the angled seat.

Juan turned off the ignition and his motor died. The rain pattered on the roof of the bus. He tapped his palms on the steering wheel for a moment and then he turned in his seat and faced his passengers. "Well," he said. "That does it."

They stared back at him, shocked at the situation. Mr. Pritchard said softly, "Can't you get us out?"

"I haven't looked yet," said Juan.

"But it seems to me like we're in pretty deep. What are you going to do?"

"I don't know," said Juan. He wanted to see Ernest Horton's face, to see if he knew the thing had been deliberate, but Ernest was hidden behind Norma. Camille showed no effect at all. She had waited too long to be impatient.

"Sit tight," Juan said. He pulled himself upright against the angled bus and pushed the door lever. The lock clicked but the door was sprung. It did not open. Juan stood up and put his foot against the door and pushed it open. They could hear the hiss of rain on the road and on the grass. Juan stepped out into the rain and walked around to the back of the bus. The slanting rain felt cold on his head.

He had done a good job. It would probably take a wrecking car or maybe even a tractor to get it out. He leaned down and looked underneath to verify something he already knew. The axles and the differential were resting on the ground. Through the windows the passengers were looking out, their faces distorted by the wet glass. Juan straightened up and climbed back into the bus.

"Well, folks, I guess you'll just have to wait. I'm sorry, but don't forget you all wanted to come this way."

"I didn't," Van Brunt said.

Juan whirled on him. "God damn it, keep out of this! Don't get me mad because I'm right on the point of getting mad."

Van Brunt saw that he meant it. He looked down at his hands, pinched up the loose skin on his knuckles, and rubbed his left hand with his right.

Juan sat sideways in the driver's seat. His eyes flicked over the Virgin. "All right, all right," he thought to her, "so I cheated a little bit. Not much, but a little. I guess you're justified now in making it pretty uncomfortable for me." Aloud he said, "I'll just have to walk on ahead and phone for a wrecking car. I'll tell them to send out a taxi for you folks. That shouldn't take very long."

Van Brunt spoke with restraint. "There isn't a place in four miles. The old Hawkins place is about a mile, but it's standing empty since the Bank of America took it over. You'll have to go to the county road and that's a good four miles."

"Well, if I have to go, I have to go," said Juan. "I can only get just so wet."

Pimples had a rush of friendliness. "I'll go," he said. "You stay here and let me go."

"No," said Juan, "this is your day off." He laughed. "You just enjoy it, Kit." He reached over to the instrument board, unlocked the glove box, and opened the little door. "There's some emergency whisky here," he said.

He paused. Should he take the pistol—a good Smith & Wesson 45-caliber revolver with a 6-inch barrel? It would be a shame to leave it. But it would be a nuisance to have it too. If he got into any kind of trouble the gun would go against him. He decided to leave it. If he was going to leave his wife, he could surely leave his gun too. He said lightly, "If you get jumped by tigers, there's a gun in here."

"I'm hungry," Camille said.

Juan smiled at her. "You take these keys and open up the back. There's a lot of pies there." He grinned at Pimples. "Don't eat 'em all, son. Now, you can stay in the bus or you can get out the tarpaulin from the back and put it on the ground up in those caves if you want. You might even build a fire in there if you can find any dry wood. I'll get a car sent out to you soon as I can."

"I'd like to go instead of you," Pimples said.

"No, you stick around and look after things," said Juan, and he saw a flash of pleasure on Pimples' face. Juan buttoned his jacket tightly over his chest. "Just sit tight," he said, and he stepped down out of the bus.

Pimples clambered down after him. He followed Juan a few steps until Juan turned and waited for him. "Mr. Chicoy," he said softly, "what is it you got on your mind?"

"On my mind?"

"Yeah. You see—well, you spun them wheels."

Juan put his hand on Pimples' shoulder. "Look, Kit, I'll tell you sometime. You just hold on for me, will you?"

"Well, sure, Mr. Chicoy, only—I'd just like to know."

"I'll tell you all about it when we get a minute alone," Juan said. "You just keep these folks from killing each other for a little while, will you?"

"Well, sure," Pimples said uneasily. "How long you think it'll be before you get back?"

"I don't know," Juan said impatiently. "How can I tell? You do like I say."

"Sure. Oh, sure," said Pimples.

"And eat all the pie you want," said Juan.

"But we'll have to pay for it, Mr. Chicoy!"

"Sure," said Juan, and he strode away along the road in the rain. He knew that Pimples was looking after him and he knew that Pimples sensed something. Pimples knew he was running out. Juan didn't feel good about it now. Not the way he thought he would. It didn't seem as good or as pleasant or as free. He stopped and looked back. Pimples was just getting into the bus.

The road went past the cliff with its eroded stone caves. Juan turned off the road and went into the shelter for a moment. The caves and their overhang were larger than they looked from outside and they were fairly dry too. In front of the entrance to the largest cave there were three fire-blackened stones and a battered tin can. Juan stepped back to the road and walked on.

The rain was thinning out. To his right, down the hill, he could see the great bend of the river and how it turned and headed back across the valley through the sodden green fields. The country was too wet. There was an odor of decay in the air, the fat green stems fermenting. The road ahead was rain-beaten and rotted by water, but not by wheels. Nothing had been over it for a long time.

Juan bowed his head into the rain and walked faster. It wasn't so good. He tried to remember the sunny sharpness of Mexico and the little girls in blue *rebozos* and the smell of cooking beans, and instead Alice came into his head. Alice, looking out of the screen door. And he thought of the bedroom with its flowered curtains. She liked things nice. She liked pretty things. The bedspread, now, a giant afghan she had knitted herself in little squares, and no two the same color. She said she could get over a hundred dollars for it. And she had knitted every bit of it herself.

And he thought of the big trees, and how nice it was to lie in a tub full of hot water in the bathroom, the first real bathroom he had ever had outside of hotels. And there was always a bar of sweet-smelling soap. "It's just a god-damned habit," he said to himself. "It's a damned trap. You get used to a thing and so you think you like it. I'll get over it the way I'd get over a cold. Sure, it'll be painful. I'll worry about Alice. I'll be sorry. I'll accuse myself, and it might be I won't sleep good. But I'll get over it. After a while I won't think about it. It's just a damned trap." And Pimples' face, trusting and warm, came up before him. "I'll tell you later. I'll tell you all about it, Kit Carson." Not many people had trusted Juan that way.

He tried to think of the lake at Chapala, and over its pale

smooth water he saw "Sweetheart," the bus, sagged down in the mud.

Ahead and down the hill to the left, in an indentation of the foothills, he saw a house and a barn and a windmill with the blades broken and hanging. That would be the old Hawkins place. Just the set-up he'd been thinking about. He would go in there, maybe in the house, but more likely in the barn. An old barn is usually cleaner than an old house. There was bound to be a little haw or stray in the barn. Juan would crawl in there and sleep. He wouldn't think about anything. He would sleep until maybe this time tomorrow, and then he'd walk on to the county road and pick up a ride. What difference did it make to him about the passengers? "They can't starve. It won't hurt them at all. It'll be good for them. It isn't any business of mine."

He hurried his steps down the hill toward the old Hawkins place. They'd look for him. Alice would think he was murdered and she'd call in a sheriff. Nobody ever thought he'd run off like this. That's what made it such a good joke. Nobody thought he could do it. Well, he'd show them. Get to San Diego, cross the border, pick up the mail truck to La Paz. Alice would have the cops out.

He stopped and looked back at the road. His footprints were clear enough, but the rain would probably wash them out, and he could cover his tracks if he wanted to. He turned in off the road toward the Hawkins place.

The old house had gone to pieces very quickly once it was abandoned. A few wandering boys broke out the windows and stole the lead pipe and the plumbing, and the doors soon banged themselves silly and fell off their hinges. The old dark wallpaper, pulled down under wind-driven rain, revealed under-sheets made from old newspapers with old cartoons— "Foxy Grandpa" and "Little Nemo" and "Happy Hooligan" and "Buster Brown." Tramps had been there and had left their litter and burned the door casings in the old black fireplace. The smell of desertion and damp and sourness was in the house. Juan looked in the doorway, walked through and smelled the odor of the vacant house, and went out the back door toward the barn.

The corral fence was down and the big door off, but inside the barn smelled fresh. The stalls were polished where the horses had rubbed against the wood. The corners were cob-webbed. Between the manure windows were still the candle-boxes with the worn brushes and rusty currycombs. And an old collar and hames and a set of tugs hung on a rack beside the door. The leather of the collar was split and the padding stuck out.

The barn had no loft. The whole central part had been used to store hay. Juan walked around the end of the last stall. It was dusky inside and the light of the sky lanced through broken shakes in the roof. The floor was covered with short straw, dark with age, and with a slightly musty smell. Standing still in the entrance, Juan could hear the squeaking of mice and he could smell the colonies of mice too. From a rafter two cream-colored barn owls looked down at him and then closed their yellow eyes again.

The rain had diminished so that there was only a faint puttering on the roof. Juan went to a corner and with his foot kicked aside a layer of the dusty top straw. He sat down and then lay back and thrust his hands behind his head. The barn was alive with secret little sounds, but Juan was very tired. His nerves itched and he felt mean. He thought perhaps if he slept he would feel better.

Back in the bus he had felt, in anticipation, a bursting, or-gasmic delight of freedom. But it was not so. He felt miserable. His shoulders ached, and now that he was relaxed and stretched out he wasn't sleepy. He wondered, "Won't I ever be happy? Isn't there anything to do?" He tried to remember old times when it seemed to him that he was happy, when he had felt pure joy, and little pictures came into his mind. There was a very early morning with chill air and the sun was coming up behind the mountains and in a muddy road little gray birds were hopping. There wasn't any reason for joy, but it had been there.

And another. It was evening and a shining horse was rubbing his lovely neck on a fence and the quail were calling and there was a sound of dropping water somewhere. His breath came short with excitement just remembering it.

And another. He rode in an old cart with a girl cousin. She was older than he—he couldn't remember what she looked like. The horse shied at a piece of paper and she fell against him, and to right herself she put out her hand and touched his leg, and delight bloomed in his stomach and his brain ached with delight.

And another. Standing at midnight in a great, dim cathedral with a sharp, barbaric smell of copal smarting his nose. He held a skinny little candle with a white silk bow tied about it halfway up. And like a dream, the sweet murmur of the mass came from far away at the high altar and the drowsy loveliness drew down over him.

Juan's muscles relaxed and he slept in the straw of the deserted barn. And the timid mice sensed his sleep and came out from under the straw and played busily and the rain whispered quietly on the barn roof.

Chapter 15

THE passengers watched Juan walk away and disappear over the brow of the hill. They didn't speak, not even when Pimples climbed back into the bus and took his place in the driver's seat. The seats were tilted and each passenger tried to get comfortable.

At last Mr. Pritchard asked, generally, "How long do you suppose it'll take him to get a car out here?"

Van Brunt rubbed his left hand nervously. "Can't possibly expect it under three hours. He's got a four-mile walk. Even if he can get a car to come out, it'll take them an hour to get started and an hour to get here. That is, if they'll come out at all. I'm not sure anybody will come over this road. We should have walked in with him and caught a ride at the county road."

"We couldn't," said Mr. Pritchard. "We've got all our baggage."

Mrs. Pritchard said, "I didn't want to say anything when you got this crazy idea, Elliott. After all, it is your vacation."

She had been wanting to explain to the other passengers how people of the obvious position of the Pritchards should come to find themselves on a bus—should put themselves in the way of this kind of thing. They must have been wondering, she thought. Now she turned and addressed them. "We came out on a train, a nice train—the City of San Francisco, a very comfortable extra-fare train. And then my funny husband had this crazy idea of coming down on a bus. He thought he would see the country better that way."

"Well, we're seeing it, little girl," he said bitterly.

She went on, "My husband said he had been out of touch. He wanted to see what the people, the real people, were talking about." A delicate malice was creeping into her voice. "I thought it was silly but it's his vacation. He's the one who's worked so hard for the war effort. The wives didn't have much to do, just trying to make out with rationing and all, and no food in the stores. Why, once for two months we didn't taste beef. Nothing but chicken."

Mr. Pritchard looked at his wife in some surprise. It was not a common thing for this edge to come into her voice and it had a strange effect on him. Suddenly he found himself getting angry, getting wildly, unreasonably angry. It was her tone that did it. "I wish we'd never come," he said. "I didn't want to come anyway. I'd have had a real rest playing a little golf and sleeping in my own bed. I never wanted to come."

The other passengers watched with curiosity and interest. They were bored. This might be good. The anger of these two was beginning to fill the bus.

Mildred said, "Mother, Dad, cut it out."

"You stay out of this," Mr. Pritchard said. "I didn't want to come. I didn't want to at all. I hate foreign countries, particularly dirty ones."

Mrs. Pritchard's mouth pinched white and her eyes were cold. "This is a fine time to tell me about it," she said. "Who made all the plans for it and bought all the tickets? Who got us on this bus, stalled in the middle of nowhere? Who did all that? Did I?"

"Mother!" Mildred cried. She had never heard this tone in her mother's voice before.

"And it seems a strange thing"—Mrs. Pritchard's voice broke a little—"I try so hard. This trip, when you get it all paid for, is going to cost three or four thousand dollars. If you didn't want to come I could have built the little orchid house I've wanted so long, just a little, tiny orchid house. You said it wouldn't be a good example, getting it during the war, but the war is over now and we take a trip you didn't want to take. Well, you spoiled it for me now too. I won't enjoy it. You spoil everything. Everything!" She covered her eyes with her hand.

Mildred stood up. "Mother, stop it. Mother, stop this right now!"

Mrs. Pritchard moaned a little.

"If you don't stop it I'm going to walk away," Mildred said.

"Go away," said Mrs. Pritchard. "Oh, go away. You don't understand anything."

Mildred's face set. She picked up her gabardine topcoat and put it on. "I'm going to walk to the county road," she said.

"That's four miles," Van Brunt said. "You'll spoil your shoes."

"I'm a good walker," said Mildred. She had to get out, her hatred for her mother was rising in her and making her sick.

Mrs. Pritchard's handkerchief was out and the scent of lavender filled the bus.

"Pull yourself together," Mildred said harshly. "I know what you're going to do. You're going to get a headache and punish us. I know you. One of your fake headaches," she said viciously. "I'm not going to sit around and see you get away with it."

Pimples watched, fascinated. He was breathing through his mouth.

Mrs. Pritchard looked up at her daughter with horror. "Dear! You don't believe that!"

"I'm beginning to," said Mildred. "Those headaches come too opportunely."

Mr. Pritchard said, "Mildred, stop it."

"I'm going on."

"Mildred, I forbid it!"

His daughter whirled on him. "Forbid and be damned!" She buttoned her coat over her chest.

Mr. Pritchard put out his hand. "Mildred, please, dear."

"I've had enough," she said. "I need the exercise." She stepped out of the bus and walked rapidly away.

"Elliott," Mrs. Pritchard cried. "Elliott, stop her. Don't let her go."

He patted her arm. "Now, little girl, she'll be all right. We're just irritable. All of us."

"Oh, Elliott," she groaned, "if only I could lie down. If only

I could get some rest. She thinks my headaches aren't true. Elliott, I'll kill myself if she believes that. Oh, if I only could stretch out."

Pimples said, "Ma'am, we got some tarpaulins in the back end. We use 'em to cover the baggage when we carry it on top. If your husband would take one of them up in that cave, why, you could lay down there."

"Why, that's a wonderful idea," said Mr. Pritchard.

"Lie on the old damp ground?" she demanded. "No."

"No, on a canvas. I could fix you a sweet little bed for a sweet little girl."

"Well, I don't know," she said.

"Look, dear," he insisted. "Look, I'm going to roll up my top-coat. Now you just put your head down there, like that. Now, in a little while I'll come and get you and take you to your own little bed."

She whimpered.

"And rest your head on the pillow and close your eyes."

Pimples said, "Mr. Chicoy told me to bring out the pies if anybody got hungry. There's four flavors and they're pretty good too. I could eat a piece right now."

"Let's get that tarpaulin first," Mr. Pritchard said. "My wife is exhausted. She's about at the end of her strength. You help me fix her a bed, will you?"

"O.K.," said Pimples. He felt that he was doing all right in Juan's absence. He felt fine and jaunty. His posture showed his mood for his shoulders were back and his pale wolf eyes were bright and confident. There was only one worry in Pimples. He wished he had had sense enough to throw an old pair of shoes into the bus. His two-toned oxfords were likely to take a beating from the mud, and that would mean a long job with a toothbrush to clean them up again. And he couldn't appear to protect his shoes for that would indicate to Camille that he was not a devil-may-care fellow. She wouldn't be impressed by a man who was careful of his shoes even if they were new white and brown oxfords.

Ernest said, "I'm going to have a look at those caves," and he got up and climbed to the door of the bus. Van Brunt grumbled and followed.

Mrs. Pritchard nestled her cheek in Mr. Pritchard's coat and closed her eyes. She was filled with dismay .How could she have fought with him in public—with her own husband? It had never happened before. When it was necessary to quarrel she always managed that they should be alone. Not even Mildred was permitted to hear a quarrel. She felt it was vulgar to fight when people could hear, and, besides, it broke a pattern she had been years building, the story that because of her sweetness her marriage was ideal. Everyone she knew believed that. She believed it herself. Through her own efforts she had built a beautiful marriage and now she had slipped. She had quarreled. She had let it get out about the little orchid house.

For a number of years she had wanted such a house. Ever since, in fact, she had seen an article in *Harper's Bazaar* about a Mrs. William O. MacKenzie who had one. The pictures had been lovely. People would say of Mrs. Pritchard that she had the darlingest little orchid house. It was precious and valuable. It was better than jewelry or furs. People she didn't even know would hear about her little orchid house. Secretly she had learned a great deal about such projects. She had studied plans. She knew costs of heating systems and humidifiers. She knew where the original stock was bought and how much it cost. She had studied books on propagation. And all of this very secretly because she knew that if and when the time came that she could have it Mr. Pritchard would want to find out these things and tell her. It was the only way. She didn't even resent it. That was simply a way of life, the way she had made her marriage successful. She would be impressed with his knowledge and she would ask his advice about everything.

But she was worried because she had let the thing slip in anger. Such a mistake might set her back six months or more. She had planned to have him suggest it, and by careful reluctance cause him to overcome her opposition. But now the subject had been mentioned in anger and he would have a block against it. Unless she was very careful in the future he might never come around. It had been stupid of her and vulgar of her.

She could hear Norma and Camille talking softly behind her. Her eyes were closed and she looked so little and so ill that they couldn't imagine she was listening.

Norma was saying, "One of the things I'd like to have you show me is how you handle—well, fellas."

Camille laughed shortly. "What do you mean?" she asked.

"Well, you take Pimples. I can see how he's been—trying, and he can't get to first base with you, and at the same time you don't even seem like you're doing it. And you take that other fella. That salesman. Well, he's pretty clever and you handled him just like nothing. I wish I knew how you did it."

Camille was pleased. Much as she might be worried by this incipient millstone, it was pleasant to have admiration. Now was the time to tell Norma she wasn't a dental nurse, to tell her about the giant wine glass and the stags, and yet she couldn't. She didn't really want to shock Norma. She wanted to be admired.

"Thing I like is you never are mean or nasty about it and still they never lay a finger on you," Norma continued.

"I never noticed," Camille said. "I guess it's kind of like an instinct." She chuckled. "I've got a girl friend that can really handle men. She just don't give a hoot and she's kind of mean with men anyway. Well, Loraine—that's her name—was—well, she was kind of engaged to this fellow and he had a good job and so he wasn't any trouble. Loraine wanted a fur coat. Of course, she had a short wolf jacket and she had couple of white fox furs because Loraine is a very popular girl. She's pretty and little and when she's with girls she'll keep you laughing all the time. So Loraine wanted a mink coat, not a short one, but a real full-length one, and they cost three, four thousand dollars."

Norma whistled between her teeth. "Jesus God!" she said.

"Well, one afternoon Loraine said, 'I guess I'll get my fur coat now.' And I said, 'You're kidding.'

"'You think I'm kidding? Eddie's going to give it to me.'

"'When did he tell you?' I asked her.

"Loraine just laughed. 'He didn't tell me. He don't even know it yet.'

"'Well,' I said. 'Look, you're nuts.'

"'You wanna bet?' Loraine will take a bet on anything.

"I don't bet on things so I said, 'How are you going to go about it?'

"'If I tell you, will you keep it to yourself?' she said. 'It's easy. I know Eddie. I'm gonna needle him tonight and keep needling him till he gets mad. And I'm gonna keep right on until he throws a punch at me. I may even have to step into one because when Eddie's a little drunk he misses pretty bad. Well, then I'm gonna let Eddie stew in his own juice. I know Eddie. He'll get to feeling mean and sorry. You want to take that bet?' she said. 'I'll even lay down a time. I'll bet you I have that coat by tomorrow night.'

"Well, I don't bet anything, so I said, 'Two bits you don't.'"

Norma's mouth was open with excitement, and a gleam of reflected light came from between Mrs. Pritchard's closed lashes.

"Did she get it?" Norma demanded.

"Well, I went over to her place Sunday morning. Loraine had a mouse all right, a real blue shiner, and she had a patch over it and her nose was cut up too."

"Well, did she get the coat?"

"She got the coat all right," Camille said. There was a frown on her face, a puzzled look. "She got the coat and it was a beauty. Well, then she took off all her clothes. There were just two of us there. She turned that coat inside out and she put it right on next her skin with the hair next her skin. And then she rolled and rolled on the floor and she laughed and giggled like she was crazy."

Norma's held breath exhaled slowly. "God," she said, "why did she do that?"

"I don't know," said Camille. "It was like she—well, it was like she was a little crazy, kinda nuts."

Mrs. Pritchard's face was glowing. She breathed very rapidly. Her skin tingled, and there was an aching, itching feeling in her legs and stomach she had never felt before, and there was an excitement in her that she had had only once in her life and that was on horseback a long time ago.

Norma said judiciously, "I don't think it was nice. If she really loved Eddie and he was going to marry her, I don't think it was a nice thing to do."

"I don't either," said Camille. "It kind of bothered me about Loraine and I told her so, but she said, 'Well, some girls just take the longer way around. I wanted it quick. It'll be the same thing in the end, anyway. Somebody was gonna work Eddie over.'"

"And did she marry him?"

"Well, no. She didn't."

"I'll bet maybe she never loved him at all," Norma said heatedly. "I'll bet she just gold-dug Eddie."

"Maybe," said Camille, "but she's been my girl friend for a long time, and if I ever needed anything she was right there. One time when I had pneumonia she sat up with me for three days and nights, and I was broke and she paid the doctor."

"I guess you just can't tell," Norma said.

"No, I guess not," said Camille. "Anyway, you asked me about how to handle men."

Mrs. Pritchard was beating herself with words. Her reaction had frightened her. She said to herself, even whispering the words, "What a horrible, vulgar story. What animals those young girls are. So this is what Elliott means by 'getting down to the people.' Oh, that's horrible. We just forget how people are, how nasty they can be. Dear Ellen," she wrote frantically, and the excitement was still tingling on the insides of her legs. "Dear Ellen, the trip was terrible between San Ysidro and San Juan de la Cruz. The bus went into a ditch and we just sat and waited for hours. My Elliott was very sweet and made me a bed in a funny cave. You said I would have adventures. Remember? You said I always would have adventures. Well, I did. There were two vulgar, illiterate girls on the bus, one of them a waitress and the other was rather pretty. She was a you-know-what. I was resting and I guess they thought I was asleep and they went right on talking. I couldn't put in a letter what they said. I'm still blushing. Gentle people just don't know how these little things live. It's incredible. I always think it's ignorance. If we only had better schools and if—well, if you want the truth—if we who should be examples were just better examples, I'm sure the whole picture might change, gradually, but certainly."

Ellen would read the letter over and over to people. "I just had a letter from Bernice. She's having the most exciting adventures. You know, she always does. Why, I want you to hear what she says. I've never known anyone who could see the good sides of people the way Bernice can."

Norma was saying, "If I liked a fella I wouldn't think of doing a thing like that to him. If he wanted to give me a present he'd have to think of it himself."

"Well, that's the way I feel about it too," said Camille. "But I haven't got a fur coat, not even a chubby. And Loraine's got three."

"Well, I don't think it's fair," said Norma. "I don't think I'd like Loraine."

"God Almighty!" Camille cried in her mind. "You don't know if you'd like Loraine. I wonder if you've got any idea what Loraine would think of you?" No, she thought, that isn't true. Loraine would probably take this girl and fix her up and help her. Whatever you could say about Loraine, nobody could say she wasn't a good scout.

Chapter 16

MILDRED put her head down to keep the rain from misting her glasses. The gravelly road felt good under her feet and the exercise made her draw her breath deeply. It seemed to her that the day was getting darker. It couldn't be very late, and still an evening light was creeping in, making light things, such as pieces of quartz and limestone, seem lighter, and dark things, such as the fence posts, seem black.

Mildred walked quickly, her feet stabbing at the ground and her heels striking into the gravel. She was trying to push the quarrel out of her mind. She did not remember having seen her mother and father fight before. But this had been a practiced thing with a routine-like quality that indicated it was a far from uncommon process. Her mother must maneuver the quarrels into the bedroom where no one could hear them. She had built up and maintained a story of the perfect marriage. This time the tension had got to a breaking point and there was no bedroom to retire to. There had been mean little drops of yellow venom in the quarrel that disturbed Mildred. It was a poison that seeped subtly in, not an open, honest rage but rather a secret, creeping anger that struck with a thin, keen blade and then concealed the weapon quickly.

And there was this endless trip to Mexico ahead. Suppose Mildred didn't come back? Suppose she walked on and caught a ride and disappeared—rented a room someplace, perhaps on the coast by the sea, and spent the time on the rocks or on the beach? The idea was very pleasant to her. She could cook for herself and get to know other people on the beach. The idea was ridiculous. She hadn't any money. Her father was very generous—but not with cash. She could charge her clothes and sign checks in restaurants, but her actual money was always very short. Her father was generous but very curious. He wanted to know what she bought and where she ate, and he could find these things out on the monthly bills.

Of course, she could go to work. She would pretty soon anyway, but not right yet. No, she had to weather it out. She had to stumble through this horrible Mexican trip, which could be so wonderful if she were alone, and then go back to college. It wouldn't be long until she would go to work, and her father would approve of that. He would say to Charlie Johnson, "I'd give her anything she wants, but no, sir, she's got too much get-up-and-go. She's making her own living." And he would say it with pride, as though some virtue of his own was involved, and he would never know that she was working for the sake of privacy, so she could have her own apartment and some spending money, for things he didn't know about.

At home, for instance, she was free to go to the liquor cabinet any time she wanted, but she knew that her father had in his memory the exact level of liquid in every bottle, that if she took three drinks he would know it immediately. He was a very curious man.

She took off her glasses and wiped them on the lining of her coat and put them on again. In the road she could see Juan's tracks, long strides. There were places where his foot had slipped on a rock, and there were muddy stretches where the whole prints of his feet were visible, with the line broken by the drives of his toes. Mildred tried to walk in his tracks, but his step was too long for her, and she felt the pull on her thighs after she had kept it up for a while.

He was a strange, compelling man, she thought. She was glad she had got out of that crazy experience of the morning. No sense in it, she knew. Irritation and functioning glands interplaying—she knew all that. And she also knew herself to be a girl of strong sexual potential. There would come a time in the not far future when she would either have to get married or make some kind of permanent arrangement. Her times of restlessness and need were growing more frequent. She thought of Juan's dark face and shining eyes and she was not affected. But there was warmth in him and honesty. She liked him.

As she cleared the hill she saw the deserted farm below and was fascinated. She could feel the despondency of the place. She knew she couldn't pass the house without looking through it. Her steps quickened. All her interest was aroused.

"Bank foreclosed," Van Brunt had said, "and the family had to move, and the bank wouldn't be interested in an old house. It was the land they were taking."

Her strides were almost as long as Juan's now. She came swinging down to the foot of the hill to the muddy entrance of the farm and suddenly she stopped. Juan's tracks turned in. She walked along the road a little to find whether they emerged and continued, but she could find no other footsteps ahead.

"He must still be in there," she said to herself. "But why? He was going out to the county road. There couldn't be a telephone here." She grew cautious as she realized she didn't know what was going on, and she didn't know much about this man. She walked slowly into the entrance and moved out on the grass so that her feet would not make a rasping sound on the gravel.

There was something dangerous about the deserted house. She recalled old newspaper stories of murders in places like this. Her throat tightened with fear. "Well," she consoled herself, "I can turn right around and go out. Nobody's stopping me. Nobody's pushing me in, but I know I must. I know I won't leave. Maybe those murdered girls could have got away too. Maybe they were asking for it."

She saw a vision of herself lying on the floor of one of the rooms, strangled or stabbed, and there was something in the vision that made her laugh—her glasses were still on. And what did she know about Juan? He had a wife and a business. Then there was a headline she remembered. "Father of three in sadist murder. Parson murders choir singer." Why are so many choir singers and organists murdered, she wondered. There seems to be a high occupational hazard about choir singing. Choristers are always being found choked behind the organ. She laughed. She knew she was going into this house.

Should she just clump on in or should she steal in and catch Juan Chicoy at whatever he was doing? Maybe he was just going to the toilet.

She put a careful foot on the step and paused when the floorboard creaked under her weight. She went through the house opening cupboards. There was an overturned pepper can in the kitchen and a coat hanger in the closet of the bedroom. She turned her head sideways to look at the old comic pages under the peeled wallpaper. She read a strip of "Happy Hooligan." The mule, Maud, drew back her legs and kicked and Cy sailed through the air, and on the seat of Cy's pants were the imprints of the mule's hoofs.

She straightened her head. Why hadn't she thought of the barn before? Mildred crept back to the front porch and looked closely at the boards. She could see the wet track of Juan's shoes. She followed the track to the living room and lost it. Then she went to the open back door and looked out. What a fool she had been, creeping about! There were the footprints going out, headed, in fact, for the barn.

She went down the broken steps and followed the trail across the lot and passed the old windmill. She entered the barn and stood listening. There was no sound. She thought of calling out and gave it up. Slowly she moved down the line of stalls and around the end stall. It had taken a little while for her eyes to adjust to the light. She stood in the entrance to the central part. All the little mice flicked out of sight. Then she saw Juan lying on his back, his hands cupped behind his head. His eyes were closed and he was breathing evenly.

"I can go away," Mildred said. "Nobody's keeping me. It will be my fault. I just want to remember that. He's minding his own business. Oh, what's this nonsense?"

She took off her glasses and put them in her pocket. The outline of the man was fuzzy to her now, to her unfocused eyes, but she could still see him. She walked slowly, carefully, across the straw-covered floor and when she was beside him she crossed her ankles and let herself down and sat on her crossed feet. The scar on his lip was white and he breathed shallowly and evenly. "He was just tired," she said to herself. "He lay down to rest a moment and he fell asleep. I shouldn't wake him up."

She thought of the people back in the bus—suppose neither

she nor Juan ever came back. What would they do? Her mother would collapse. Her father would wire the governor—two or three governors. He would call the FBI. There would be hell to pay. Yet what could they do? She was twenty-one. When they caught up with her she could say, "I'm twenty-one and doing what I want to do. Whose business is it?" And suppose she went to Mexico with Juan? That would be quite a different story, quite a different thing.

And now little irrelevancies invaded her mind. If he's an Indian or has Indian blood, how is it someone can creep up on him? She held her eye corners back to bring his face into focus. It was a scarred, leathery face, but it was a good face, she thought. The lips were full and humorous, but they were kind. He would be gentle while he was with a woman. He might not stay with her for very long, but he would be nice to her. But he had that wife, that horrid wife, and he stayed with her. God knows how long. She must have been pretty when he married her, but she was ugly now. What had happened there? How did that horrid woman hold him? Maybe he was just like everyone else, like her father. Maybe he was just held in line by fears and by habit. Mildred didn't see how it could happen to anyone, but she knew it did. When people got old they grew frightened of smaller and smaller things. Her father was frightened of a strange bed or a foreign language or a political party he didn't belong to. Her father truly believed that the Democratic party was a subversive organization whose design would destroy the United States and put it in the hands of bearded communists. He was afraid of his friends and his friends were afraid of him. A rat race, she thought.

She moved her eyes down over Juan's body, a tough, stringy body that would get tougher and stringier as he got older. His trousers were a little wet from the rain and they hugged close to his legs. There was a neatness about him—a neatness of a mechanic who has just washed up. She looked at his flat stomach and at his broad chest. She saw no change in his breathing, no muscular change, but his eyes were open and he was looking at her. And his eyes were not sleep-heavy but bright.

Mildred started. Perhaps he hadn't been asleep at all. He might have watched her come into the barn. She found herself explaining, "I needed exercise. You know, I've been sitting a long time. I thought I'd walk to the county road and pick up the car there. And then I saw this old place. I like old places."

Her feet were going to sleep. She leaned sideways and, supporting herself with one hand, moved her legs and feet to one side and covered her knee carefully with her skirt. Her feet buzzed and burned with returning blood.

Juan did not answer. His eyes were on her face. Slowly he rolled on his side and supported his head with a hand under his ear. A dark gleam came into his eyes, and his mouth curled up a little at the corners. His face was hard, she thought. No way of getting past the eyes into the head. It was either all on the surface or else it was too completely protected ever to get at.

"What are you doing here?" she asked.

His lips parted a little. "What are you doing here?"

"I told you, I needed exercise. I told you."

"Yes, you told me."

"But what are you doing here?"

He didn't seem really awake. "Me? Oh, I sat down to rest. I went to sleep. No sleep last night."

"Yes, I remember," she said. She had to go on talking. She was wound up. "I wondered about you. You don't belong here. I mean, driving a bus. You belong someplace else."

"Like where?" he asked playfully. His eyes dropped to where the lapels of her coat crossed.

"Well," she said uneasily, "I had a funny kind of a thought while I was walking. I thought maybe you wouldn't come back. You might just keep going and maybe go back to Mexico. I could see how I might do that if I were you."

His eyes squinted and he peered into her face. "Are you nuts? What made you think that?"

"Well, it was just something that came to me. Your life, driving the bus, I mean, must be pretty dull after—well, after Mexico."

"You haven't been in Mexico?"

"No."

"Then you don't know how dull it is there."

"No."

He raised his head and straightened his arm and put his head down on his arm. "What do you think would happen to those people back there?"

"Oh, they'd get back somehow," she said. "It isn't far. They wouldn't starve."

"And what do you think would happen to my wife?"

"Well—" She was confused. "I hadn't thought of that."

"Yes, you did," said Juan. "You don't like her. I'll tell you something. Nobody likes her except me. One of the reasons I like her is because nobody likes her." He grinned. "What a liar," he said to himself.

"It was just a crazy thought I had," she said. "I even thought I might run away too. I thought I would disappear and live by myself and—well, never see anyone again that I knew." She rose up on her knees and sat down again on the other side.

Juan looked at her knee. He put out his hand and pulled her skirt down over it. She flinched when his hand came toward her and then relaxed uneasily.

"I don't want you to think I followed you in here," she said.

"You don't want me to think it, but you did," said Juan.

"Well, what if I did?"

His hand came out again and rested on her covered knee and fire raced through her.

"It's not you," she said. Her throat was dry. "I don't want you to think it's you. It's me. I know what I want. I don't even like you. You smell like a goat." Her voice staggered along. "You don't know the kind of life I lead. I'm all alone. I can't tell anyone anything."

His eyes were hot and shiny and they seemed to bathe her in heat.

"Maybe I'm not like anyone else," she went on. "How do I know? But it's not you. I don't even like you."

"You give yourself a hell of an argument, don't you?" said Juan.

"Look, what are you going to do about the bus?" she demanded. "Are you going to the road?"

The weight of his hand on her knee increased and then he took his hand away. "I'm going back and pull the bus out, pull those people through," he said.

"Then why did you come here?"

"Something went haywire," he said. "Something I figured out went haywire."

"When are you going back?"

"Pretty soon."

She looked at his hand, relaxed on the straw in front of her, its skin dark and shiny and a little wrinkled. "Aren't you going to make a pass at me?"

Juan smiled and it was a good, open smile. "Yes, I guess so. After you get through arguing with yourself. You're on both sides now. Maybe pretty soon you'll decide whether you're for or against and I'll have something to work on."

"Don't you—don't you want me?"

"Sure," said Juan. "Sure."

"Is it that you know I'll fall into your lap anyway, so you won't have to take any trouble?"

"Don't get me into your argument," said Juan. "I'm older than you are. I like this thing very much. I like it so much that I can wait. I can even go without for a while."

"I could dislike you very much," she said. "You don't give me any pride. You don't give me any violence to fall back on later."

"I thought you'd have more pride to be left to make up your own mind."

"Well, I don't."

"I guess not," he said. "The women in my country are like that too. They have to be begged or forced. Then they feel good about it."

"Well, are you always this way?"

"No," said Juan, "only with you. You came here for something. You said yourself it didn't have anything to do with me."

She looked at her fingers. "It's funny," she said. "I'm what you'd call an intellectual girl. I read things. I'm not a virgin. I know thousands of case histories, but I can't make the advances." She smiled quickly and warmly. "Can't you force me a little?"

His arms stretched out and she fell into place beside him in the straw.

"You won't hurry me?"

"We've got all day," he said.

"Will you despise me or laugh at me?"

"What do you care?"

"Well, I do, whether I want to or not."

"You talk too much," he said. "You just talk too much."

"I know it and it goes on all the time. Will you take me away? Maybe to Mexico?"

"No," said Juan. "Let's see if you can shut up for a little while."

Chapter 17

PIMPLES took the keys from the ignition lock on the instrument board and went to the rear of the bus. He unlocked the padlock which defended the luggage and threw up the lid. The smell of pies came sweetly to his nose. Mr. Pritchard looked in over his shoulder. The luggage was stacked tightly in the compartment.

"I guess I'll have to take it all out to get those tarps," said Pimples, and he began to pull at the wedged suitcases.

"Wait," said Mr. Pritchard. "Let me lift and you pull and we can leave them all in." He stood on the bumper and strained upward at the bottom suitcase while Pimples yanked at the heavy fold of canvas. Pimples worked it from side to side and gradually it came free from under the luggage.

"Maybe we'd better get a couple of pies while we got it open," Pimples said. "There's raspberry and lemon cream and raisin and caramel custard cream. A piece of caramel custard cream would go pretty good now."

"Later," said Mr. Pritchard. "Let's get my wife settled first." He took one side of the heavy cloth and Pimples the other and they proceeded toward the cliff with its caves.

It was a fairly common formation. The side of the little hill had dropped away in some old time, leaving a smooth surface of soft limestone. Gradually wind and rain cut under from below, while the top of the cliff was held in place by topsoil and grass roots. And over the ages several caves were formed under the overhanging cliff. Here a coyote littered her pups, and here, in the old days when there were such things, a grizzly bear came to sleep. And in the higher caves the owls sat during the day.

Three deep, dark caves developed at the bottom of the cliff and a few small ones higher up. All the cave entrances were now protected from the rain by the high overhang of the cliff itself. The caves were not entirely the inventions of nature, for bands of Indians hunting antelopes had rested here and lived here, and had even fought forgotten battles here. Later it became a stopping place for white men riding through the country, and the men had enlarged the caves and built their fires under the overhang.

The smoke stains on the sandstone were old and some fairly new, and the floors of the caves were comparatively dry, for this little hill, one side of which had dropped away, did not receive the drainage from other, higher hills. A few initials had been scratched on the sandstone cliff, but the surface was so soft that they soon became illegible. Only the large, weathering word "Repent" was still clear. The wandering preacher had let himself down with a rope to put up that great word in black paint, and he had gone away rejoicing at how he was spreading God's word in a sinful world.

Mr. Pritchard, carrying his end of the tarpaulin, looked up at the word "Repent." "Somebody went to a lot of trouble," he said, "a lot of trouble." And he wondered who had financed such a venture. Some missionary, he thought.

He and Pimples dropped the tarpaulin under the cliff's overhang while they went to inspect the caves. The shallow holes were nearly alike, about five feet high and eight or nine feet wide and ten or twelve feet deep. Mr. Pritchard chose the cave the farthest toward the right because it seemed to be drier and because it was a little darker inside. He thought the darkness would be good for his wife's coming headache. Pimples helped him spread the tarpaulin.

"I wish we could get some pine boughs or some straw to put underneath the canvas," Mr. Pritchard said.

"Grass is too wet," said Pimples, "and there ain't a pine tree in fifty miles."

Mr. Pritchard rubbed the canvas with the butt of his hand to see whether the cloth was dirty. "She can lie on my overcoat," he said, "and she can put her fur coat over her."

Ernest and Van Brunt came in to look at the cave.

"We could stay here for weeks if we had anything to eat," Ernest said.

"Well, we may be quite a time at that," said Van Brunt. "If that bus driver isn't back by tomorrow morning I'm going to walk in. I've had about all the nonsense I can take."

Pimples said, "I can break out a couple of pies if you folks want."

"That might be a good idea," said Ernest.

"What kind you like?" Pimples asked.

"Oh, any kind."

"The caramel custard cream is nice. It's got graham crackers instead of crust."

"That'll be fine," said Ernest.

Mr. Pritchard went back to the bus for his wife. He was feeling ashamed about his anger of a little time ago. He had the hard knot in his stomach he got when things were not going well, a fistlike knot. Charlie Johnson said he must have an ulcer, and Charlie was pretty funny about it. He said no one under twenty-five thousand dollars a year got an ulcer. It was a symptom of a bank account, Charlie said. And unconsciously Mr. Pritchard was a little proud of the pain in his stomach.

When he climbed into the bus, Mrs. Pritchard's eyes were closed.

"We've got your little bed all fixed," Mr. Pritchard said.

Her eyes opened and she stared wildly about.

"Oh!"

"Were you asleep?" he said. "I shouldn't have wakened you. I'm sorry."

"No, dear. It's all right. I was just dozing."

He helped her to her feet. "You can lie on my overcoat and put your little fur coat over you."

She smiled weakly at his tone.

He helped her down the steps. "I'm sorry I was rude, little girl," he said.

"It's all right. You're just tired. I know you didn't mean it."

"Well, I'm going to buy you a great big dinner in Hollywood to make up for it, maybe at Romanoff's, with champagne. Would you like that?"

"You can't be trusted with money," she said playfully. "It's all forgotten now. You were just tired."—"Dear Ellen, we had the nicest dinner at Romanoff's and you'll never guess who was at the next table."—"Why, it's hardly raining at all," she said.

"No, and I want my little girl to get some sleep so she'll be well and strong."

"Are you sure it's not damp and there aren't any snakes?"

"No, we looked around."

"And no spiders?"

"Well, there weren't any spider webs."

"But how about big, hairy tarantulas? They don't have webs."

"We can look around some more," he said. "The walls are smooth. There's no place for them to hide." He conducted her to the little cave. "See how nice? And you can lie with your head up this way so you can look out if you want to."

He spread his coat and she sat down on it.

"Now, lie down and I'll cover you up."

She was very docile.

"How's my girl's head?"

"Well, it's not as bad as I was afraid it would be."

"That's good," he said. "You get a little nap. Are you comfy?"

She made a little moan of comfort.

"If you want anything just call out. I'll be near."

Pimples came to the cave entrance. His mouth was full and he carried a pie tin in his hand. "You like to have a piece of pie, ma'am?"

Mrs. Pritchard raised her head and then she shivered and put her head down. "No, thank you," she said. "It was nice of you to think of me, but I couldn't eat pie."—"Elliott just treated me like a queen, Ellen. How many people can say that after they've been married twenty-three years? I just feel lucky all the time."

Mr. Pritchard looked down at her. Her eyes were closed and there was a small smile on her lips. He felt the sudden lonely sorrow that came so often. He remembered, really remembered, the first time it had happened. He had been five when his little sister was born, and suddenly there were doors closed against him and he couldn't go into the nursery and he couldn't touch the baby and the feeling came on him that he was always a little dirty and noisy and unworthy and his mother was always busy. And then the cold loneliness had fallen on him, the cold loneliness that still came to him sometimes, that came to him now. The little smile meant that Bernice had retired from the world into her own room, and he couldn't follow her.

He took his gold nail pick from his pocket and opened it and cleaned his nails as he walked away. He saw Ernest Horton sitting against the cliff on the other side of the overhang. The high cave was over his head. Ernest was sitting on some newspapers and as Mr. Pritchard approached he slipped a double sheet of paper from under him and held it out.

"Most useful things in the world," he said. "You can do anything with them except read them."

Mr. Pritchard chuckled, took the paper, and sat down on it beside Ernest. "If you read it in the paper it isn't true," he said, quoting Charlie Johnson. "Well, here we are. Two days ago I was in a suite in the Hotel Oakland and now we're in a cave. It just shows, you can't make plans."

He stared at the bus. Through the window he could see that Pimples was in there with the two girls and they were eating pie. He felt a strong urge to join them. He could eat a piece of pie.

Ernest said, "Everything goes to show something. I have to laugh sometimes. You know, we're supposed to be a mechanical people. Everybody drives a car and has an icebox and a radio. I suppose people really think they are mechanical minded, but let a little dirt get in the carburetor and—well, a car has to stand there until a mechanic comes and takes out the screen. Let a light go off, and an electrician has to come and put in a new fuse. Let an elevator stop, and there's a panic."

"Well, I don't know," said Mr. Pritchard. "Americans are pretty mechanical people all in all. Our ancestors did pretty well for themselves."

"Sure, they did. So could we if we had to. Can you set the timer on your car?"

"Well, I—"

"Go further," said Ernest. "Suppose you had to stay out here two weeks. Could you keep from starving to death? Or would you get pneumonia and die?"

"Well," said Mr. Pritchard, "you see, people specialize now."

"Could you kill a cow?" Ernest insisted. "Could you cut it up and cook it?"

Mr. Pritchard found that he was getting impatient with this young man. "There's a kind of cynicism running around the country," he said sharply. "It seems to me young people have lost their faith in America. Our ancestors had faith."

"They had to eat," Ernest said. "They didn't have time for faith. People don't work much any more. They've got time for faith."

"But they haven't any faith," Mr. Pritchard cried. "What's got into them?"

"I wonder," Ernest said. "I've even tried to figure it out. My old man had two faiths. One was that honesty got rewarded some way or other. He thought that if a man was honest he somehow got along, and he thought if a man worked hard and saved he could pile up a little money and feel safe. Teapot Dome and a lot of stuff like that fixed him on the first, and nineteen-thirty fixed him on the other. He found out that the most admired people weren't honest at all. And he died wondering, a kind of an awful wondering, because the two things he believed in didn't work out—honesty and thrift. It kind of struck me that nobody has put anything in place of those two."

Mr. Pritchard shook this out of his head. "You can't be thrifty because of taxes," he said. "There was a time when a man could build up an estate, but now he can't. Taxes take it all. You're just working for the government. I tell you, it knocks initiative on the head. No one has any ambition any more."

"It don't make a lot of difference who you work for if you believe in it," said Ernest. "The government or anybody else."

Mr. Pritchard interrupted him. "The returning soldiers," he said, "they're the ones I'm worrying about. They don't want to settle down and go to work. They think the government owes them a living for life and we can't afford it."

Ernest's forehead was beaded with perspiration now, and there was a white line around his mouth and a sick look in his eyes. "I was in it," he said softly. "No, no, don't worry. I'm not going to tell you about it. I wouldn't do that. I don't want to."

Mr. Pritchard said, "Of course, I've got the greatest respect for our soldiers, and I think they should have a voice."

Ernest's fingers crept to his lapel buttonhole. "Sure," he said, "sure, I know." He spoke as though he addressed a child. "I read in the papers about our best men. They must be our best men 'cause they got the biggest jobs. I read what they say and do, and I've got a lot of friends that you might call bums, and there's awful little difference between them. I've heard some of the bums get off stuff that sounded even better than the stuff that the Secretary of State gets off—Oh, what the hell!" He laughed. "I've got an invention, and it's a rubber drum that you beat with a sponge. It's for the drunks that want to play traps in the orchestra. I'm going to take a little walk."

"You're nervous," said Mr. Pritchard.

"Yeah, I'm nervous," Ernest said. "Everybody's nervous. And I'll tell you something. If we've got to fight somebody again, you know what's the most awful thing? I'll go too. That's the most awful thing." And he got up and walked away, back in the direction from which the bus had come.

His head was down and his hands were in his pockets and his feet beat against the gravel of the road and he was holding his mouth very tight and he couldn't stop. "I'm nervous," he said, "I'm just nervous. That's all it is."

Mr. Pritchard stared after him and then he lowered his eyes to his hands and got out his nail file again and cleaned his nails. Mr. Pritchard was shaken and he didn't know why. With all Mr. Pritchard's pessimism about government interference with business, there was always in the back of his mind a great hopefulness. Somewhere there was a man like Coolidge or like Hoover, who would come along and take the government out of the hands of these fools in the administration, and then everything would be all right. The strikes would stop and everybody would make money and be happy. It was just around the corner. Mr. Pritchard believed it. He had no idea that the world had changed. It has just made a few mistakes and the right man would come along—say, Bob Taft—and everything would get on an even keel again and these damned experiments would stop.

But this young man bothered him because this was a bright young man, and he had a feeling of hopelessness. Although he hadn't said it, Mr. Pritchard knew that Ernest Horton wouldn't even vote for Bob Taft if he were nominated. And Mr. Pritchard, like most of his associates, believed in miracles, but he was deeply shaken. Horton hadn't attacked Mr. Pritchard directly but—now, about the carburetor. Mr. Pritchard let his mind create the shape of a carburetor. Could he take it apart? Vaguely he knew that there was a little float in a carburetor, and in his mind he could see the brass screen and the gaskets.

But he had more important things to think about, he told himself. Horton had said "if the lights went out"—and Mr. Pritchard tried to think where the fuse boxes were in his house, and he didn't know. Horton had been attacking him. Horton didn't like him. Suppose they were stranded as the young man had said.

Mr. Pritchard closed his eyes and he was standing in the aisle of the bus. "Don't worry," he said to the other passengers, "I'm going to take care of everything. I haven't built a big business organization without some ability, you know. Let's reason this out," he said. "We need food first. There's some cows in that field back there." And Horton had said he didn't know how to kill a cow. Well, he'd show him. Probably Horton didn't know there was a pistol in the compartment on the instrument board. But Mr. Pritchard knew.

Mr. Pritchard took out the pistol. He got out of the bus and walked away toward the field and climbed a fence. He held the big black pistol in his hand. Mr. Pritchard had been to a great many movies. His mind unconsciously made a dissolve. He didn't see himself kill the cow or cut it up, but he saw himself come to the overhang again with a great slab of red meat. "There's food for you," he said. "Now for a fire." And again he dissolved, and the fire was leaping and a big piece of meat hung on a stick over the blaze.

And Camille said, "But what about that animal? It belongs to someone."

Mr. Pritchard answered, "Expediency knows no law. The law of survival comes first. Nobody could expect me to let you people starve."

And suddenly he dissolved again and he shook his head and opened his eyes. "Stay off that," he whispered to himself. "Keep away from that." Where had he seen her? If he could just talk to her a little while he ought to be able to place it. He knew he wasn't wrong because her face had given him a clutching sensation in his chest. He must not only have seen her, but something must have happened. He looked toward the bus. Pimples and the two girls were still inside.

He got to his feet and brushed the seat of his trousers as though the paper had not protected him from dust. The rain was only misting a little now, and in the west there were patches of blue sky. Everything was going to be all right. He walked over to the bus and climbed the steps. Van Brunt was stretched out on the seat at the rear which went across the width of the bus. Van Brunt seemed to be asleep. Pimples and the girls were talking softly so that they wouldn't disturb him.

"What I want in a wife is to be true," Pimples said.

"How about you?" Camille asked. "You figure to be true too?"

"Sure," said Pimples, "if she's the right kind of wife I will."

"Well, suppose she isn't?"

"Well, then I'll show her a thing or two. I'll show her two can play that game, like Cary Grant done in that movie."

An empty pie tin and another with only a quarter of a pie left were on the seat across from the group. The two girls sat together and Pimples, sitting sideways on the seat ahead of them, dropped his arm over the back.

They all looked up as Mr. Pritchard came. "You mind if I sit in?" he said.

"Sure, come on in," said Pimples. "You like to have a piece of pie? Here's a piece right here." And he handed the pie to Mr. Pritchard and moved the empty tins so he could sit down.

"Have you got a girl now?" Camille continued.

"Well, kind of a one. But she's—er—well, she's kind of silly."

"Is she true to you?"

"Sure," said Pimples.

"How do you know?"

"Well, I never could—I mean—yeah, I'm sure."

"I guess you'll be getting married pretty soon," Mr. Pritchard said playfully, "and going in business for yourself."

"No, not for a while," said Pimples, "I'm studying by mail. There's a big future in radar. Make up to seventy-five dollars a week inside of a year."

"You don't say?"

"There's fellas that took that course that wrote in and said that's what they're making," said Pimples. "One of them is a district manager already, after one year."

"District manager of what?" Mr. Pritchard asked.

"Just district manager. That's what he said in his letter, and it's printed right in the ad."

Mr. Pritchard was beginning to feel good again. Here was ambition. Not everybody was cynical.

Camille said, "When do you think you'll get married?"

"Oh, not right yet," said Pimples. "I think a fella ought to see the world a little before he settled down. He ought to get around some. I might get on a ship. If you know radar, why, you know radio too. I thought I might get on a ship and be a radio operator for a while."

"But when are you going to finish your course?" Mr. Pritchard asked.

"Well, the lessons are going to start pretty soon now. I've got the coupon all made out and I'm saving up for the down payment. I took a test and they say I got plenty of talent. I had three or four letters from them."

Camille's eyes were very weary. Mr. Pritchard looked at her face. He knew his eyes were shielded by his glasses. He thought she had a fine face when you looked at it closely. Her lips were so full and friendly now, and only her eyes were tired. All the way from Chicago on a bus, he thought. She didn't look strong enough. He could see the fullness of her breasts under her suit and the suit was wrinkled. She had turned the French cuffs of her shirt inside out so that the edges would be clean. Mr. Pritchard noticed this. It meant neatness to him. He studied little details.

He felt this girl almost like a perfume. He felt an excitement and a hunger. It's just that you don't often see a girl like this, so attractive and so nice, he told himself. And then he heard himself talking and he hadn't even known he was going to talk.

"Miss Oaks," he said, "I've been thinking, and it occurred to me that you might like to listen to a little business idea I had. I'm president of quite a large corporation and I thought —well, I'm sure these young people would excuse us for a little while if you'd care to hear my ideas. Would you step over to the cliff there? I have some newspapers to sit on." He was astonished at his own words.

"Oh, Jesus!" Camille said to herself. "Here it comes."

Mr. Pritchard got down first and gallantly helped Camille off the bus. He held her elbow as she stepped across the ditch and he guided her gently to the spread newspapers where he and Ernest had sat. He pointed downward.

"Oh, I don't know," Camille said. "I've been sitting a long time."

"Well, maybe the change in position will rest you," said Mr. Pritchard. "You know, when I'm working long hours at my desk I change the height of my chair about every hour, and I find it keeps me fresh." He helped her to sit down on the newspapers. She covered her knees with her skirt and sat hugging her knees against her breast.

Mr. Pritchard sat down beside her. He took off his glasses. "I've been thinking," he said. "You know, a man in my position has to look ahead and plan. Now, technically, I'm on a vacation." He smiled. "Vacation—I wonder what a real vacation would be like."

Camille smiled. The ground felt very hard. She wondered how long this was going to take.

"Now the main raw product of a successful company is human beings," Mr. Pritchard said. "I'm always looking for human beings. You can get steel and rubber any time, but brains, talent, beauty, ambition—that's the difficult product."

"Look, mister," Camille said, "I'm awful tired."

"I know, my dear, and I'll come to the point. I want to employ you. That's as simply as I can say it."

"As what?"

"As a receptionist. It's quite a specialized job, and from there you could become—well, you might even become my personal secretary."

Camille was played out. She looked toward the cave entrance where Mrs. Pritchard was. She couldn't see anything. "What'll your wife have to say about that?"

"Well, what's she got to do with it? She doesn't run my business."

"Mister, like I said, I'm tired. We don't have to go through all that. I'd like to be married. I'd be a good wife, and with a settlement so I wouldn't have to worry for a while, why, I could even be good to a man."

"I don't see what you're getting at," Mr. Pritchard said.

"Yes, you do," said Camille. "You won't like me because I don't play it your way. You'd like to take months to get around to it and surprise me with it, but I'm nearly broke. You say your wife doesn't run your business, but I say she does. You and your business and everything about you. I'm trying to be nice but I'm tired. She probably picks your secretaries and you don't even know it. That's a tough woman."

"I don't know what you're talking about."

"Yes, you do," Camille said. "Who bought your tie?"

"Well—"

"She would know about me in a minute. She would. Now let me talk a little bit. You couldn't ask a girl outright. You'd have to go round about. But there's only two ways, mister. You either fall in love or you make a business proposition. If you'd said, 'Here's the way it is. So much for an apartment and so much for clothes,' why, I could have thought it out and I could have come to a conclusion, and it might have worked. But I'm not going to be nibbled to death by ducks. Did you want to surprise me after two, three months of me sitting at a desk? I'm getting too old to play."

Mr. Pritchard's chin was stuck out. "My wife does not run my business," he said. "I don't know where you got that idea."

"Oh, skip it," said Camille. "But I'd just as soon come up against a nest of rattlesnakes as your wife if she didn't like me."

"I'm a little surprised at your attitude," Mr. Pritchard said. "I hadn't thought of any of these things. I was just trying to offer you a job. You can take it or leave it."

"Oh, brother!" said Camille. "If you can kid yourself into believing that, God help any girl you get. She'll never know where she stands."

Mr. Pritchard smiled at her. "You're just tired," he said. "Maybe when you get rested you'll think it over."

The enthusiasm was gone out of his voice and Camille was relieved. She thought maybe she had made a mistake because he'd be very easy to handle, a real sucker. Loraine could have taken his shirt in one day.

Mr. Pritchard saw her face differently now. He saw hardness in it and defiance, and now that he was this close he saw the make-up and how it was put on, and he felt naked before this girl. It bothered him to have her talk this way. He had thought if everything worked out—well, he would—well—but the trouble was that she knew. Only he wouldn't have called it—

well, there was such a thing as being a lady about such things.

He was confused, and in his confusion he was getting angry again. Twice in one day to be angry was unusual with him. His neck was getting red with anger. He had to cover up. He had to for his own sake. He said crisply, "I simply offered you a job. You don't want it—all right. There's no reason to be vulgar about it. There's such a thing as being a lady."

An edge came into her voice. "Look, Mac," she said, "I can play rough too. This lady business does it. I'm going to tell you something. You thought you recognized me. Now, do you belong to any clubs like The Octagon International or The Birds of the World or The Two Fifty—Three Thousand Club?"

"I'm an Octagon," Mr. Pritchard said stiffly.

"You remember the girl that sits in the wine glass? I've seen what you boys look like. I don't know what you get out of it and I don't want to know. But I know it isn't pretty, mister. And maybe you'd know a lady if you saw one. I don't know." Her voice came in little breaks and there was almost a hysteria of weariness in her. She jumped to her feet. "I'm going to take a stroll now, Mac. Don't give me any trouble because I know you, and I know your wife."

She walked away quickly. Mr. Pritchard watched her go. His eyes were wide and there was a heavy weight in his chest, a kind of played-out, physical horror. He watched her pretty body swaying as she went, and he saw her pretty legs, and his mind took her clothes off, and she was standing beside the huge glass and the wine was running down in red streams over her stomach and thighs and buttocks.

Mr. Pritchard's mouth was open and his neck was very red. He looked away from her and studied his hands. He took out his gold nail file and put it back in his pocket again. A dizziness came over him. He stood up uncertainly and walked down under the cliff to the little cave where Mrs. Pritchard lay.

She opened her eyes and smiled as he entered. Mr. Pritchard lay down beside her quickly. He pulled up her coat and crawled under it.

"Dear, you're tired," she said. "Elliott! what are you doing? Elliott!"

"Shut up," he said. "You hear me? Shut up! You're my wife, aren't you? Hasn't a man got any rights with his wife?"

"Elliott, you're mad! Someone'll—someone'll see you." She fought him in panic. "I don't know you," she said. "Elliott, you're tearing my dress."

"I bought it, didn't I? I'm tired of being treated like a sick cat."

Bernice cried softly in fear and in horror.

When he left her she cried with her face nestled close to her fur coat. Gradually her crying stopped and she sat up and looked out the cave entrance. Her eyes were ferocious. She raised her hand and set her nails against her cheek. She drew them down experimentally once and then she bit her lower lip and slashed downward with her fingernails. She could feel the blood oozing from the scratches. She put out her hand and dirtied it on the cave floor and rubbed the dirt into her bleeding cheek. The blood flowed down through the dirt and down her neck to the collar of her waist.

Chapter 18

MILDRED and Juan came out of the barn and she said, "Look, the rain has stopped. Look at the sun on the mountains. It's going to be beautiful."

Juan grinned.

"You know, I feel wonderful," she said. "I feel wonderful."

"Sure," said Juan.

"Do you feel wonderful enough to hold my mirror? I couldn't see in there." She took a little square mirror from her purse. "Here. No, a little higher." She combed her hair quickly and patted some powder on her cheeks and put on lipstick. She peered very closely in the mirror because she could see only at short range. "Do you think I'm flippant for a violated girl?"

"You're all right," he said. "I like you."

"But just that? No more?"

"Do you want me to lie?"

She laughed. "I guess I do a little. No, I don't. And you won't take me to Mexico?"

"No."

"This is the end then? There isn't any more?"

"How do I know?" Juan asked.

She put the mirror and the lipstick back in her purse and smoothed the lipstick on, one lip over the other. "Brush the straw off my coat, will you?"

She turned as he brushed her coat with his hand. "Because," she went on, "my father and mother don't know about these things. I'm sure I was conceived immaculately. My mother planted me, a number one bulb, before the snow came and covered me with soil and sand and manure." She was giddy. "Can't go to Mexico. What do we do now?"

"Go back and dig out the bus and drive to San Juan." He walked toward the entrance gate of the old farm.

"Can I take your hand just for a little?"

He looked at the hand with the amputated finger and started to move to the other side to give her his whole hand.

"No," she said, "I like that one." She took his hand and rubbed her finger over the smooth skin of the amputation.

"Don't do that," he said. "It makes me nervous."

She clutched his hand tightly. "I won't have to put on my glasses," she said.

The ranges to the east of them were glowing and gold with the setting sun. Juan and Mildred turned to the right and started up the hill toward the bus.

"Will you tell me something as—well, as a payment for my whoring?"

Juan laughed. "What do you want?"

"Why did you come down here? Did you think I'd follow you?"

"You want the truth or do you want to play games?" he asked.

"Well, I'd like both. But no—er—I guess I want the truth first."

"Well, I was running away," said Juan. "I was going to beat my way back to Mexico and disappear and let the passengers take care of themselves."

"Oh, and why don't you?"

"I don't know," he said. "It went sour. The Virgin of Guadalupe let me down. I thought I fooled her. She doesn't like fooling. She cut the heart out of it."

"You don't believe that," she said seriously. "I don't believe it either. What was the real reason?"

"For what?"

"For you coming down to that old place?"

Juan walked along and his face broke into a wide smile and the scar on his lip made the smile off-center. He looked down at her and his black eyes were warm. "I came down here because I hoped you would go for a walk, and then I thought I might —I might even get you."

She wrapped her arm around his arm and pulled her cheek hard against the sleeve of his jacket. "I wish it could go on a little more," she said, "but I know it can't. Good-by, Juan."

"'Good-by," he said. And they walked slowly back toward the bus.

Chapter 19

VAN BRUNT lay outstretched on the back seat of the bus. His eyes were closed but he was not sleeping. His head rested on his right arm and the weight of his head cut off the full flow of blood to his right hand.

When Camille and Mr. Pritchard left the bus Pimples and Norma were silent for a while.

Van Brunt listened to age creeping in his veins. He could almost feel the rustle of blood in his papery arteries, and he could hear his heart beat with a creaking whistle in it. His right hand was going to sleep, but it was his left hand that worried him. There wasn't much feeling in his left hand. The skin was insensitive, as though it were a thick rubber. He rubbed and massaged his hand when he was alone to bring the circulation back, and he really knew what was the matter although he hardly admitted it even to himself.

A few months ago he had fainted, just for a moment, and the doctor had read his blood pressure and told him to take it easy and he'd be all right. And two weeks ago another thing had happened. There had been an electric flash in his head behind his eyes, a feeling like a blinding blue-white glare for a second, and now he couldn't read any more. It wasn't that he couldn't see. He saw clearly enough, but the words on a page swam and ran together and squirmed like snakes, and he couldn't make out what they said.

He knew very well he had had two little strokes, but it was a secret he kept from his wife and she kept from him and the doctor kept from both. And he waited, waited for another one, the one that would flash in his mind, would flash through his body, and if it didn't kill him, it would numb out all feeling. Knowing it had made him angry, angry at everyone. Physical hatred of everyone around him crowded in his throat.

He tried on all possible glasses. He used magnifying glasses on the newspapers because he himself, with half of his mind, was trying to keep his condition secret from himself. His angers had a habit now of bursting from him without warning, but the real horror to him was that he cried, uncontrollably sometimes, and couldn't stop. Recently he had awakened early in the morning saying to himself, "Why should I wait for it?"

His father had died of the same thing, but before he died he had lain like a gray, helpless worm in a bed for eleven months, and all the money he had saved for his old age was spent on doctor bills. Van Brunt knew that if the same thing happened to him the eight thousand dollars he had in the bank would be gone, and his old wife would have nothing after she buried him.

As soon as the drugstores opened that day, he went in to see his friend Milton Boston of the Boston Drug Store.

"I've got to poison some squirrels, Milton," he said. "Give me a little cyanide, will you?"

"That's damn dangerous stuff," Milton said. "I kinda hate to sell it. Let me give you some strychnine. "It'll do the job just as well."

"No," Van Brunt said, "I've got a government bulletin with a new formula and it calls for cyanide."

Milton said, "Well, all right. You'll have to sign the poison book, of course. But look out for that stuff, Van. Look out for it. Don't leave it around."

They'd been friends for many years. They'd gone in the Blue Lodge together and had been through the Chairs, and in succeeding years they had been Worshipful Master of the San

Ysidro Lodge, and then Milton went into the Royal Arch and the Scottish Rite and Van Brunt never went beyond the third degree. But they had remained friends.

"How much of the stuff do you want?"

"About an ounce, I guess."

"That's an awful lot, Van."

"I'll bring back what I don't use."

Milton was worried. "Don't touch it at all with your hands, will you?"

"I know how to handle it," Van Brunt said.

Then he went into his office in the basement of his house, and with a sharp pocketknife he pricked the back of his hand. When there was a little blood coming out, he opened the glass tube of crystals. And then he stopped. He couldn't do it. He just couldn't tip the crystals into the cut.

After an hour he took the tube to the bank and put it in his safety-deposit box along with his will and his insurance policies. He thought of buying a little ampule to wear around his neck. Then, if the big one came, he could maybe get it to his mouth the way those people in Europe did. But he couldn't take it now. Maybe it wouldn't happen.

There was a weight of disappointment on him, and there was anger in him too. All the people around him who weren't going to die angered him. And there was another thing that bothered him. The stroke had knocked the cap off one set of his inhibitions. He had suddenly reachieved powerful desires. He was pantingly drawn toward young women, even little girls. He couldn't keep his eyes and his thoughts from them, and in the midst of his sick desires he would burst into tears. He was afraid, as a child's afraid of a strange house.

He was too old to accommodate the personality change of his stroke and the new nature it gave him. He had never been a reader, but now that he could not read he was famished for reading. And his temper grew sharper and more violent all the time until people he had known for years began to avoid him.

He listened to time passing in his veins and he wanted death to come and he was afraid of it. Through half-shut eyes he saw the golden light of the sunset come into the bus. His lips moved a little and he said, "Evening, evening, evening." The word was very beautiful, and he could hear the whistling in his heart. A fullness of feeling came on him, swelled in his chest, swelled in his throat, pulsed in his head. He thought he was going to cry again. He tried to clench his right hand, but it was asleep and it wouldn't clench.

And then he became rigid with tension. His body seemed distended, like a blown-up rubber glove. The evening light blazed in. In back of his eyes a terrible flickering flash came. He felt himself tumbling and tumbling toward grayness and toward darkness and into black, black. . . .

The sun touched the western hills and flattened itself, and its light was yellow and clear. The saturated valley glittered under the level light. The clean, washed air was crisp. In the fields the flattened grain and the thick, torpid stems of the wild oats tightened themselves, and the sheathed petals of the golden poppies loosened a little. The yellow river boiled and swirled and cut viciously at the banks. In the back seat of the bus Van Brunt snored hoarsely against his palate. His forehead was wet. His mouth was open and so were his eyes.

Chapter 20

PIMPLES moved into the seat beside Norma and she gathered her skirts daintily against her and slid a little toward the window.

"What do you suppose that old guy wants with that girl?" he asked suspiciously.

"I don't know," said Norma. "But I tell you one thing. She can handle him. She's a wonderful girl."

Pimples said, "Oh, I don't know. There's other wonderful girls."

Norma flared up. "Like who?" she said, derisively.

"Like you," said Pimples.

"Oh!" She hadn't expected this. She put her head down and stared at her laced fingers, trying to regain her balance.

"What did you have to go and quit for?" Pimples said.

"Well, Mrs. Chicoy wasn't nice to me."

"I know. She isn't nice to anybody. But I wish you didn't quit. We could have got together, maybe."

Norma didn't answer. Pimples said, "If you say the word I'll get out one of the raisin pies. They're pretty nice."

"No. No, thanks. I couldn't eat anything."

"You sick?"

"No."

"Well, if you'd only come back to work at the Corners we could maybe go into San Ysidro Saturday nights and dance and stuff like that."

"You didn't think of that before," she said.

"I didn't think you liked me."

She became a little arch now. This was a delightful game. "What makes you think I like you now?" she said.

"Well, you're different now. You kinda changed. I like the way you done your hair."

"Oh, that," she said. "Well, there wasn't any reason to kinda fix myself up back at the lunchroom. Who'd see me?"

"I would," Pimples said gallantly. "Come on back. They'll give you your job again. I guarantee that."

She shook her head. "No, when I quit, I quit. I don't go crawling back. Besides, there's a future. We've got plans."

"What kind of plans?"

Norma wondered whether she ought to tell. In some ways it was bad luck, but she found she couldn't help herself. "We're going to get a little apartment with a nice davenport and a radio. And we're going to have a stove and an icebox and I'm going to study to be a dental nurse." Her eyes were shining.

"Who's 'we'?"

"Me and Miss Camille Oaks, that's who. When I'm a dental nurse I can dress good and we'll go to shows and maybe give little dinners."

"Nuts," he said. "You won't never do that."

"What makes you say that?"

"You just won't. Now, why don't you come back to the Corners? I'm studying radar and we'll go out together sometimes and you can't tell—we might get together. You take a girl—she's gonna want to get married. I'm a young guy. It's—er —it's good for a young guy to have a wife. It gives him kind of—ambition."

Norma looked into his face, a level, questioning look, to see whether he was making fun of her. And there was something so direct in her look that Pimples misinterpreted it and glanced away in embarrassment.

"I know," he said bitterly. "You think you couldn't go with a guy that's got these things. I done everything. I spent over a hundred dollars going to doctors and for stuff at the drugstore. But it don't do no good. There was one doctor says they won't last. He says they'll go away in a couple more years. But I don't know if that's the truth. Go ahead," he said fiercely. "Get your damn apartment. Maybe I got ways of having fun you never heard of. I don't have to take no guff from nobody." His voice was completely miserable and he stared down into his lap.

Norma looked at him in amazement. She had never known this kind of abject pain in anyone but herself. No one ever needed Norma for sympathy or reassurance. A bubble of warmth burst in her and a kind of gratefulness.

She said, "Don't you think like that. You don't have to, because if a girl cared for you she wouldn't think like that. The doctor knew what he was talking about. I knew three other young fellows, and them things went away after a while."

Pimples kept his head down. There was still misery in him but an imp was stirring too. He felt the advantage coming to his side and he began to use it, and it was a new thing to him, a new discovery. Always he had blustered with girls and bragged, and this was so easy. A sly imp began to operate.

"Well, it just gets so you can't stand it," he said. "Sometimes I think I'll just kill myself." He forced a half sob.

"Now don't you say like that," said Norma. This was a new function for her too, but one she fitted into probably better than any other.

"Nobody likes me," Pimples said. "Nobody won't have nothing to do with me."

"Don't you say like that," Norma repeated. "It's not true. I always liked you."

"No, you never."

"I did too." She laid her hand on his arm in reassurance.

Blindly he reached up and held her hand against his arm. And then his hand clasped hers and he squeezed her fingers and automatically she squeezed back. He turned in his seat and flung his arms about her and pushed his face into hers.

"Don't!" she cried. "Stop that!"

He gripped her more tightly.

"Stop it," she said. "Stop it. That old man back there."

Pimples whispered, "Listen to the old bastard snore. He's pounding his ear. Come on, come on."

She wedged her elbows against his chest to hold him away. His hands began plucking at her skirt. "Stop," she whispered. "You just stop." She knew now that she had been tricked. "Stop it! Let me get out of here!"

"Come on," he said frantically. "Please come on." Pimples' eyes were glazed and he was fighting with her skirt.

"Stop it, please stop. Suppose—suppose Camille came in? Suppose she saw what you're—"

Pimples' eyes cleared for a moment. He looked at her evilly. "Suppose she did. What do you care what that god-damned tramp sees?"

Norma's mouth fell open and her muscles relaxed. She looked at him in unbelief. She looked at him as though she hadn't heard what he said. Then her rage was cold and murderous. Her work-hardened muscles set rigidly. She tore her hand free and hit him in the mouth. She leaped to her feet and swung at him with both her fists, and he was so startled that he covered his face with his hands to protect himself.

She was spitting at him like a cat. "You skunk!" she said. "Oh, you dirty little skunk." And she kicked and shoved and pushed him out into the aisle, and she ran up the aisle and out of the bus. His feet were tangled in the stanchions of the seats and he tried to roll over.

A sickness and a weakness came over Norma. Her lips were quivering and her eyes were streaming. "Oh, the dirty skunk," she cried. "The filthy, dirty skunk."

She crossed the ditch and flung herself down in the grass and put her head down on her arms. Pimples got to his feet and peeked out the window. He didn't know what in the world to do.

Camille, walking slowly back along the road, saw Norma lying face down in the grass. She stepped across the ditch and leaned over her. "What's the matter? Did you fall down? What's the matter with you?"

Norma raised her tearful face. "I'm all right," she said.

"Get up," said Camille shortly. "Get up out of that wet

grass." She reached down and jerked Norma to her feet and led led her under the cliff and sat her down on the folded newspapers. "Now, what in the hell is the matter with you?"

Norma wiped her wet face with her sleeve and destroyed the last of her lipstick. "I don't want to talk about it."

"Well, that's your business," said Camille.

"That Pimples. He grabbed me."

"Well, can't you take care of yourself? Do you have to pull a nosedive?"

"That wasn't why."

"Well, what was why?" Camille wasn't really interested. She had her own troubles.

Norma rubbed her red eyes with her fingers. "I hit him," she said. "I hit him because he said you was a tramp."

Camille looked quickly away. She stared across the valley where the last of the sun was disappearing behind the mountains and she rubbed her cheek with her hand. Her eyes were dull. And then she forced them to take on life and she forced them to smile and she gave the smile to Norma.

"Look, kid," she said. "You'll just have to believe this until you find it out for yourself—everybody's a tramp some time or other. Everybody. And the worst tramps of all are the ones that call it something else."

"But you aren't."

"Let it lay," said Camille. "Just let it lay. Come on, let's try to do something with your face. New lipstick isn't as good as a bath but it's better than nothing."

Camille opened her purse and dug into it and got out a comb.

Chapter 21

JUAN quickened his footsteps so that Mildred had trouble keeping up with him.

"Do we have to run?" she asked.

"It'll be a lot easier digging the bus out while it's still light than floundering around in the dark."

She trotted along beside him. "Do you think you can get it out?"

"Yes."

"Well, why didn't you do that in the first place instead of walking away?"

He slowed his footsteps for a moment. "I told you," he said. "I told you twice."

"Oh, yes. You really meant that, then."

"I really mean everything," said Juan.

They came to the bus after the sun had slipped below the range. But the high clouds were lighted with rose and they threw a rose transparency over the land and the hills.

Pimples skulked out from behind the bus when Juan approached. There was a hostile cringing about him. "When are they coming out?" he asked.

"I can't get anyone," Juan said shortly. "We'll have to do it ourselves. We're going to need help. Where the hell is everybody?"

"Scattered around," said Pimples.

"Well, get out the tarpaulin."

"That lady's got it laying down up there."

"Well, get her up. I want rocks if you can find any and I want planks or some posts. We may have to tear down some fence. But leave the barbed wire up so the stock won't get out. And, Pimples—"

Pimples' mouth dropped open and his shoulders sagged. "You said—"

"Get all the men. I'm going to need help. I'll get the big jack out from under the back seat."

Juan climbed into the bus. It was a little dark in the bus now. He saw Van Brunt lying on the seat. "You'll have to move so I can get the jack," he said.

Suddenly Juan leaned close. The eyes of the old man were open and rolled up, and a harsh, labored snoring came from his mouth, and there was spittle around the corners of his mouth. Juan turned him over on his back and his tongue fell into his throat and his in-breathing was plugged. Juan reached into his open mouth with his fingers and pushed the tongue down and forward. He shouted, "Pimples! Pimples!" and with his free hand he knocked on the window with his gold wedding ring.

Pimples climbed into the bus.

"This man's sick, goddammit. Call some help. Blow the horn."

It was Mr. Pritchard who took over Van Brunt. He hated it and yet he had to do it. Juan cut a little piece of stick and showed him how to hold down the tongue and wedge the stick against the roof of the mouth so that the old man could breathe. Mr. Pritchard was revolted by the look of the man, and the sour odor that came from the laboring chest sickened him. But he had to do it. He didn't want to think about anything. His mind wanted to stop. A series of chilling agonies ran through him. His wife came into the bus and saw him and took the first seat inside the door, as far from him as possible. And even in the dusky light he could see the scratches and the blood on her collar. She didn't speak to him.

He said in his mind, "I must have been crazy. I don't know how I could have done it. Dear, can't you just think I was sick, out of my head?" He said it in his head. He would give her the little orchid house, and not such a little one. He'd build her the finest orchid house money could buy. But he couldn't even mention it for a long time. And the Mexican trip—they would have to go through with it. It would be horrible, but they would have to go through with it. How long would it be before the look would go out of her eyes, the reproach, the hurt, the accusation? She wouldn't speak for several days, he knew, or when she did it would be with perfect politeness; short replies and a sweet voice, and her eyes would not meet his. "Oh, God," he thought, "how do I get into these things? Why can't it be me here, dying, instead of this old man? He's never going to have to go through anything again."

He felt the men working under him on the bus. He heard the shovel bite and the suck of the mud and he heard the stone thrown under the wheels. His wife sat stiffly and her lips were set in a tolerant smile. He didn't know yet how she was going to handle the situation, but it would come to her.

She was sad and she said to herself, "I must think no evil. Just because Elliott went down under a bruitishness is no reason for me to lose beauty and toleration." There was a flicker of triumph in her. "I have conquered anger," she whispered, "and I have conquered disgust. I can forgive him, I know I can. But for his own sake it must not be too soon—for his own good. I'll have to wait." Her face was full of dignity and hurt.

Outside, Pimples was performing miracles of muscle and fortitude. His two-toned oxfords were destroyed with mud. Almost purposely he destroyed them. There was a layer of mud on his chocolate trousers. He violated his fine clothes. He drove his shovel into the earth and dug down behind the wheels and underneath the sides and he threw the mud out. He got on his knees in the mud to use his hands. His wolf eyes glittered with effort and the sweat stood out on his forehead. Out of the corner of his eye he watched Juan. Juan had forgotten, and just at a time when Pimples needed him most. Pimples drove his shovel into the ground with gusty bursts of strength.

Ernest Horton took a pickax and crossed the ditch. He picked away the turf and roots and topsoil until he found what he wanted. The broken stone from the ancient crash of the hill. He lifted the stones out and piled them on the grass beside his hole.

Camille came over to him. "I'll help you carry some of these down."

"You'll get all dirty," said Ernest.

"You think I can get any dirtier than I am?" she asked.

He rested the pick on the ground. "You wouldn't like to give me your phone number? I'd take you out."

"That was the truth," said Camille. "I don't live any place yet. I haven't got a number."

"Have it your own way," said Ernest.

"No, this is straight. Where are you going to stay?"

"Hollywood Plaza," said Ernest.

"Well, if you're in the lobby about seven o'clock day after tomorrow, I might come by."

"Fair enough," said Ernest. "I'll take you to Musso-Franck's for dinner."

"I didn't say I would," she said. "I said I might. I don't know how I'm going to feel. If I don't show up, don't drop your watch. I'm too pooped to figure anything out."

"Fair enough," said Ernest. "I'll stick around till seven-thirty."

"You're a good guy," said Camille.

"I'm just another sucker," said Ernest. "Don't take those big ones. I'll bring those. You take the little ones."

She picked a rock up in each hand and walked toward the bus.

Juan went to the old fence and tore the posts out of the earth. He tore down eight of them, but alternate posts, so that the barbed wire would not fall down. He carried the posts down and went back for more.

The rose afterglow was turning pale pink and a duskiness settled on the valley. Juan set his jack against a post and under the flange of the wheel rim, and he lifted one side of the bus. As the wheel rose, Pimples filled the hole under the tires with rocks.

Juan took another bite and lifted again, and gradually one side of the bus rose out of the mud. Juan moved his jack to the other side and raised the other wheel.

Camille and Norma were carrying rocks to fill the holes while Ernest dug them out.

Mildred asked, "What can I do?"

"Steady this post while I get a new pinch," said Juan. He was working furiously against the coming dark. His forehead was glistening with sweat. Pimples, on his knees in the mud, packed rocks under the wheels, and the other side of the bus rose out of the mud.

"Let's get it extra high," said Juan, "so we won't have to do it all over again. I'd like to have these posts in under the wheels."

It was almost dark when they were ready. Juan said, "I want everybody to give a push when I start. If we can just make three feet we'll be all right."

"How's the road ahead?" Pimples asked.

"It looked all right to me. God! You raised hell with your clothes."

Pimples' face was sick with disappointment. "It don't amount to nothing," he said. "What good is clothes?" His tone was so despondent that Juan stared at him in the half darkness.

A tight smile raised Juan's lips. "You'll have to take charge back here, Kit, while I drive. Make them throw their weight on it when I go ahead. You know how. You take charge back here, Kit."

Pimples threw down his shovel. "Come on, everybody," he shouted. "Come on, snap into it! I'll take the right side. Girls too. Everybody got to shove." He marshaled his people at the back of the bus. For a second he looked hungrily at Mrs. Pritchard sitting inside. "She'd just be in the way, I guess," he said.

Juan climbed into the bus. "Get out and give a shove," he said to Mr. Pritchard.

The engine started easily enough. Juan let it turn over for a moment. He eased it into compound-low and then he knocked twice on the side of the bus and heard Pimples knock back twice on the rear wall. He speeded his engine a little and let his clutch in. The wheels caught, slipped, groaned, and caught, and "Sweetheart" waddled drunkenly over the bed of rocks and climbed out onto the road. Juan pulled ahead out of the mud on the road and then he set his hand brake. He stood up and looked out the doorway.

"Just pile the tools in here on the floor," he said. "Come on, let's get moving."

He turned on his lights and the beam lighted the gravel road as far as the top of the little hill.

Chapter 22

JUAN took the bus very slowly over the hill and down the water-scarred gravel road past the deserted house. As he turned, his headlights picked out the eyeless house and the broken windmill and the barn.

The night was very black, but a new breeze had come up, bearing the semenous smell of grass and the spice of lupine. The headlights tunneled the night over the road and an owl flew flashing in and out of the light. Far ahead a rabbit crossing the road looked into the lights so that its eyes glowed red, and then it hopped clear into the ditch.

Juan kept the bus in second gear and missed the water-scored ruts with his wheels. The inside of the bus was dark except for the dash lights. Juan let his eyes dart to the Virgin. "I ask only one thing," he said in his mind. "I gave up the other, but it would be nice if you could make it so she was sober when I get back."

Mrs. Pritchard was not rigid any more. Her head swayed with the movement of the bus and she was dreaming. She was dressed in—what—what would she have on? Something light. It would have to be white. And she was taking Ellen through her little orchid house. "You wonder why I keep a few purple orchids?" she asked Ellen. "Well, everybody has relatives who like purple ones. Even you have, Ellen, you know that. But look over here. These are just coming—the lovely browns and greens. Elliott ordered those from Brazil. They came from a thousand miles up the Amazon."

On the floor of the bus the pickax clinked against the shovel.

Pimples leaned close to Juan's ear. "I could take her over, Mr. Chicoy. You're tired out. I'll drive if you want."

"No, thanks, Kit, you've had enough."

"But I ain't tired."

"It's all right," said Juan.

Mildred could see Juan's profile against the lighted road. "I wonder how long I can make the day last. Like a peppermint stick. I'll have to hold onto today until I can get another one as good."

Over the banging and the bouncing of the bus Mr. Pritchard listened for the breathing of Van Brunt. He could just barely see the face against the seat. He found that he hated this man because he was dying. He inspected his hatred in amazement. He felt that he could strangle this man easily and get it over with. "What kind of a thing am I?" he cried. "What makes these horrible things in me? Am I going crazy? Maybe I've been working too hard. Maybe this is a nervous breakdown."

He leaned close to make sure that the breathing of the sick man was not cut off. There would be a bad bruise in the roof of his mouth where the stick was wedged. He heard a little stir and saw that Ernest Horton had come back and taken the next seat.

"You want me to take over?"

"No," said Mr. Pritchard. "I guess everything's all right. What do you suppose it is?"

"It's a stroke," said Ernest. "I didn't mean to blast you today. I was just nervous."

"Just one of those days," said Mr. Pritchard. "When things are pretty bad my wife says, 'It'll be funny some time.'"

"Well, that's a good way to look at it if you can do it," said Ernest. "I'll be at the Hollywood Plaza if you want to give me a call. Or try that apartment some night—that number I gave you."

"I'm going to be all tied up, I'm afraid," said Mr. Pritchard. "I wish you'd look in at the plant some time, though. We might do business yet."

"We might at that," said Ernest.

Norma sat next to the window now and Camille was by her side. Norma leaned her elbow on the window sill and looked out at the fluttering dark. There was a little rim of lighter sky around the edge of a great dark cloud over the western mountains, and then as the cloud lifted the evening star shone out of it, clear and washed and steady.

"Star light, star bright, first star I see tonight, wish I may, wish I might, get the wish I wish tonight."

Camille turned her head sleepily. "What did you say?"

Norma was silent for a moment. Then she asked softly, "We'll see how it goes?"

"Yeah, we'll see how it goes," said Camille.

Far ahead and a little to the left a cluster of lights came into view—little lights winking with distance, lost and lonely in the night, remote and cold and winking, strung on chains.

Juan looked at them and called, "That's San Juan up ahead."

A Sensible Plan for Busy Men and Women
who "can't find time to read books"
BOOKS ABRIDGED

Four-books-in-one-volume... shortened, never rewritten, exactly like the full-length books offered in magazines ... each one readable at a sitting ... published in a fine hard-bound library edition at a very low price

Books Abridged is a new and sensible service for busy men and women directed straight at the cause of a common problem—*lack of time for reading.*

A GREAT SAVING ALSO—The price is only $2.19 per volume, plus a small charge for postage and handling. The combined price of the original publishers' editions of the four books in each volume of *Books Abridged* will run from $14 to $16.

YOU MAY REJECT ANY BOOK AND CANCEL WHEN YOU PLEASE—An advance description of each monthly volume is sent to you with a return form to send in if it doesn't interest you. You may reject any volume *before* receiving it. You do not have to take a specified number of volumes, and you may withdraw from membership at any time.

NO OBLIGATION—May we send you the current volume—at no expense to you—so that you may *demonstrate to yourself* how much good reading you can absorb in just one month—and also how satisfying these shortened versions can be. You may keep this volume without obligation, but please fill in and mail the coupon promptly as our supply of this particular volume is limited.

THE FIRST VOLUME
FREE
TO DEMONSTRATE
...how much good reading you can enjoy in a single month, and how thorough and satisfying these shortened versions are...

Only the most outstanding books from the hundreds published every month in hard-cover editions are chosen for the Bantam trademark.

That's why the book which carries the Bantam rooster is often one that has been a book club selection, a nationally listed bestseller, the basis for a great motion picture, and the choice of leading literary critics.

That's why Bantam's list of authors includes so many of the foremost writers of our time—novelists like Hemingway, Steinbeck, A. J. Cronin, Maugham, Costain, McCullers; mystery writers like Rex Stout, John Dickson Carr; Western writers like Luke Short, Peter Dawson; writers of science-fiction like Ray Bradbury, Fredric Brown.

Whether your choice is a mystery, a novel, a Western, or a work of non-fiction—if it carries the symbol of the Bantam rooster, you can be sure it is a book of exceptional merit, attractively printed, economically priced.